"I've always been of the opinion that a woman would be far more satisfied lying in bed with the devil than with a saint."

—Lady Catherine Mabry

They call him the Devil Earl—a scoundrel and accused murderer who grew up on the violent London streets. A proper young lady risks more than her reputation when consorting with the roguishly handsome Lucian Langdon, but Lady Catherine Mabry believes she has no choice. To protect those she loves, she would do anything—even strike a bargain with the devil himself.

Lucian desires respectability and a wife above all else, but the woman of his choosing lacks the social graces to be accepted by the aristocracy. Catherine can help Lucian gain everything he wants. But what she asks for in exchange will put their very lives in jeopardy. When danger closes in, Catherine discovers a man of immense passion and he discovers a woman of immeasurable courage. As secrets from his dark past are revealed, Lucian begins to question everything he knows to be true, including the yearnings of his own heart.

By **Lorraine Heath**

In Bed with the Devil
Just Wicked Enough
A Duke of Her Own
Promise Me Forever
A Matter of Temptation
As an Earl Desires
An Invitation to Seduction
Love with a Scandalous Lord
To Marry an Heiress
The Outlaw and the Lady
Never Marry a Cowboy
Never Love a Cowboy
A Rogue in Texas

If You've Enjoyed This Book,
Be Sure to Read These Other
AVON ROMANTIC TREASURES

How to Propose to a Prince *by Kathryn Caskie*
Never Trust a Scoundrel *by Gayle Callen*
A Notorious Proposition *by Adele Ashworth*
The Perils of Pleasure *by Julie Anne Long*
Under Your Spell *by Lois Greiman*

Coming Soon

The Mistress Diaries *by Julianne MacLean*

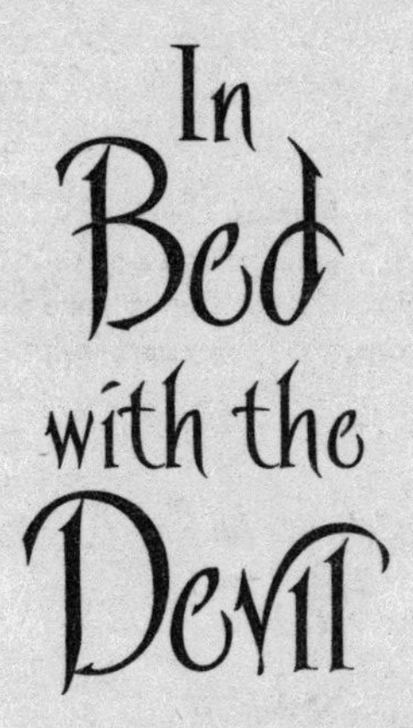

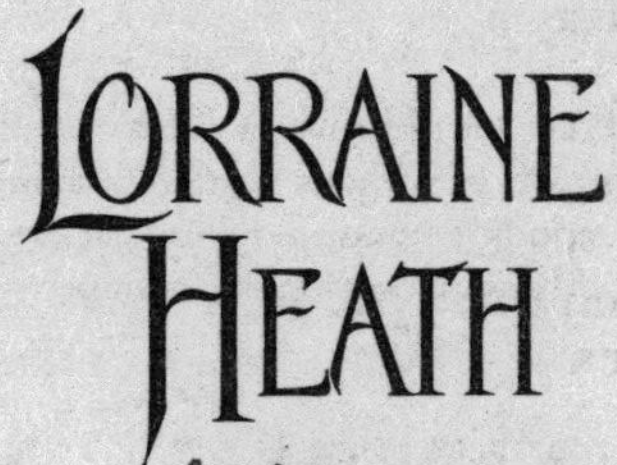

An Avon Romantic Treasure

AVON
An Imprint of HarperCollins*Publishers*

This is a work of fiction. Names, characters, places, and incidents are drawn from the author's imagination or are used fictitiously and are not to be construed as real. Any resemblance to actual events, locales, organizations, or persons, living or dead, is entirely coincidental.

AVON BOOKS
An Imprint of HarperCollins*Publishers*
10 East 53rd Street
New York, New York 10022-5299

ISBN 978-0-06-135557-8
www.avonromance.com

First Avon Books paperback printing: July 2008

Printed in the U.S.A.

10 9 8 7 6 5 4 3 2 1

For Auntie Jean
Thank you for always being there.

In
Bed
with the
Devil

Prologue

From the Journal of Lucian Langdon

They say my parents were murdered in the London streets by a gang of ruffians. I have no memory of it, yet it has always seemed to me that I should.

After all, I was supposedly there, but only if I truly am who the world recognizes me to be.

The Earl of Claybourne.

It is not a pleasant thing to always doubt one's identity. I often study the portrait of my father hanging above the massive fireplace in the grand library of my London residence and catalogue the similarities in our appearance.

The hair—black as the soot that lined the inside of a chimney.

The eyes—the shade of pewter that brought a fair price from fences.

The nose—a slender knife-like shape, a fine-honed blade, aristocratic. Although that similarity might be merely wishful thinking on my part. It's difficult to tell if our noses are truly the same, as mine was severely broken at an early age, the result of an encounter that left me nearly dead. I have always attributed my escape from death's clutches to Jack Dodger, who offered himself up as a target for the abuse being delivered to me. Things went much worse for him. Not that we ever speak of it.

When you grow up on the streets of London you learn about a great many things of which people never speak.

It's my eyes that convinced the old gent who called himself my grandfather that I was indeed his grandson.

"You've got the Claybourne eyes," he'd said with conviction.

And I readily admit that looking into his was very much like looking into a mirror at my own, but still it seemed a rather trite thing upon which to base so grand a decision.

I was fourteen at the time. Awaiting trial for committing murder. I must confess it was a rather fortuitous moment to be declared a future lord of the realm, as the judicial system was not opposed to hanging young lads who were considered troublesome. I'd developed quite a reputation in that regard. Considering the circumstances of my arrest, I have no doubt I was traveling a swift path straight to Newgate and then the gallows. Having a fondness for breathing, I was determined to do whatever was necessary to escape the hangman's noose.

Because I was brought up under the tutelage of Feagan, the kidsman who managed our rather notorious den of child thieves, I was adept at deceiving people, at pretending to remember things of which I truly had no memory. During a rather intensive inquisition, observed by inspectors of Scotland Yard, I was quite the showman, and the old gent not only declared me to be his grandson, but appealed to the Crown to take the unfortunate circumstances of my life into consideration and to show extreme leniency. After all, I'd witnessed my parents' murder, been stolen and sold into near slavery. Certainly it was understandable that I'd engage in a bit of misbehavior. If returned to his keeping, he vowed to set me back on the righteous path to being a proper gentleman. His request was granted.

And I found myself traveling a far different—and more difficult—road than I'd expected, always looking for the familiar, the evidence that I truly belonged where I now resided. By the time I grew to manhood, by all appearances, I was an aristocrat.

But beneath the surface . . . I remained a scoundrel at heart.

Chapter 1

London
1851

It was common knowledge that one never spoke of the devil for fear that in so doing one would attract his ardent attention. So it was that few among the aristocracy spoke of Lucian Langdon, the Earl of Claybourne.

Yet, as Lady Catherine Mabry stood in the midnight shadows near his residence, she couldn't deny that she'd been fascinated with the Devil Earl ever since he'd dared to appear at a ball uninvited.

He'd danced with no one. He'd spoken with no one. But he had prowled through the ballroom as though taking measure of each and every person within its confines and finding them all sadly lacking.

She'd found it particularly distressing when his gaze had settled on her and lingered a second or two longer than was proper. She'd neither flinched nor looked away—although she'd dearly wanted to do both—but she'd held his gaze with all the innocent audacity that a young lady of seventeen could muster.

She'd taken some satisfaction in his being the first to look away, but not before his strangely silver eyes had begun to darken, to appear as though they were heated by the fiery depths of the very hell from which he was supposedly spawned.

Few believed him to be the rightful heir, but none dared question his status. After all, it was well known that he was quite capable of committing murder. He'd never denied that he'd killed the previous earl's remaining son and heir.

That night at the ball, it had been as if the entire throng of guests had taken a solitary breath and held it, waiting to see where he might strike, upon whom he might vent his displeasure, because it had been quite obvious he was not one to exhibit gaiety. And it could only be assumed that he'd arrived with some nefarious purpose in mind, for surely he was aware that no lady in attendance would dare risk her reputation by dancing with him nor would any gentleman have his respectability questioned by openly and willingly conversing with Claybourne in so public a venue.

Then he'd sauntered out, as though he'd been searching for someone, and failing to find him—or her—had decided the rest of them weren't worth the bother.

That irritated Catherine most of all.

To her immense shame, she'd desperately wanted to dance with him, to be held within the circle of his arms, and to gaze once more into those smoldering silver eyes, that even now, five years later, continued to haunt her dreams.

Bringing up the hood of her pelisse, covering her head in an attempt to warm herself as the damp fog thickened, she studied the earl's residence more closely, searching for some clue to indicate that he was home. She wasn't certain that her fascination with him was entirely healthy. As a matter of fact, she was fairly certain it wasn't.

She couldn't say exactly what it was about him that drew her; she knew only that she was irrevocably drawn. Clandestinely, unknown to her family, after her first encounter with Clabourne, she'd even dared to have invitations to her balls and dinners hand-delivered to him by a faithful servant. Not that he'd ever bothered to acknowledge her overtures or attend her social functions.

As far as she knew, save for that one night, he'd never made an appearance at any other soiree. He was not openly welcomed in the best of homes, and she was quite insulted that he'd rebuffed her attempts to include him in her life. Although she had to admit that her reasons for wanting him there were quite selfish and not entirely respectable.

She no longer had the luxury of trying to entice him nearer with gilded invitations. She was quite determined to have a word with him, and if not within the safety of a crowded ballroom, then she would do it within the privacy of his own residence.

An icy shudder skittered down her spine, and

she tried to attribute it to the chill of the fog, rather than her own cowardice. She'd been standing in the shadows for quite some time and the dampness had seeped into her bones. If she didn't approach soon, she'd be a shivering mess and that would hardly suit her purpose. She had to appear as though she had no qualms whatsoever about approaching him, otherwise, she'd no doubt garner his disdain and that wouldn't do at all.

Cautiously she glanced around. It was so very late, and the night was very quiet. Ominously so.

No one was about to witness her approaching his door, no one would be aware of her scandalous midnight visit. Her reputation would remain unscathed. Still she hesitated. Once she set foot on this path, there would be no turning back, but she didn't see that she had any other choice.

With renewed resolve, she stepped into the street and began marching forward, fearing that, before this night was done, her reputation would remain the only thing untouched by the Devil Earl.

None would ever dare claim that Lucian Langdon, the Earl of Claybourne, was a coward. Yet as he sat at the gaming table, he knew the truth of it. He was there only because he hadn't the courage to press his suit with the lovely Frannie Darling. He'd come to Dodger's Drawing Room with the specific intent of finally asking Frannie for her hand in marriage, and just before he'd reached the door to the office where she kept track of Jack Dodger's accounts, he'd decided to take a quick detour by the gaming tables. Just to give his hands an opportunity to stop quaking and his mind the chance to rehearse once again the words he'd been practicing.

That had been six hours ago.

He could blame his delay on the fact that he was winning. But then he always won.

The next set of cards was dealt. He gave his a passing glance. It wasn't the cards he was dealt that assured his victory, but rather his ability to accurately determine what the other gents were holding.

The Earl of Chesney's eyes bugged slightly when he received a nicely matched set of cards, as though he were taken by surprise by his good fortune. This round, his eyes remained noticeably *un*bugged. Viscount Milner kept rearranging the order of his cards, never finding satisfaction there. The Earl of Canton always took a sip of his brandy when he was pleased. His glass remained untouched. The Duke of Avendale sat forward as though ready to pounce upon the winnings when he thought they would be his. He lounged back when the outcome was doubtful. Presently, he looked as though he were in danger of sliding out of his chair onto the floor. A monstrously bad hand that he no doubt thought he could bluff his way through.

The game continued, with each man betting or passing. When this particular round of brag was completed, with all the other lords groaning and moaning, Claybourne took his winnings and added them to the stack of wooden chips already resting in front of him.

"I believe, gentlemen, that I shall call it a night," he said, coming to his feet.

A young lad, dressed in the purple livery for which Dodger's was so well known, rushed over with a copper bowl. He held it at the edge of the table while Claybourne slid his abundant winnings into it.

"See here, Claybourne," Avendale said, "you're hardly being sporting about this. You should at least give us an opportunity to win it back."

Removing a crown from his pocket, Claybourne took the bowl from the lad, flipping him the coin as he did so. The boy, who was probably no more than eight, touched his fingers to his brow and dashed off.

"I've given you most of the night, gentlemen. Trust me when I assure you that you'll come out ahead if I leave now."

The gentlemen did a bit more grumbling, but Claybourne knew they weren't sorry to see him go. He made them uncomfortable. No more so than they made him. But that was his secret. Unlike them, he never allowed his emotions, thoughts, or feelings to rise to the surface. Not even when it came to Frannie. He doubted that she had any idea how deeply his affection for her ran.

He stopped by the exchange window and swapped his chips for coins, relishing the additional weight of the bowl.

As he strode through the gaming establishment, he realized that Frannie had no doubt already retired for the evening, in which case, he'd have to wait until tomorrow to proclaim his feelings. But as he neared the back, he saw the door to her office was open. Most likely he'd find Jack inside. The man gave fewer hours to sleep than Claybourne did. But what if it wasn't Jack? Claybourne could get this bothersome matter over with. So he walked down the hallway, peered around the door frame . . .

And there was Frannie. Lovely Frannie. Her red hair pulled back and tucked neatly into a tight bun, the dusting of freckles across her nose and cheeks barely visible beneath the glow from the lamp on the desk behind which she sat, diligently marking numbers in a column. Her dress had a high collar, every button, all the way up to her chin, securely in place. The long sleeves left only her hands visible. Her delicate brow was pleated. When she became his wife, she'd have no worries.

She glanced up, released a tiny squeak, jerked back, and pressed a hand to her chest. "Dear God, Luke! You gave me quite a start. How long have you been standing there spying on me?"

"Not nearly long enough," he said laconically, striding into the room with a confidence he didn't quite feel. He set the bowl on the desk. "For you and your children's home."

The home was a small place she was in the process of establishing with hopes of making life easier for orphans. She looked at him through narrowed eyes. "Are these ill-gotten gains?"

"Of course."

Snatching up the bowl, she smiled at him. The impish upward curve of her lips hit him as it always did, like a powerful punch to the gut. "Then I shall take them gladly and do good works with them to absolve you of your sins."

Her voice held a bit of teasing, but a sadness marred her eyes.

"No one can absolve me of my sins, Frannie, you know that." With a wave of his hand to stop her from even attempting to argue with him on the matter, he sat in the thickly padded chair in front of her desk. "You're up rather late."

"The amount of work necessary to keep track of Jack's finances is unbelievable. His profits are astounding."

"He's always said if you wish to die rich, invest in vice."

"Well, he shall no doubt die rich, and in a way that's rather sad. He should spend the money on something that brings him pleasure."

"I think he finds his pleasure in taking money from rich blokes." His accent dipped at the end to reveal his street origins. It was always so easy to slip around Frannie, because they shared the same origins.

"But is he happy?" she asked.

"Are any of us?"

Tears welled in her eyes—

"Dammit, Frannie—"

She held up her hand. "It's all right. I'm in one of my moods is all, and while I can't claim to be happy, I do believe I'm content."

Now was the perfect opportunity to promise her unending happiness. But her office suddenly seemed like such a ghastly unromantic place. Whatever had he been thinking to consider asking her here? The setting for the proposal should be as memorable as the proposal itself.

Tomorrow. He would ask her tomorrow. Clearing his throat, he came to his feet. "Well, it's rather late. I'd best be off."

She gave him another impish smile. "It was kind of you to stop by and visit." She touched the copper bowl containing his winnings. "I thank you for your contribution."

"I'd give you more—legitimate funds—if you'd take them."

"You've done more than enough for me, Luke."

Again, it seemed like the perfect opportunity to tell her that he'd not done nearly as much as he planned to do for her. But the words lodged in his throat. Why was he always so damned tongue-tied around her when it came to speaking from his heart? Was it because, as he feared, he truly had no heart, just a black hole that reflected the darkness of his soul?

Telling her anything at all should come easily. After all, they knew the worst of each other's lives. Why was that so much easier to share than what should be the best?

He took a step back. "I'll probably see you tomorrow."

"I'll let you know then exactly how I plan to use this money you've given me."

"Use it however it pleases you, Frannie. It comes with no attachments. You owe me no explanations."

"You've never been comfortable around orphans, have you?"

"Whatever are you about? All my best friends are orphans."

"Feagan's merry little band of ne'er-do-wells. We're an odd assortment, aren't we?"

"Only because we overcame the circumstances of our youths and are all quite successful."

"We have your grandfather to thank for our change in fortunes. He lifted us all up when he lifted you."

"If he was my grandfather."

"How can you still doubt it?"

He almost told her the truth, but he didn't think she'd approve of the lie he was certain he was living. He gave her what he hoped was one of his more charming smiles. "Good night, Frannie. Sweet dreams."

As for himself, he had only nightmares when he drifted into slumber.

He strode from the room before she could pester him for more answers. His former life was an area that he didn't relish reliving. Sometimes it struck him as strange that he wanted to marry someone who was so ensconced in his past. With her at his side, he'd never be able to run from it, but perhaps he could better face it.

He was nearly to the front door when he heard, "You owe me five quid, Luke."

Coming to an abrupt halt, he turned and watched as Jack Dodger swaggered toward him, a confident grin on his darkly rugged face.

"You don't know that," Luke said when Jack stopped in front of him.

"So you did ask Frannie to marry you?"

With a sigh, Luke removed his wallet from inside his jacket and handed Jack the requested amount. "I never should have told you my intentions."

"No, you never should have accepted the wager

that you'd actually do it." Jack tucked away the money. "Did you want to take one of my girls home with you tonight"—he winked—"for a bit of comfort?"

Luke cursed Jack soundly for tempting him, cursed himself for finding it so difficult to resist temptation. He'd never availed himself of one of Jack's girls.

"I'm not going to let Frannie see me walking out with one of your girls."

"I'll send her 'round the back. Frannie'll never know."

"You don't think your girls talk?"

"They're very discreet. I insist on it."

Luke considered, then shook his head. "No, I'll not risk causing her to doubt my affection."

"Are you saying you've been celibate all these years?"

"Of course not, but like your girls, I am extremely discreet." Dodger's was not the only place to offer female companionship. Besides, Frannie was less likely to hear of Luke's liaisons if he sought them out elsewhere. For a few years, he'd even had a mistress, but they had parted ways when Luke had decided that it was time to ask Frannie to be his wife.

"For God's sake, Frannie works here. She knows men have urges."

"I'm not going to have her wonder about mine. You might understand if you had someone you favored."

"I prefer my women bought. Ensures no misunderstandings."

And in Luke's experience, no real passion.

"So shall we make the usual wager for tomorrow?" Jack asked.

"By all means."

"It's been almost a year since you set yourself this task. I don't relish getting rich off my friends, so take care of the matter tomorrow, will you?"

"If you don't relish it then stop making the blasted wagers!"

"You know I have a weakness where wagering is concerned." A corner of his mouth hitched up. "And I can seldom beat you at cards."

"Tomorrow. I'll ask her tomorrow," Luke said with renewed conviction.

Jack clapped him on the shoulder. "Bring another fiver just in case."

It was all Luke could do to not punch that knowing smirk off Jack's face. But just as Frannie owed Luke, so he owed Jack a debt he could never repay.

Luke strode out of the building into the fog-shrouded night. His bones immediately began to ache, a reminder from too many nights sleeping in the cold. Now he kept the rooms of his residences unbearably warm simply because he could. Having spent his youth without many comforts, he indulged in all of them now. He'd developed a reputation for being eccentric and extravagant, for spending foolishly. But he could well afford to spend however he damned well pleased. Being in partnership with Jack ensured it.

Yes, investing in the vices paid handsomely.

Before he reached his coach, his liveried footman opened the door with a slight bow.

"Home straightaway," Luke said, as he climbed inside.

"Aye, m'lord."

The door closed, and Luke sat back against the plush seat. The well-sprung coach lurched forward. Gazing out the window, Luke could see little save the gray swirling mist. He didn't care for it much as it had a permanent place in his dreams.

Not that he dreamed often. In order to dream, one needed to sleep, and Luke seldom slept for any great length of time. He wasn't certain any of them did. Feagan's children. They were bound together by the things they'd done. Things the nobility could never comprehend being desperate enough to do.

It was one of the many reasons that he wasn't entirely comfortable with his place in the world. Shortly after the old gent's demise, Luke had attended a ball to publicly take his place as the new Earl of Claybourne, and a hush had descended over the crowd as soon as he'd been announced at the top of the stairs. He'd sauntered through the room, daring anyone to question his presence. No one had been able to meet his gaze.

An image flittered at the edge of his memory. One young lady had not only dared to hold his gaze, but had fairly challenged him. He wasn't certain why, but he thought of her on occasion. She was nothing like Frannie. Standing there in her elegant evening gown, with every strand of her blond hair tucked perfectly into place, she appeared spoiled and pampered. It was one of the reasons he abhorred the idea that he was now part of the aristocracy. They knew nothing of suffering. They knew nothing of the humiliation of scrounging for morsels of food. They weren't familiar with the sharp bite of the cane when begging didn't bring in enough coins or slipping hands into pockets didn't acquire enough handkerchiefs. They didn't know the fear of being caught. Even children were sent to prison, sometimes transported on great hulking ships to Australia or New Zealand, and on rare occasions, hanged.

The coach came to a halt, the door opened, and Luke alighted. He always felt a tad guilty upon first arriving at his London residence. Two dozen families could live there comfortably. Instead it was only he and two dozen servants. Of course, that would change once he married Frannie. Children would roam these hallways soon afterward. They'd experience a far gentler life than their parents had known.

The massive front door opened. He was surprised to find his butler still awake. Luke kept all hours, came and went as he pleased, when he pleased. He didn't expect his servants to live their lives according to his late-night habits.

Fitzsimmons had seen after the residence long before Luke ever came to live there with the old gent. The butler had been fiercely loyal to the previous earl, and not once—as far as Luke knew—had Fitzsimmons ever questioned the old gent's contention that Luke was his grandson.

Once the door was closed, Luke removed his hat and handed it to the butler. "I've told you before that you need not stay up until I return home."

"Yes, my lord, but I thought it best to do so this evening."

"And why is that?" Luke asked, tugging off his gloves.

"A lady arrived earlier."

Luke stilled. "Who?"

"She wouldn't say. She knocked at the servants' entrance, said it was of paramount importance—a matter of life and death were her precise words—that she speak with you. She's been waiting in the library ever since."

Luke glanced toward the hallway. "And you have no idea who she is?"

"No, my lord, although I would venture to guess she is a lady of the utmost quality. She has that air about her."

Over the years a few ladies of quality had sought out Luke's bed. He lived a life of abundance that many had wanted to embrace, but he always made it clear that he offered nothing permanent. Some had simply wanted to play with the devil for a time. But none had ever claimed visiting him was a matter of *life and death*. How dramatic. The remainder of his evening promised to be entertaining.

He handed his gloves to Fitzsimmons. "See that we're not disturbed."

"Yes, my lord."

His curiosity piqued, Luke strode down the hallway. No footman waited outside the door. He had no reason to believe his services would be required at this ungodly hour. Luke entered the library, slamming the door behind him, a grand entrance to disarm his visitor.

The woman standing at the window, gazing onto a garden hidden by darkness and fog, jerked around. The hood of her pelisse lay against her shoulders, its clasp interfering with what would have been a lovely show of skin from throat to bosom. Beneath the cloak, she'd dressed to seduce and for reasons he couldn't fathom, he was suddenly very much in the mood for seduction.

"Lady Catherine Mabry, as I recall," he drawled, sauntering nearer until he could smell the expensive perfume that wafted over her skin like the fragrance of a delicate rose.

Her blue eyes widened slightly. "I'd not realized you knew who I was."

"I make it my business to know who everyone is."

"You consider me your business?"

"Ah, yes, Lady Catherine. Isn't that what you wanted when you challenged me that night at the ball?"

"Not particularly, no," she muttered.

Mesmerized, he watched as her delicate throat moved ever so slightly as she swallowed—the only indication she gave that she was having second thoughts about being there. She was lovelier than he remembered—or perhaps it was simply that maturity agreed with her—and she still possessed the courage to hold his gaze. Or perhaps not. It wavered for a heartbeat as she glanced away while licking her lips. An invitation for something more intimate.

He trailed his finger along the soft flesh beneath her chin and her gaze jumped back to his. Beneath his touch, he could feel her pulse quickening, fluttering like a tiny moth that had dared to approach the flame and now realized it was left with no means of escape. It was obvious she was a novice when it came to the art of seduction, but no matter. He had enough experience to see them through.

"I know why you're here," he said, his voice low, provocative, a prelude to their lying beneath the silken sheets that adorned his bed.

She furrowed her delicate brow. Her features were exquisite perfection, carved by nature with obvious care and never altered by the harshness of life.

"How—" she began.

"Do not think you're the first to try to trap me into marriage. I'm not easily caught." He slid his finger along her flesh, down to the clasp at her throat. "I have little doubt your guardian stands just beyond the window, watching, waiting until the perfect moment to make his presence known." With nimble fingers, he loosened the clasp and carefully slid the cloak off her shoulders until it pooled on the floor.

His body tightened with his unobstructed view of all she had to offer. He'd gone too damned long without a woman beneath him. Even if he were snared by her trap he would escape it easily enough. Cradling her face, he leaned nearer until his breath mingled with hers. "But even if he witnesses my removing your clothing, even if he sees you welcoming me with open arms and crying out in ecstasy, I will not marry you," he whispered.

He heard her breath catch.

"I will not restore your reputation once tarnished." He brushed his lips over hers. "If you get with child, I will not give you respectability. The price you pay for waltzing with the devil is residing in hell."

He settled his mouth firmly over hers, not at all surprised that she acquiesced so easily. Even if she'd not come here to trap him, he knew what he was to her. A curiosity, nothing more. A bit of misbehavior before she settled into a respectable marriage with a lord whose lineage was never questioned behind his back.

She didn't resist when he urged her lips to part. She moaned when he swept his tongue through her mouth, leaving nothing unexplored. Her hands gripped the lapels of his jacket, and he thought for a moment that she swayed. He reacted with a need so strong that it almost brought him to his knees.

Even as he cursed her and his own weakness, he recognized that he had no will to resist temptation. He would have her. She'd brought this moment upon herself by arriving at his doorstep. He was a man who always took advantage of opportunities presented, and she was presenting him with an opportunity for passion. It had been too long since he'd unleashed his desires. She would benefit from all that he had to offer this night, but no more than that. In the morning, she'd take nothing from him except the memories.

Tearing his mouth from hers, he bracketed her face between his hands and held her gaze. "Be sure this is what you want, my lady, for there will be no undoing once this is done."

Her breaths coming in short gasps, she shook her head. "You misunderstand my purpose in coming here."

"Do I?" he asked mockingly.

She nodded. "I want someone dispensed with. And I hear you're just the man to do it."

Chapter 2

If Catherine hadn't been standing so extremely close to Claybourne that their hearts fairly beat in the same erratic rhythm, she'd have thought he'd received a brutal blow. Although he seemed to recover quickly enough as he released his hold on her and stepped back, his face once more an unreadable mask.

His expression had been just as inscrutable when he'd first walked into the room. While she was certain his butler had told him that a lady had come to call, Claybourne had not even looked surprised to discover *she* was the one waiting for him. It was only when he'd drawn back from the kiss that she'd seen any emotion at all, and she could have sworn it was desire. Desire for her specifically? Hardly likely. It was no doubt nothing more than lust unleashed and the particular woman standing before him of no consequence.

He was known for flirting at the edge of respectability, and he was no doubt accustomed to dragging others over the precipice with him.

But to her immense shame, she couldn't help but think it would be a lovely way to go. In the secret recesses of her mind where wickedness lurked, she'd dreamed of him kissing her, but never in her wildest fantasies had she imagined that his lips would be so soft, his mouth so hot, his tongue so determined to have its way. What their mouths had been doing was quite uncivilized, and even though she knew she should have stepped away, she should have objected, she should have slapped him, all she'd wanted was to deepen the intimacy. He tasted of a flavor she'd never before experienced. He was bold with his explorations, enticing her to forget all she'd learned of decorum.

With his mouth playing over hers, he'd succeeded in making her body thrum madly and burn with desire as it never had. She'd been halfway tempted to follow where he was leading, but more was at stake than satisfying her own yearnings. His earlier words had convinced her that he'd hold no respect for her if she succumbed to his charms, as no doubt many a woman had before her, and at this stage of the game she needed to have the upper hand.

Giving her his back, he walked to a small table where an assortment of crystal decanters rested. He took the top off one and poured amber liquid into one glass, and then another.

"Dispensed with? Such gentle words. I assume you mean you want someone killed," he stated flatly.

"Yes." Reaching down, she gathered up her pelisse, holding it close as though it had the power to stop her trembling. Dear God, but she wanted to reach out to him, run her hands over his back, his shoulders. She wanted to comb her fingers through his thick, black hair. She wanted to press her body against his. Waltz with the devil, indeed. Lord save her, she wanted to lie with him.

Turning from the table, he held a glass toward her. Swallowing hard, forcing her body not to reveal its inner quivering, she reached for the glass, pausing as her gaze fell on the inside of his right thumb, scarred with a series of raised welts as though someone had repeatedly slashed at him. Upon further inspection, she realized more than a knife had been used. He'd been burned as well.

"Staring at it won't make it look any prettier," he said.

She snapped her gaze up to his. "My apologies. I—" She could say nothing to make the matter right, so she simply took the glass he offered. "Thank you."

His gaze roamed over her. Disdainfully. It was all she could do to keep holding her head high, but hold it high she did.

He brushed past her and dropped into a chair, lounging insolently. Gone was any semblance of him being a gentleman, any hint that he viewed her as a lady. Although in truth, he'd ceased to be a gentleman the moment his warm, pliant lips had met hers. Even now her body heated with the memory of his mouth urging hers to open for him, to welcome the thrust of his tongue. And in the welcoming she'd ceased to be a lady, but she could regain her footing easily enough by simply reverting back to her upbringing.

He took a long swallow, then with the hand holding the glass, indicated the chair opposite him. Not certain how much longer her quaking legs could support her, she gracefully sat, ever mindful of her posture, determined to remain a lady, even if he were no longer acting the gentleman. Since that first night, at least a thousand times, she'd imagined being in his presence, but not like this. They were always in a ballroom, their gazes meeting across the crowded room—

"Who?" he asked.

The brusqueness of his tone brought her back to the moment. She wrapped both hands around the glass. "Pardon?"

He sighed with impatience. "Who do you want killed?"

"I won't tell you until I know for certain that you're willing to do it."

"Why?"

"Because I don't want you warning him if you're not going to take care of the matter—"

"No," he interrupted brusquely.

Disappointment slammed into her. She considered arguing, but she felt almost undone by the kiss and his complete disregard for her plight. Despising the small tremors cascading through her and determined to make as dignified an exit as possible, she stood. "Thank you for your time then."

"No," he ground out. "I wasn't saying I wouldn't do it. I said no because you're answering the wrong question."

"Pardon?"

"I wasn't asking why you wouldn't tell me

who he was. I was inquiring as to the reason you wanted him killed."

"Oh." She sat back down. Hope returned like a fledgling bird learning to fly. "I'm afraid I can't tell you that either."

He took another swallow of his brandy, studying her over the rim of his glass. It was all she could do not to squirm. He wasn't what she'd call classically handsome. His nose was slightly bent and uneven across the top as though at one time it might have been smashed. Oddly, it added strength to a face that might have appeared a bit too elegant otherwise. He was in need of a shave, but at this time of night, she suspected most men were. She could still feel where his dark whiskers had abraded her chin and cheeks as he'd kissed her.

She closed her eyes and fought back those carnal images and her body's embarrassing reaction to them. Her lips were still tingling and swollen. She wondered if they'd ever again feel normal. Apparently being spawned from the depths of hell caused everything about a man to be exceedingly hot. She was surprised she'd not burned to a cinder.

"How many men have you kissed?" he suddenly asked.

Her eyes flew open, and—*Drat it!*—she squirmed. She considered lying, but what was to be gained by deception? She suspected he did enough deceiving for both of them. "Only tonight."

He took another long swallow, scrutinizing her again. She didn't like when he studied her. She didn't like it at all. She was reminded of that first night, at the ball, when she'd felt as though he'd been measuring her worth—and had decided she was worth very little.

"But I'm not here to discuss kisses. I'm here to discuss—"

"Yes, yes, whether I'll kill someone for you. And you expect me to take you at your word that he deserves killing without even telling me what he's done. For all I know perhaps he neglected to ask you for a dance."

"Surely, you don't think I'm as trite as all that."

"I know little about you, Lady Catherine, except that you have no qualms about visiting a gentleman in the dead of night. Perhaps you visited this gent, he rebuffed you, and you took offense."

"I'm not in the habit of visiting gentlemen in the dead of night."

"Your actions would speak otherwise."

"Do you judge all by their actions?"

"They are more telling than their words."

"And you no doubt have considerable experience with false words."

One corner of his mouth eased up slightly, a mocking imitation of a smile. "Most women fawn over a gentleman when they wish him to do their bidding."

She glanced down at the glass in her hands. She wondered if she drank its contents if she'd find her retreating courage at its bottom. "I meant no insult."

"Did you not?"

She lifted her gaze back to his. "Yes, I suppose I did."

His eyes widening slightly, he seemed surprised by the truth of her answer.

"So what did the gentleman do to earn your displeasure? Mock your gown? Step on your toes while waltzing? Present you with wilted flowers?"

"My reasons are my own, my lord. You'll not goad me into telling you. Our arrangement will involve nothing more than you're agreeing to take care of the matter at which point I'll tell you who is to be taken care of."

"Why should I agree to this? What is the benefit to me?"

"I shall pay you handsomely for this service."

His harsh laughter, echoing between the walls lined with shelves laden with books, somehow seemed at home here. As though masculinity ruled and no space was allowed for anything of a kinder nature. "Lady Catherine, money is the one thing of which I have absolutely no need."

She'd feared that would be the case, leaving her in a weak bargaining position. What could she offer him? She'd heard enough rumors to know he wasn't a man who did anything as a result of having a charitable heart. "What are you in need of then, my lord?"

"From you—nothing."

"Surely you are in need of something that your present circumstance can't provide."

He stood. "Nothing that would cause me to kill a man simply because you wish him dead. You've wasted your time by coming here. Please see yourself out."

Dismissing her, he walked back to the corner

and began refilling his glass. She wouldn't beg, but neither would she give up quite so easily. She rose to her feet. "Is there nothing you want so desperately that you'd be willing to do anything in order to acquire it?"

"If you want him dead that badly, kill him yourself."

"I fear I'll botch it. I suspect it takes a certain type of individual to complete the act when the reality of it comes rushing home."

"A man like me perhaps? A coldhearted bastard?"

"Did you—did you kill him? Did you kill your uncle?" She couldn't believe she'd asked the impudent question. The words had rushed out before she'd had a chance to stop them.

He downed the amber liquid and poured more into his glass. "What answer would satisfy you, Lady Catherine?"

"An honest one."

Turning slightly, he met her gaze. "No, I did not kill my uncle."

And in spite of his answer, which his unwavering gaze revealed to be the absolute truth, the fine hairs on the nape of her neck prickled, and she no longer had any wish to linger in his presence. She'd been a fool to come here, but then desperation often created fools.

"I'm sorry to have bothered you, my lord."

"No bother, Lady Catherine. The kiss was well worth the intrusion on my evening."

She angled her chin haughtily. "A pity I cannot claim the same."

His dark laughter followed her out of the library,

and she had little doubt that the sound of it would filter into her dreams, along with the memory of his lips pressed against hers. Visiting the devil had been a mistake, and she could only pray that her actions wouldn't return to haunt her.

Damn her. Damn her. Damn her.

Lounging in the stuffed, brocade armchair, Luke drained the last of the whiskey from the bottle, before hurling it against the wall. Breathing heavily, he dropped his head back. The room was swirling around him, the darkness closing in. It was the third bottle he'd finished. One more should do it. One more should numb him to the gruesome images of innocence lost that were bombarding him. One more should shove them back into the darkest corners of his mind. One more should swallow the remorse, the guilt, the regret.

While others had prayed to God, he'd given his soul to the devil to find the strength to do what needed to be done. And now a stupid chit was asking him to do it again.

Damn her!

She'd sent him invitations to her silly balls as though they were important, as though an evening spent in her company was well worth his time. What did she know of torment? What did she know of hell? Doing her bidding would only serve to drag her down into it, and once there, she'd find no escape. He knew that truth well enough.

Reaching down, he grabbed another bottle from the little army he'd lined up on the floor beside his chair. He'd had too many nights like this one not to know where to turn for comfort when a woman wasn't near.

Damn, he should have brought one of Jack's girls home. Not even Frannie would be able to offer him solace. He'd never be able to take her with the desperation that clawed at him now. What he needed was a woman strong enough to meet his powerful thrusts without flinching, a woman who wouldn't cower, a woman who could call to the beast in him and have no desire to tame it.

An image of Lady Catherine Mabry writhing beneath him filled his mind, and he flung the half-emptied bottle across the room. He cursed her yet again. He fought so hard to remain civilized, not to revert to his roots, and she'd managed to completely undo him. He should have lifted her into his arms and carried her to his bedchamber; he should have shown her exactly what he was capable of.

Murder? Dear God, as he'd proven, he was capable of far worse than that.

From the Journal of Lucian Langdon

I did not know the name of the man I killed. I did not know that destiny had proclaimed him to be heir to a title.

I knew only that he had harmed Frannie—cruelly and without mercy. So I took it upon myself to be his judge, jury, and executioner.

Unfortunately in my haste to see justice delivered, I did not take proper precautions. There was a witness, and I was promptly arrested.

In hindsight, I can see that I was arrogant to believe that I alone had the wisdom to determine his fate. But I was intimately familiar with the judicial system, having been arrested at the age of eight. I served three months in prison. I bore the mark of my crime upon my right thumb. A T, for thief, burned into the tender flesh.

A year after my incarceration, it was determined that the practice of marking criminals in that cruel manner should be stopped. And so it was.

I knew prison was not a pleasant place. I knew some criminals were transported on great hulking ships away from England's shore, but I didn't know the particulars and so I could not judge the fairness of it.

I'd attended a public hanging or two. It seemed a harsh way to go.

But still I was not willing to risk that the man who'd hurt Frannie would go unpunished or that his punishment would not fit his crime. So I killed him.

The policeman who arrested me assured me that I'd soon find myself dancing upon the wind. I listened to his grave predictions with stoicism for I had no regrets. When someone harms those whom we love, we must do as we must. And I had always loved Frannie.

I was waiting in an interrogation room at Whitehall Place when they brought in an old gent. Vengeance burned in his eyes and I knew, without being told, that it was his son I had killed. By his dress and manner, I recognized that he was a man with the power to see me delivered into hell.

He stared at me for the longest, and I stared back. Since my arrest, I'd spoken not one word, other than my name. I neither denied nor confirmed the charges.

"Always 'old yer tongue," Feagan had advised us on the matter of being arrested. "No matter wot ye tell 'em, truth or lie, they'll twist it around to suit their own purposes."

I'd learned early on that Feagan's words were not to be dismissed. He knew of what he spoke.

Then the old gent did the strangest thing. He stepped forward, clamped his gloved hand around my chin, and turned my face one way and then the other. "I need more light," he declared.

More lamps were brought in and set upon the table, until I felt completely exposed. The anger in the old gent's eyes changed into something softer, an emotion I didn't recognize.

"What is it, my lord?" an inspector asked.

"I think he's my grandson," the old gent rasped.

"The one that went missing?"

The old gent nodded once, and I saw a way out of my predicament. Already I had learned how to read people. I knew what the old gent wanted. With my answers to his questions, I deceived him into believing it was me.

When he was convinced that I was his grandson, he told the inspectors to give us a moment alone. He sat in a chair across from me.

"Did you kill my son?" he asked.

I nodded once.

"Why?"

For the first time that night, I spoke the truth. In the end, it was the truth that convinced the old man that I was redeemable. It would be some time before he forgave me completely.

My salvation and my punishment were to live my life as his grandson.

Chapter 3

"It's so monstrously difficult to decide," the Duchess of Avendale said. "I don't know which one would be best."

Looking across the small table in her garden, she caught Catherine in the midst of an embarrassing yawn, not that the duchess seemed to notice. She pushed the selections across the table. "Which do you favor?"

"Winnie, you're selecting parchment for invitations," Catherine told her. "Great Britain will not fall because of your decision. Which one do you like best?"

Winnie gnawed on her lower lip. "I don't know. I think I like the look of the cream, but it's more expensive. Is it worth it?"

"If it pleases you then it's worth the extra expense."

"It's not I who has to be pleased, it's my husband. The stationer is expecting me this afternoon. Will you come with me to make sure I do the invitations properly?"

Winnie had been Catherine's dearest friend

since they were small girls. It bothered Catherine immeasurably to see Winnie's confidence waning. "You've given balls before. You know how to properly order invitations."

"But Avendale is always disappointed in some aspect of the affair. I want everything to be perfect."

Catherine couldn't believe there were many men in London who truly gave a fig about ball preparations. It was Winnie's misfortune that she'd married one of them. Always striving for perfection, he made her life miserable and took the joy out of every task.

"There's no such thing as perfection, and even if there were, I think it'd be rather boring. Still, let's go with the cream color," Catherine said. "I think it looks a bit more elegant and I'll purchase the invitations."

"That's not necessary."

"It's the least I can do. You're letting me host the ball with you, at your lovely home, since Father's ill and it wouldn't be proper to have a ball in mine. So I'll see to the invitations."

"If you're sure you don't mind."

"I don't mind at all."

Winnie released a deep breath. "Thank you. That's one less thing to worry about."

"I'll stop by the stationers on my way home."

"You're such a dear."

Catherine yawned again. "Sorry."

"I don't recall there being any balls last night, and yet since the moment you arrived, I've had the distinct impression you were out rather late," Winnie said.

"I simply didn't sleep well."

"Is it your father? Has his condition worsened?"

It should have been her father keeping her from sleep. It had been almost a year since his last bout with apoplexy had left him a bed-ridden invalid. Now he was little more than a shell of a man. She spent her afternoons and often her evenings reading to him, trying to bring him what comfort she could. She'd hired nurses to see after him when she couldn't be there, because she'd known he'd feel guilty if he thought she was devoting all her time to him. She was young. He'd want her to enjoy life. But of late, that was very difficult to accomplish.

"No, Father seems to be the same, although it's difficult to tell since he can't speak."

"What's pressing on your mind then?"

A certain irritating lord. Somehow he'd managed to cast some sort of spell over her body to make it writhe unsatisfied for the remainder of the night, not that there had been much remaining after she'd finally gone to bed. What sort of debauchery had he been engaged in to return home so late? And to immediately assume that a woman such as she was there for carnal purposes? Only the worst of blackguards would view women in such a way. Catherine wasn't a trollop. She was chaste and pure and proper. Although after tasting his kiss, she realized her life was rather dull. Still, his actions had resulted in her finally comprehending why ladies were discouraged from experiencing such intimacies until they were wed. Did all men hold such power over women—to make them burn with desire? Or was it only those like Claybourne, who loitered at the gates of hell?

"Winnie, you've been married for five years now."

She'd attracted the Duke of Avendale's attention their very first Season and had married him at Christmas that same year.

Winnie furrowed her brow. "Is that a question?"

"No, it's an observation that I felt compelled to make before asking: Does he kiss you?"

"That's an odd question."

"I'm a maiden and I have no mother to ask about the questions that cause me curiosity, and so I must turn to my married friend for the answers. Does he kiss you?"

Winnie sipped her tea as though mulling over her answer. "On occasion."

"Does it leave you wanting?"

"Wanting what?"

Catherine almost laughed. If she had to explain it, well, then he wasn't kissing as Claybourne did. But Avendale had been born a gentleman, while Claybourne was little more than a scoundrel dressed in lord's clothing.

She watched as Winnie leaned forward ever so slightly to pour them more tea. It was ironic that such beauty as found in this garden surrounded a house where incredible ugliness lurked. Her movements explained so much about her unnecessary worry over the invitations. "He's beaten you again, hasn't he, Winnie?"

"Don't be silly."

Reaching out, Catherine placed her hand over her friend's, stilling her actions. "I see how gingerly you move—as though the smallest of movements causes you the greatest of pain. You can confide in me. I won't tell a soul. You know that."

Tears welled in Winnie's expressive eyes. "He came home late last night in a fit of temper. I'm not sure what I did wrong—"

"I doubt you did anything wrong, and even if you did, he has no right to strike you."

"The law disagrees."

"Damn the law."

Gasping, Winnie widened her eyes. "Catherine, your language."

"You chastise me for my language and yet I wager you take his beatings in silence."

"I'm his wife, his property. The law gives him leave to do with me as he pleases, even force his attentions on me when I might not want them. A day will come when you'll learn the truth of marriage."

"I doubt I shall ever marry. But if I should, I'll not give a man control over me."

"You've only managed to escape marriage because your father is infirmed and your brother traipses over the continents. Once he returns and settles into his responsibilities, including those toward you, everything will change."

No, it wouldn't. Catherine was stronger than Winnie. Although she had to readily admit she'd grown more independent after Sterling left. Her father had begun to teach her things, for fear that her wanderlust brother might not return from his travels. Since her father had fallen ill, she'd taken it upon herself to step into his shoes as much as possible. She knew her forceful nature no doubt intimidated some and was whispered about by others. But she'd not let her father's legacy fall into decay or disarray.

"I'm all of two and twenty, Winnie, and no man has indicated an interest in having me as a wife."

"It's because of the way the Devil Earl looked at you that night as though he was singling you out—and the way you peered back. You should have lowered your gaze as any decent woman would. Now you are tainted by him."

Catherine forced herself to laugh. If Winnie knew that Catherine had done a good deal more than look at him recently, had actually welcomed his kiss, she'd no doubt expire on the spot.

"He was striving to intimidate. I'm not one to be intimidated. It seemed the perfect opportunity to demonstrate that part of my character," Catherine said.

"What you demonstrated was that you are willful. No man wants a willful wife."

"Then no man shall have me, for I'll not change to please him."

"When you love a man, you will do anything to gain his favor."

"Even allow him to beat you?"

Winnie flinched, and while Catherine regretted the harshness of her words, she didn't know how else to make her dear friend listen—for her own good. "Leave him, Winnie. Come with me. We'll go to my father's house in the country. You'll find sanctuary there."

"Do you have any idea how furious my husband would be? He would find me, Catherine, and he would kill me for so blatant a betrayal. I have no doubt. He is a proud man, and when his pride is threatened—"

"He strikes out at you, because he hasn't the courage to face his own weaknesses."

"You think so poorly of him."

"Why should I think otherwise? I see what he does to you. You strive to hide it, but I fear a day will come when it can't be hidden."

"Not five minutes ago, you were asking if he kissed me. He does and sometimes it's very lovely."

"Lovely? No. A kiss should be all-consuming, make your knees weaken, your heart pound . . ." Her voice trailed off as she shook her head. She was getting carried away, remembering Claybourne's kiss.

"Catherine, what have you done?"

"Nothing."

"You're acting most peculiar and your description . . . Have you had a dalliance?"

"Don't be ridiculous."

"Then why this sudden interest in kisses?"

"I'm simply trying to determine why you put up with all that you do. What does he give you that makes any of it worth it?"

"It is a woman's place to stand by her husband."

Catherine squeezed Winnie's hand. "Winnie, I'm not your family who insists you be the good daughter and the good wife. It breaks my heart to see you suffer like this."

Tears rolled from Winnie's eyes. "Oh, Catherine, sometimes he terrifies me so. They say his first wife was clumsy and fell down the stairs. And his second slipped in the bedchamber and banged her head so hard on the floor that it killed her. I knew these tales, but I didn't doubt the veracity of them, not until after I was wed. He is so charming when he is not angry. Oh, but when he is displeased, he is most frightening."

"Then leave him."

"I can't!" she ground out. "The law will not protect me. He can claim that I abandoned him and the law will give him my son. My family will be mortified and not stand beside me, and my husband, dear God, Catherine, the fury he will exhibit will pale in comparison to anything he has revealed before. I know it as surely as I know that our tea has grown cold. It will be miserable for everyone. It's best if I simply accept my fate and strive to appease him in all matters."

Catherine released Winnie's hand and leaned back. "Oh, Winnie, I hate what he has done to you. The physical abuse is bad enough, but what he has done to ruin the lovely woman who resided inside you—I shall never forgive him for that."

Grimacing, Winnie reached across the table and took Catherine's hand. "I know how headstrong you can be. You must never confront him about this matter, you must never let on that you know. If he feels threatened, Catherine, dear Lord, save us both."

"He will never know from me how much I despise him."

Winnie seemed to physically relax, her deathgrip on Catherine's hand easing. "Can we change the subject now? It serves to only burden my heart further to know that I cause you such worry."

"Don't be concerned with my feelings, Winnie. I love you. No matter what happens, that will not change."

"Mummy!"

A small boy of four raced across the garden, leaving his nanny behind. He slammed into Winnie. Gasping, she paled considerably. "Darling, you mustn't jostle Mummy so."

The boy looked wounded at the sharp reprimand. Catherine realized that Winnie was hurt much worse than she was letting on. She never scolded her child. Never.

"Whit, come see Auntie Catherine," Catherine said. "My lap is in need of a child."

He rushed over and Catherine pulled him close. She wondered how long before his father took his frustrations out on him.

It was late in the afternoon when Catherine finally returned home. How would she ever live with the guilt if Avendale killed Winnie? How would she be able to look at herself in the mirror if she did nothing—knowing all that was happening?

She had an abundance of acquaintances, friends, servants, and yet sometimes she felt so alone. She had no one other than Winnie in whom she felt she could confide all that troubled her. Yet, she dared not tell Winnie everything, because her dear friend was already weighted down with her own troubles, so Catherine carried her worries and her burdens alone.

Weary, with a heavy heart, she climbed the stairs and stopped outside her father's bedchamber.

Since he'd fallen ill, she'd achieved an independence that few ladies ever did. Without her brother here to serve as her guardian, she could do as she pleased and answer to no one.

Was Winnie right? Would she lose this freedom if she ever did marry? Or was Catherine right—and no man would ever consider her?

Even as a child, she'd been a bit willful. *All right,* she scolded herself. *A lot willful.* Her brother had called her spoiled on more than one occasion. Not that he was one to point fingers. He was the one off touring the world, having his fun, sewing his wild oats, while she was left here to tend to their father. Although to be fair, Sterling didn't know their father had taken ill.

After her father's first apoplectic fit, he'd still been able to talk. He'd told her then that she wasn't to contact Sterling for any reason. The next fit had left him unable to speak, to communicate at all. He was now simply withering away.

She took a moment to shore up her emotions. She'd not add to her father's problems by weeping for her friend, weeping for him, weeping for everything she didn't have the strength or power to change. She took a deep breath, opened the door, and stepped inside. She was immediately hit with the stench of illness.

His nurse rose from her chair near his bed, where she'd been embroidering. She curtsied. "My lady."

"How is he?"

"All bathed and tidied up, awaiting your afternoon visit."

Catherine walked to the foot of the bed and smiled down on her father. She thought she saw pleasure in his blue eyes, but perhaps it was only wishful thinking on her part. "It's a lovely day. I should have a servant carry you into the garden."

He didn't react to her suggestion, other than to blink.

She wondered if he'd be embarrassed—or grateful—to be carted down. It was so difficult to know what to do.

"Temperance, before you take some time for yourself, please have the servants move the chaise longue from the morning room to the garden and then send a footman up to carry my father down."

"If I may be so bold, my lady, I'm not certain his physician would agree with that action. It may do more harm than good."

Then Catherine might have her father's death on her conscience. Avendale's she could live with, but her father's—

She sighed. "Ask his physician the next time he comes to check on the duke."

"Yes, my lady."

It seemed as though Catherine could do so little to make her father comfortable.

"I'll be visiting with my father for the next hour," Catherine told her. "Take some time for yourself."

"Thank you, my lady."

Catherine sat in the chair and took her father's hand. He moved his head only slightly to look at her. He awkwardly rubbed the ring she'd begun wearing on her right hand.

"I've taken to wearing Mother's wedding ring. Is that all right?"

He made a sound deep in his throat. Taking a linen handkerchief from a stack on the bedside table, she wiped the spittle from the corner of his mouth.

"I wish you could tell me what you wanted." She brushed her fingers through his thinning silver hair. "I hope you're not in pain."

With a sigh, she sat back and lifted a book from the bedside table. "Let's see what sort of trouble Oliver and the Artful Dodger are going to get into today, shall we?"

"Expected to be collecting from you sooner," Jack said as he welcomed Luke into their establishment that evening.

"I went away for a bit."

Three days to be exact. The worst part was when he returned from the brink of despair, when the liquor had served its purpose and its effect began fading. His head hurt, his stomach roiled, and he felt like bloody hell. It was a strange thing for a man such as he, a man who'd done the things he'd done, to be hit with a bit of conscience. It was always worse at night, when he faced his own demons alone. All that would change once he married Frannie. She'd distract him from his somber musings. She'd bring light into his darkness. She'd be his salvation.

"Into a bottle?" Jack asked.

"I don't see that it's any of your concern."

Jack shrugged. "It's not. I just wondered if I should send another case of my finest Irish whiskey round to your residence."

Luke hated admitting his weakness, even to Jack. "Yes, see to it. Tonight if possible."

"Consider it done."

Luke was well aware of Jack studying him. He also knew his friend wouldn't ask what had prompted his latest fall, so Luke was surprised when he heard himself blurt, "I had a visit from Lady Catherine Mabry."

Jack furrowed his brow. "Mabry?"

"Daughter to the Duke of Greystone."

One of Jack's eyebrows shot up. "My, my. Aren't we keeping distinguished company of a sudden?"

"She wanted me to kill someone."

His other brow shot up. "Who's the unlucky bloke?"

"She wouldn't say."

"I assume you declined to do her bidding."

"You assume correctly."

"Were you bothered that she had little doubt you could carry out her request?"

He was bothered by the fact that she thought he *would* carry it out. With no explanation, no justification as though he was a man accustomed to washing blood off his hands. But he wasn't going to confess all that to Jack so he held his silence.

Jack slapped him on the shoulder. "Don't be troubled, my friend. They're no better than we are; the only difference is we know it, recognize our faults, and readily admit to having them."

"I'm supposed to be one of them, Jack." But he'd never felt comfortable around them, never felt as though he belonged.

"But we both know you're not."

Jack was the only one who knew the truth of Luke's deceptions, knew he'd pretended to recall what the old gent wanted him to.

"No, I'm not."

"Don't know why you feel so damned guilty about it."

"I grew fond of the old gent. It didn't seem quite right to deceive him."

The old gent had loved Luke because he'd thought Luke was his grandson. It was one thing to fool someone into giving him a coin so his stomach wouldn't ache when he went to sleep that night. It wasn't quite as easy to swallow the notion that he had tricked someone into giving him his heart.

"You made him happy, Luke. It's not often that we're able to do something that causes a person to die as the old gent did, content and satisfied, knowing that his kingdom was safe in your hands—and believing that in your hands it rightfully belonged. Draw some comfort in that."

He tried. He really did. "I'm taking Frannie out for a while."

Jack grinned cockily, but then everything about him was cocky and self-assured. He'd even swaggered when they were in prison, as though it were all a grand joke, when Luke had never been more terrified in his entire life.

"Finally going to do it, huh?" Jack asked.

"I think you've made enough money off me."

"I'll never have enough, but you're right. I'm tired of collecting on this wager. It's grown boring. Go make her—and yourself—happy."

That was Luke's plan as he strode through the establishment, briefly acknowledging those of his acquaintance, until he made his way to the back where he knew he'd find Frannie. She did her good works during the daylight hours, but at night she saw to Jack's books. She was sitting at the desk, with her hair pinned up in a no-nonsense type of bun. She wore her usual non-enticing clothing and yet he was enticed, as always.

"Good evening, Frannie."

She glanced up, without being startled this time. He'd no doubt caught her before she'd immersed herself fully in the numbers.

"I expected you to come by sooner for an accounting of how I spent your donation."

"I was occupied with other business. Besides, I told you that you didn't owe me an accounting. I was wondering, however, if you might be willing to take a ride with me in the coach."

"Whatever for?"

"I just thought it would be nice to get away from Jack's books for a while. There's no fog yet and London at night can be quite breathtaking. I'd like to share it with you."

"You sound so mysterious."

"We've not had much time together of late, and I always enjoy your company, as you well know."

"I could show you the children's home. The building is almost completed."

"I'd like that."

As she stood, she gave him the same sweet smile that always warmed him. He snatched her shawl from the hat rack near the door and draped it around her shoulders. Then he extended his arm. Shyly, she placed her hand on his forearm. Neither spoke a word until they reached his coach and the footman opened the door. She halted as Luke was assisting her inside. Her smile bright, she looked back over her shoulder at him. "It's filled with flowers."

"Yes, I thought they'd bring you pleasure."

"They must have cost you a fortune."

He heard the gentle scolding in her voice. She didn't believe in frivolous spending, and her attitude only served to diminish his pleasure at giving her a gift.

"I can well afford it, Frannie."

"You're far too generous, Luke."

Sometimes he didn't think he was generous enough. She climbed inside, and he followed, sitting opposite her, the fragrance of the flowers almost nauseating. An abundance of bouquets were arranged on either side of her. He'd have his footman carry them to her living quarters when they returned.

As the coach rolled along the street, the dim light of the lantern inside allowed him to have a shadowy view of her. He always took such delight in watching her, and the confines of the conveyance created an intimacy that he'd not been able to achieve while she sat at her desk with her ledgers before her. Leaning forward, he took her bare hands in his. While he knew it was improper for his bare skin to touch hers, it somehow seemed appropriate at this moment. He'd memorized Shakespeare's twenty-ninth sonnet to recite to her, but he suddenly felt that he should rely on his own words, as inadequate as they might be. "Frannie, I adore you. I always have. Will you honor me by becoming my wife?"

Her smile withered, her fingers tightened around his. She shook her head jerkily. "Luke, I can't," she whispered hoarsely, and he heard the terror in her voice.

He closed his hands more firmly around hers. "Frannie—"

"Luke, please—"

"Frannie, allow me to finish."

She nodded.

"I know your only experience"—how to say it without terrifying her more—"with a man was nothing short of brutal, but I assure you that in my bed you'll find nothing except tenderness. I will be as gentle as a man can possibly be. I will never force you, nor will I rush you. I'll wait until you're ready. It will be good between us, Frannie. I swear to you."

He saw tears brimming in her eyes. "Please don't cry, sweetheart."

She lifted his hands and pressed her lips to his knuckles. "I know you would never harm me, Luke, but you are a lord and I"—she released a bitter laugh—"I don't even know my real name. Do you think there is actually a family somewhere in London named Darling who has no idea what happened to their daughter? I'm Frannie Darling because that's how Feagan referred to me. 'Frannie, darling, rub my feet.' 'Frannie, darling, fetch me a cuppa gin.' And so when your grandfather asked me my name, I said Frannie Darling. I was a child. What did I know?"

"I don't care about your origins," he said roughly.

"You know who your family is. I have no idea, and a lady who becomes a peer should know."

He could confess to her that he didn't know who his family was any more than she did hers, but to know of his deceit wouldn't endear him to her. If anything it could cause him to lose her completely. While she'd always known he harbored doubts about the old gent, she'd never known that his doubts were justified, that he'd done all in his power to convince the old gent he was his grandson. She'd never known that he'd lied, deceived, tricked the old gent into seeing what he wanted to see. Death waiting in the shadows was a powerful motivator, but even then he didn't think she'd forgive him for taking so much that didn't belong to him. But he was spoiled now from having. He didn't want to give it back. He wouldn't give it back.

"Frannie, don't think of yourself as becoming a peer. Think of yourself as becoming my wife. That's all that matters to me."

"How can you say that, Luke? Good Lord, you sit in the House of Lords. The responsibility that comes with your position is overwhelming. And it falls to the wife to know all manner of etiquette and rules. When we have people over for dinner—"

"We won't have dinners."

"And when I'm presented to the queen? Do you

know how I am to dress? Do you know what behavior I must and must not exhibit?"

"You could learn. The old gent gave you lessons. He hired tutors."

"They taught me to read, write, cipher, and speak properly. But dear God, Luke, your grandfather never expected me to become a peer. He saw that I was taught to serve, not to be served.

"Please don't ask this of me. I owe you everything. You saved my life." Tears rolled along her cheeks. "But please don't ask this of me. Please don't ask me to step into your world. The very thought of it terrifies me. It would be such a lonely place."

The very reason he wanted her there. Because he was so damned lonely. There were times when he thought he'd die of the loneliness, times when he could imagine no worse hell than to be caught between two worlds. To live in one, but belong in the other.

"Frannie—"

"Please, Luke, I don't want to hurt you, but I can't marry you. I simply can't. It will destroy me."

"You're stronger than you give yourself credit for."

"But I'm not as strong as you. I could never do the things you've done."

Sometimes, he thought that he'd have been better off letting them drop the noose around his neck.

"Is there nothing I can say to sway you?" he asked.

Slowly she shook her head.

With a sigh, he released her hands, leaned back, and gazed out the window. The fog was rolling in. It somehow seemed symbolic. "I hope you don't mind if I'd rather not go see your children's home."

"I'm so frightfully sorry—"

"Don't, Frannie, don't keep apologizing. It only makes matters worse."

"I do love you, you know," she said softly.

Which only served to make everything all the more unbearable.

Luke lined up his little soldiers, grateful for the bottles of whiskey that Jack had seen delivered tonight as promised. Then Luke sat in his chair and began gulping the contents of the first bottle.

Frannie had refused him and cut him to the core by doing it. He'd put off asking her to marry him not because he'd thought she'd deny him, but because he couldn't quite convince himself that he was deserving of her—that he was deserving of any woman.

But to have her refuse him because she feared this life . . . Had living here been that hard on her?

The old gent had taken her and a few of Feagan's lads in when he'd discovered Luke sneaking them into the house to feed them and give them a warm place for the night. He'd watched them closely, not quite trusting them. He'd hired tutors. He'd seen that they were taught proper behavior.

So what was Frannie afraid of? What did she think she didn't know? Or was there more to her refusal than he wanted to accept? Was it the darkness that resided within him that she couldn't live with and she was simply too kind to admit it?

Luke tossed the empty bottle aside. He reached for another and something beneath the far chair caught his eye. He stood and the room spun. Dropping to his knees, he crawled to the chair, reached beneath it, and folded his fingers around the object. Turning, he put his back against the chair and studied the clasp.

Lady Catherine's clasp. It must have fallen from her pelisse. One of his servants wasn't taking as much care with the floor as she should, but he wasn't particularly upset about her shoddy work. He felt the smallest movement of his mouth as though a smile were forming as he remembered Catherine's bravado, remembered her surprise that he knew her name.

Oh, yes, he'd known who she was. He'd uncovered that little truth the first night he'd set eyes on her. Even the most loyal of servants favored their pockets over their masters. Offering a few coins, he'd found someone willing to hide in the bushes, peer through the window with him, and identify the lady Luke pointed out.

He'd not been surprised to find her in his library. He'd been surprised only that it had taken her so long to make an appearance. That night at the ball he'd felt an immediate attraction, the intensity greater than any he'd experienced before or since.

He'd always assumed that if he'd first met Frannie as a young woman, his attraction for her would have hit him as hard, if not harder. But they were children when they'd first been introduced and they'd grown into affection.

He rubbed his thumb over the clasp. Catherine was different. Catherine was—

He heard the laughter echoing around him, only vaguely aware that he was responsible for the sound.

Catherine was the answer to his acquiring what he wanted more than anything else.

Chapter 4

Very deliberately and carefully, Catherine dipped the gold nub of her pen into the inkwell. Her father wouldn't be pleased by her actions, but she didn't see that she had any choice.

My dearest brother,
I hope my letter finds you well—

I hope it finds you at all, she thought wearily.

—and enjoying your travels.
However, I have desperate need of you at home.

Her hand was shaking when she again dipped into the inkwell. She had Sterling's traveling schedule, but she had no idea if he was following it diligently. Still she didn't see that she had much choice except to try to get in touch with him. But then the doubts surfaced.

How could she even consider asking of her

brother what she'd asked of Claybourne? He didn't possess Claybourne's dark soul. Her brother was kind and generous. She loved him dearly—except for the fact that being several years older he seemed to be of the opinion that his was the only one of any importance. That attitude had no doubt led to the row with her father, bless him.

How might her request change Sterling? Would it turn him into a man like Claybourne? Did she want to be responsible for turning an angel into a devil? But she was so worried that the next time Avendale took his fists to Winnie he'd kill her.

Claybourne was right. She should see to the matter herself. But oh, dear Lord, where would she find the strength? And how would she do it? A pistol? A knife? Poison?

How many times would she need to shoot him or stab him? She'd never even seen a dead person—at least not so she'd remember. Her mother had died giving birth to a babe who didn't survive. Catherine had been a child at the time. Her mother had simply appeared to be sleeping. Was all death as peaceful?

Catherine was startled from her morose thoughts by a light tapping at her door. Her maid, Jenny, peered inside. "My lady, a missive has been delivered."

Catherine's heart fairly stopped beating. Was it from Winnie? Had the worst finally happened? Or was it from her brother? Was he on his way home at last? Were her prayers to be answered?

"Bring it here quickly." Her trembling worsened as she reached for the letter. It bore no seal. Just a glob of wax to hold it closed. How strange. She slipped her silver letter opener beneath the wax, parting it from the parchment. Then she unfolded the letter.

We need to meet.
Midnight.
Your garden.

—C

C? Who the devil—

She nearly gasped.

Claybourne?

She quickly folded up the letter and looked at Jenny. "Who brought this?"

"A young lad."

"Did he say anything?"

"Only that it concerned an urgent matter and should be delivered to you straightaway. Is everything all right, my lady?"

Catherine cleared her throat. "Yes, all is well. I'm feeling a bit restless tonight. I shall take a stroll later, around midnight, after which you may help me prepare for bed."

"Yes, my lady." Jenny curtsied and left the room.

Catherine unfolded and reread the missive. Oh, dear Lord, she'd called at the devil's door and now he was calling at hers. This did not bode well, this did not bode well at all.

She refolded the letter and slipped it inside a book. Then she got up and began pacing. What should she wear for this midnight encounter? A cloak, perhaps, something to hide her from watchful eyes. Although with the meeting being held in her garden, the only watchful eyes would be those of her servants, and she'd simply forbid them from going in the garden at that time.

She looked at the clock ticking on the mantel. She had two hours of waiting, two hours of worrying. She'd no doubt be wise to ignore his summons.

We need to meet.

Need. Had he not indicated that he had everything he could ever need? Then what could she possibly provide?

Another kiss perhaps? Had he lain tossing and turning every night as she had? Had he been unable to sleep? Had she haunted his dreams as he haunted hers?

She couldn't deny that she was anticipating his visit. She actually *wanted* to see him again. Maybe the next time she invited him to a ball, he'd attend.

She sat down, watched the clock, and waited. At precisely five minutes before midnight, she got up and slipped her cloak around her shoulders. She looked at her reflection in the mirror, tucked a few stray strands of her hair back into place, then laughed at her silliness. He'd barely be able to see her in the darkness. And she certainly didn't care what he thought of her appearance.

She considered donning her gloves, but this wasn't a formal outing. They'd have no reason to touch. With a calming breath, she lifted the lamp from her desk and walked out of her room.

It was very quiet, most of the lights in the household doused by now. She was almost to the morning room where doors would lead her into the garden when she heard—

"My lady, may I be of service?"

She swung around and smiled at the butler. "No, thank you, Jeffers. I'm having difficulty sleeping. I'm simply going to take a walk in the garden."

"Alone?"

"Yes, it's our garden. I should be quite safe."

"Would you like me to have a footman accompany you?"

"No, thank you. I welcome the solitude. As a matter of fact, please see to it that none of the servants disturb me."

He bowed slightly. "As you wish."

She headed to the morning room. Once there, she took a moment to gather her resolve as closely around her as her cloak and stepped out through the doors into the garden.

When they had parties, they lit the lanterns that lined the walk, but she didn't see the need for that much trouble or that much light, yet as she wandered along the path she began to second-guess her decision. She hadn't realized how very dark it was among the hedgerows and the flowers and the ivy-covered trestles, how very ominous, how very—

"Lady Catherine."

With a little squeak, she jerked around. How had she not seen him standing there? He seemed to emerge from the night shadows like the prince of darkness himself.

"You startled me, sir." Then she cursed herself for speaking before her heart had returned to a normal beat. Her voice sounded like the warbling tones her brother had exhibited when he was on the cusp of manhood.

"My apologies," Claybourne said.

"Your tone lacks any contrition. I daresay you did it on purpose."

"Perhaps. I wasn't certain you'd meet me."

"Your missive indicated you had a 'need.' Unlike you, I'm not one to generally ignore those in need."

"Indeed."

His voice had grown husky and she wondered if she'd inadvertently sent him a message she'd not meant to send. She was upset by his calm and her lack of it. She took a deep breath and asked tartly, "What was it that you needed, my lord?"

"Let's walk, shall we?"

"Not beyond the garden."

"Certainly not. But farther away from prying eyes and ears."

He began walking without waiting for her. She hurried to catch up. "I've instructed my servants not to disturb us."

He came to an abrupt halt, and she nearly bashed her nose into his shoulder when he turned to face her. He was so incredibly tall and broad. His mere presence made her heart gallop.

"You told your servants you were meeting me here?" he asked, his voice laced with incredulity.

"No, of course not. I misspoke. I told them not to disturb *me.* As far as they're concerned I'm having difficulty sleeping."

"Is that common for you? To have difficulty sleeping?"

He actually sounded curious, as though he had a care for her.

"No, not usually," she said. Unless she was thinking of him, then it was nigh on impossible.

"I daresay you will."

Whatever did he mean by that?

He began walking again, and against her better judgment she fell into step beside him. She was grateful she'd brought the lamp. While it didn't provide an abundance of light, it did provide enough that she could see him clearly.

"I wish to speak with you about your . . . proposition," Claybourne said with as much emotion as a lump of coal.

"I didn't think you were interested." She didn't quite trust him. He'd rebuffed her offer and made her feel quite silly in making it.

"I wasn't."

"But now you are."

"You sound annoyed. Have you found someone else to do your bidding?"

Oh, she wished she had. She wished she could turn on her heel and walk away. He unsettled her. She thought of his warm fingers trailing over the pulse at her throat, making it jump. She remembered his hot mouth devouring hers. . .

"No, I've not found someone else."

"Have you taken care of the matter?"

"No."

"Then perhaps we can strike a bargain. There is a young lady who I wish very much to make my wife."

Catherine stumbled to a stop, schooling her features not to reveal how the shock of those words had struck her as a blow. What did she care if he took a wife? She didn't. She absolutely did not care, and yet, she couldn't deny the disappointment. She'd spent so many years dreaming of him, although not by choice. He simply invaded her dreams as though he belonged there.

He was studying her now as though she was a curiosity. What did her face show? Nothing she hoped. Or perhaps he was simply trying to determine how much to reveal. He was as closed as a casket before it was lowered into the earth.

"She, however, has qualms about marrying me," he continued.

"Because of the wicked things you do?"

His mocking smile was all the more visible in the darkness. "The wicked things I do, Lady Catherine, are the very reason you're drawn to me."

"I'm not *drawn* to you."

"Are you not? I don't recall you're being overly upset that I kissed you. I suspect you were hoping for a taste of wickedness."

"You know nothing at all about my hopes, my lord." She swallowed, striving to regain her frigid composure. "The young lady has qualms. I can hardly blame her."

"In negotiations, Lady Catherine, it doesn't serve one well to insult the one from whom you require a favor."

"Yes, so you explained the other night. My apologies if I gave insult. She will not marry you and that has caused you to summon me because . . ."

"She fears our world. She doesn't feel that she'll fit in with the nobility."

A commoner? He was going to marry a commoner? On the other hand, what choice remained to him? She could think of no woman who would welcome his attentions, no father who would seriously consider allowing Claybourne to pursue his daughter's hand in matrimony.

"I'd not noticed you particularly trying to fit in."

"Quite honestly, Lady Catherine, until recently I'd not given a damn if I fit in or not. But Frannie and I will no doubt have children, and I don't want them whispered about as I am."

Frannie. He'd wrapped a wealth of warmth around the name as he'd spoken it. Who'd have thought he'd be capable of so grand an emotion as love?

"You are not whispered about, my lord. People do not speak of the devil."

"Now, Catherine, I know that to be untrue. Otherwise, how would you have known to come to my door?"

He purred her name with an intimacy that caused honeyed heat to pool in her belly. How quickly he gained the upper hand. How desperately she needed to reacquire it.

She angled her head and met his smile with one of her own. "Point made. So you want to ensure your children are accepted among the aristocracy." She could hardly imagine him as a father, much less a husband.

"Indeed. But before I jump forward to that problem, I must give Frannie the confidence to honor me with her hand in marriage. And that is where you come in."

"Me?"

"Yes. I need you to teach her all she needs to know to walk confidently among us. Once you've accomplished that task, I'll dispense with the person of your choosing."

"I no longer have confidence in your ability to carry out my request, my lord. You said you'd not killed."

"No, I said I'd not killed my uncle."

She studied him and the familiar features that had haunted her dreams for so long. "Dear Lord! You don't believe you're truly the Earl of Claybourne."

"What I believe or do not believe is of no consequence. The old gent believed and the Crown believed." He held out his hands. "And so here I am."

"You have an odd sort of honesty about you."

"So have we a bargain?"

"You said that you'd see to your end once I'd seen to mine. But my task could take months. How do I know when I'm finished, that you'll carry out yours?"

"You have my word on it."

"As a gentleman?"

"As a scoundrel. Have you not heard that there is honor among thieves?"

Oh, dear Lord, she feared she was playing a very dangerous game here.

"Still, you are asking a good deal more of me than I'm asking of—"

With his gloved hand, he gripped her chin and

leaned near. She could see the muscles in his jaw tightening. "You are asking me to surrender the last of my soul. Once it's done, it can't be undone. All I'm asking of you is that you teach someone how to properly host an afternoon tea."

Swallowing hard, she nodded, speaking through clenched teeth. "You're quite right. Now if you'll be so kind as to unhand me."

He seemed surprised to discover that he was holding her. He lowered his hand. "My apologies. I—"

"Not to worry. I don't believe you bruised me."

He turned away, and if she didn't know he was a fraud, she might have thought he was struggling with his conscience. "Quite honestly, my lord, I'm not certain that what I require of you can wait months to be carried out."

He glanced over his shoulder at her, and the light of her lantern caught the silver of his eyes, giving them an unholy gleam. "Frannie is quite bright. I do not question her ability to learn, rather your ability to teach. Once I see that you're able to fulfill your part of the bargain, I shall see to mine."

"I will not tell you the name until you are ready for the undertaking."

"I'm agreeable to those terms."

"And I shall never tell you why."

"It seems I should at least know what he's done to deserve to die."

His last few words caused her stomach to tighten painfully. She knew what she was asking, knew what the consequences would be. If she could think of another way to save Winnie, she'd turn to it. But she knew threats would not sway Avendale. And Winnie was right. The law was of no use to them. So Catherine strengthened her resolve before saying, "It's a private matter."

"This particular part of our arrangement does not sit well with me."

"The man you killed—Geoffrey Langdon—why did you kill him?"

"My reasons are my own."

"Did he deserve what you did to him?"

"No, he deserved much worse."

"I believe you."

"I don't give a bloody damn if you believe me or not."

She took a step forward. "I mean, I take you at your word that he deserved it, so why can you not take me at mine that this other gentleman is deserving of death?"

"Because, Lady Catherine, you live in a world where ladies weep because they didn't receive an invitation to a ball. What you might consider insult, I would merely consider inconvenience."

"You think because you grew up on the streets that you alone are privy to the dark nature of man? How terribly conceited you are."

"I have seen the worst of men and I have seen the best. Can you say the same?"

Could she? Could she even begin to fathom what horrors he might have witnessed?

"On this matter, I believe I have seen the worst."

He nodded very slowly. "Very well then. I'll take you at your word that he deserves what I shall deliver."

She thought she should have been relieved. Instead doubts plagued her. She shoved them aside. Now was not the time to get squeamish about her actions. "Then we have a bargain. Shall I have papers drawn up?"

The man who rarely exhibited emotion looked horrified. "Good God, no! There is to be no evidence, nothing written anywhere that will lead me to Newgate. Even the missive I sent earlier should be burned."

"Then how do we signify that we're both in agreement?"

"We'll shake on it." He removed his glove and extended his right hand toward her.

On her skirt, she wiped her palm—which had suddenly dampened—before pressing it against his. His long fingers closed over hers, and he drew her near, so near that she could see the narrow black outline that circled the silver of his eyes. "You are now in league with the devil, my lady. May you rest easier at night than I."

Her heart hammered as he released his hold, turned away slightly, and began to tug back on his glove. "We shall need to be discreet. I'll have my coach waiting in the alley at midnight tomorrow. Meet me there, and I'll escort you to Frannie."

"You must love her very much to be willing to do all this."

He twisted his head slightly and held her gaze. "I'm not doing anything for her that I've not done for her before."

Chapter 5

Damnation, what was it about the woman that had him confessing things he'd never confessed to anyone else? What was it about her that filled him with shame about his past? What made him want to shock her down to her very toes? What made him want to appear as evil as she believed him to be?

The thoughts had been tormenting him ever since he'd left her garden. He was no doubt a fool for getting involved in this matter without more information. She wouldn't reveal who she wanted killed until he was ready to carry out her bidding. For all he knew, he was the one she wanted done in. Not that he could think of a single reason why she would. A wise man never went into a situation without knowing all the details. He was sadly lacking in details.

He banged on the door of the simple lodging. He waited a minute, banged again. He saw a light flicker in a lower window and banged once more.

The door opened and an elderly woman held

up her lamp. "Are you daft? Are you not aware of the hour?"

"I need to see James Swindler."

"He's abed."

"Then get him up."

She glared at him. "Have you no decency? I'll do no such thing."

Footsteps echoed on the stairs and then a tall man with broad shoulders was easing the lady aside, lifting his lamp for a clearer view.

"Luke? Good God, what's wrong? Is it Frannie?"

In a way it was.

"We need to talk."

"Of course, come on up." Jim patted the woman's shoulder. "It's all right, Mrs. Whitten. He's a friend."

"No, doubt, one in trouble. Calling on an inspector of Scotland Yard this time of night. It's not what decent folks do."

"Not to worry. Go back to sleep, madam. I'll keep an eye on things."

The woman harrumphed and shuffled back toward what Luke assumed was her bedchamber.

"Your landlady is a most unpleasant woman."

Jim chuckled. "It has been my experience that few people are pleasant when they're awakened in the middle of the night. Come on up."

Luke followed him up the narrow stairs to a flat that had a sitting room and a sleeping area off to the side. He wasn't surprised to see a small fire going in the fireplace. Regardless of the season, he and his friends relished warmth now that they could afford it.

Jim poured whiskey into two glasses and

handed one to Luke. "Make yourself comfortable."

Luke sat in one of two chairs set before the fireplace while Jim sat in the other.

"An inspector? When did that happen?" Luke asked.

"Some time back."

"You're moving up in the world."

"Hardly. It's an impressive title, but it simply means I no longer walk the streets but oversee those who do."

Jim had always been humble to a fault. Luke suspected if he were suddenly crowned king of England, he'd brush it off, saying that it simply meant he sat in a fancier chair than anyone else.

"Why did you think my reason for being here had something to do with Frannie?" Luke asked.

"Because she's what we all have in common."

"No, Feagan is what we all have in common."

"But Frannie is the one we all circle around to protect." Jim leaned forward, pressing his elbows against his thighs, holding his glass with two hands, as though he expected bad news. "So if she's not what brought you to my door in the middle of the night, what is?"

"I need you to gather some information for me."

Jim leaned back, smiling confidently. "That's where my true talent lies."

Luke was well aware of that fact, and he intended to put James Swindler's skills to good use. He was determined to learn the truth behind

Lady Catherine Mabry's request long before she revealed it. Knowledge was strength, and where she was concerned, Luke needed all the strength he could summon.

A gaming hell. Claybourne had brought her through the back door of a gaming hell.

Catherine was still reeling from that realization as she stood in the office doorway watching while Claybourne sought to convince a red-haired lady—who seemed determined not to be convinced—that everything would be all right.

"Frannie, she's going to teach you that being married to a lord is not something to be feared," Claybourne said.

Unless one was married to the Duke of Avendale, Catherine thought wryly.

"But I don't want this."

They continued on, going back and forth. Catherine listened with half an ear, more intrigued by her surroundings than the conversation, even though she couldn't see the main portion of the inside of the building. She was halfway tempted to ask for a tour.

Claybourne wanted to marry a woman who worked in a gaming hell. Who *worked*. In a *gambling establishment*. Society would never accept her. The entire situation had disaster written all over it. Still, Catherine embraced the challenge. She would not only teach her, but she would see that she was accepted into Society. It was worth it to see that Winnie was safe.

The dress Catherine wore was one she used when calling on ladies of quality. It seemed entirely inappropriate all of a sudden. What did one wear when going to a gaming establishment? She struggled not to laugh maniacally. The entire situation was simply absurd and at the same time incredibly fascinating. Winnie would absolutely die if she knew where Catherine was spending her evening.

The owner of the establishment, to whom she'd been introduced upon entering, also stood in the doorway, leaning back insolently, his arms folded across his chest, his gaze running from the top of her head to her toes and back up. Even though she wasn't looking at him, she could feel his impudent perusal, as though it was a soft touch. Twisting her head, she glared at Jack Dodger. "Are you pleased with what you see?"

He snapped his gaze up to hers. "Immensely."

She allowed her gaze to wander over him, stopping for a heartbeat at the burn in the shape of a T that marred the inside of his thumb until she finally settled her gaze on his dark eyes once more. "I can't say the same."

His chuckle was a low thrumming purr, like that of a large cat preparing to strike. A shiver went slowly down Catherine's spine.

"How is it that a lady of the nobility ended up with a backbone?" he asked.

"It appears you know little of the nobility, sir."

"I know a great deal about them." He leaned forward slightly, satisfaction in his dark eyes. "They are some of my best customers."

She knew his sort—a troublemaker—the reason decent women needed an escort when traveling on the streets. He was attempting to shock her.

She was not easily shocked. She turned her attention back to the arguing couple. "We all have our vices."

"And what is yours, Lady Catherine?"

"None of your concern."

"Perhaps not, but it has occurred to me that I might have a position for you in my employ."

She glared at him once more. "Do tell."

"I believe you would fulfill a fantasy for my customers who are not of the nobility that my present girls can't. I suspect many a gent fantasizes about bedding a woman of your . . . ilk."

"And what of a lady's fantasies? Are you well equipped to see to those?"

He seemed taken aback. Good. She didn't much like him.

"Do ladies fantasize about bedding?"

She arched a brow.

A lazy grin spread over his face. "What do you fantasize?"

She gave him a slow smile in return and shifted her attention back to the arguing couple. Frannie was obviously agitated. Dear God, at this rate, they'd be here all night. Catherine was already tired. She'd spent a good deal of the afternoon with her father's man of business and she'd been too anxious about tonight's meeting with Claybourne to rest earlier that evening.

"That's quite enough already!" Catherine shouted.

Claybourne spun around, clearly irritated with her. Not that she cared a whit about his irritation one way or another.

"You can't bully her into this," she said.

"I'm not bullying her."

"You're bullying her. Can't you see that she's terrified by the thought of marriage to you? Not that I can blame her if this is the way you plan to treat her once you're married."

"No," Frannie said. "No, not marriage to Luke, but marriage to what he represents."

"The nobility, the peerage, the upper crust of society. Do you really believe we're so different?"

"Yes. You have all these rules—"

"Which can be learned, and Lord Claybourne assures me you're extremely bright and will pick up on the subtle nuances of our society in no time. So shall we get to it?"

Frannie looked at Claybourne, looked at Catherine. She appeared to be completely defeated. "Yes, of course."

Catherine stepped into the room, wondering why in the world Claybourne would want a mouse for a wife. It seemed that more than lessons on etiquette were in order. "You, Lord Claybourne, may leave."

He took a step nearer and leaned toward her. "Be gentle with her."

"I shall do what needs to be done in order to gain what I want."

"If you bring her tears—"

"For God's sake, I'm not a monster."

He started to open his mouth.

"Shh! I'll not tolerate your interference in this matter. Take Mr. Dodger with you as I don't much care for him. Be sure to close the door smartly on your way out."

A muscle in his jaw jumped, and she thought

she should be frightened by the dark look he gave her. But for some strange reason she wasn't afraid of the Devil Earl. She never had been.

He spun on his heel, strode from the room, and slammed the door in his wake. She did take perverse satisfaction in pricking his temper. She turned her attention to the woman who was no doubt older than she, but somehow seemed younger. "Hello, Frannie. I'm Catherine."

"Lady Catherine."

"Only in formal situations. Among friends I'm Catherine."

"And you expect us to be friends?"

"I do indeed." She sat in a nearby chair. "Now, tell me the true reason you don't want to marry Claybourne."

"I like her," Jack said. "I like her a lot."

Luke tossed back the whiskey Jack had poured for him before pressing the glass and his ear to the wall in Jack's sanctuary—a room nestled beside Frannie's. Damnation, he couldn't hear a bloody word.

Jack took the glass from him, refilled it, and handed it back. "She has a lot of spunk."

"She's damned irritating is what she is. I'm already regretting the bargain."

"She's a beauty."

Luke slumped down into a chair. "I hadn't noticed."

"She'd make a dead man sit up in his coffin. Damn, I might even be willing to kill a bloke myself to earn her favor."

"I'm not doing it to earn her favor."

"I know. You're doing it to earn Frannie's."

They fell into contemplative silence until Jack asked, "Do you think unmarried women fantasize?"

Luke looked up. "About what?"

"About bedding."

"No. They wouldn't know where to begin."

"Why?"

"Why what?"

"Why wouldn't they know where to begin?"

"Because they don't know the first thing about what goes on between a man and a woman."

"Once they've learned they could fantasize."

"Possibly."

"So Lady Catherine isn't a virgin."

Luke had a strange reaction. His entire body tightened and he felt a need to . . . what? Defend the lady's honor? Strike out at whoever had taken her innocence? Had someone forced his attentions on her? Was that the reason she wanted him killed?

"Why do you say that?" he asked.

"She indicated that she fantasized about men. Now I'm left to wonder if women would pay to have their fantasies realized. Perhaps we should expand our business to include offerings for ladies."

"Don't be ridiculous. Men have a need that women don't."

"I spend a good deal of my day contemplating various tantalizing aspects of women, not to mention all the various exciting things I could do with them. You don't believe they think about men?"

"No, they ponder gowns and tea and needlework."

"I'm not so certain. Maybe I'll ask Catherine—"

"She's Lady Catherine to you—and stay away from her, Jack."

"A bit difficult to manage when you bring her into my establishment."

"I have no choice. Frannie lives here and works here, and she seldom leaves. As you well know, night works best for clandestine encounters."

"You ordered me to stay away from Frannie, and I have done so. I flirt with her not at all. You can have only one woman, Luke, and you have claimed Frannie. I will do with Catherine as I please."

Luke came to his feet with such force that his whiskey sloshed over the sides of his glass as he towered over Jack. "You will leave her be."

He didn't like the way Jack was studying him, with a speculative gleam in his eye. Nor did he particularly like the fury emanating from him at the thought of Jack giving Catherine any attention at all. What was the matter with him? What did he care who gave her attention? But just the thought of her with someone else set his blood to boiling.

"As you wish," Jack said. "For now. Because you are my friend. But never make the mistake of thinking that you are my master."

Luke eased back and set the glass on the desk. "I'm off to play cards."

He needed something to distract himself from his unsettling thoughts. He'd almost smashed his fist into Jack's face, almost ground out that Catherine was his. He'd never had such a visceral reaction where Frannie was concerned, so why did he feel so possessive of Catherine?

She was nothing, simply a means to an end. While Frannie was everything.

"You need to be wary of Jack Dodger."

It was nearly three in the morning, and Catherine was completely drained of all energy. They were traveling in the coach without benefit of light so they had little risk of being seen and recognized, not that she thought there was any chance of anyone she knew being about this time of night. He'd also drawn curtains over the windows. She thought the precautions extreme, but then she suspected he was accustomed to lurking about and knew best how to achieve anonymity.

"Why is that, my lord?"

"You intrigue him, and like me, he would ruin you without remorse."

"And you think I'd fall under his charms?"

"If he sets his mind to it, yes. Many a woman has."

She laughed lightly. "I assure you he doesn't interest me in the least."

"He's a handsome devil."

"Again, my lord, I'm amazed you'd think me so shallow. My opinion of a man is not influenced by something over which he has no control—such as comely features. I base my opinion solely on his character." Which was the reason that she had such a low opinion of Claybourne. His character was questionable—in the extreme. But in spite of that, he still fascinated her—*Drat him!* "How is it that you know Mr. Dodger?"

"How much do you know of my past?"

"I know you were orphaned. I know you spent

a part of your youth living in the streets. Other than that, and what you've so kindly revealed, very little." Still, a shiver went up her back. Here she was in a coach, in the dark, with a man who'd admitted to murder and deception, a man who'd taken her to a gaming hell as though it was the proper place for a woman.

"He was one of Feagan's lads," Claybourne said. "As was I."

"And who was Feagan?"

"The kidsman who managed our little band of child thieves, taught us our craft."

"How many of you were there?"

"A dozen or so. It changed, depending on who was caught and who was recruited."

"And Frannie?"

"She's one of us as well."

"You've had a very different upbringing than most lords."

"Indeed."

"Is that where you learned to kill?"

"No, it's where I learned to steal."

"To pick pockets?"

"I was more prone to fleecing. Jack was the pickpocket."

"And Frannie?"

"The distraction."

"Do you miss it?"

"What? Living on the streets? Being filthy, cold, and hungry? No. Never."

She wished she could see him more clearly in the shadows. She knew she shouldn't be intrigued by him, and yet she was. While she'd accused him of bullying Frannie, he'd not really been unkind or forceful with her. He'd only dared to let his frustration show.

That more than anything reinforced to her his strong feelings for the woman. He guarded his emotions so carefully, but around Frannie he'd revealed them.

"I deduced that you don't believe you're the true heir to Claybourne. Forgive me for my naiveté, but why let the previous earl believe you were?"

He slipped his finger beneath the curtain, moved it aside slightly, and gazed out. She wondered if he was trying to determine their location. Or perhaps he was searching for an answer to her question.

"They were going to hang me," he said quietly, releasing the curtain. It fluttered back into place.

Her stomach knotted at the thought of him facing the gallows. "I can understand that under the circumstances, anyone would have done the same, pretended to be someone he wasn't. But once you were free, why not run back to where you belonged? You stole the title and all that came with it."

"It was more than trying to save my neck," he said quietly, almost as though he was lost in the moment. "Have you ever wanted something so badly that you would do anything, believe anything in order to acquire it?"

"I would think our present arrangement would confirm that indeed I have."

"No, I'm talking about wanting something more badly than that, wanting it with such yearning that you would be willing to deceive yourself in order to acquire it. That was how the old gent was. I saw in his eyes how desperate he was to find his grandson, how desperate he was that I be that child—"

"And you took advantage."

"That is one way to look upon it—and I readily admit that there are nights when I view my actions in that way."

"How else could you look at it?"

"I gave him what all of us want and few of us acquire: our deepest desires. There was nothing he wanted more than to once again have in his life the son of his first-born. And so I became what he wanted."

"There is that odd honesty in you again. You make it sound almost noble."

"No, not noble. Not in the least. He provided me with an opportunity to live, and I snatched it as quickly and as humbly as I could. I wish I had been his grandson. He showered me with love that rightfully belonged to another, and that I was never comfortable with."

"The love he gave you was yours. Even if he thought you were another, what he felt for you came about because he came to care for you."

"He cared for me only because he believed I was his grandson. If he believed otherwise, I have little doubt that he'd have slipped the noose around my neck himself. After all, I killed his remaining son."

A son who had a son: Marcus Langdon. The man who should be earl. Catherine knew him, because he, rather than his notorious cousin, was often invited to balls as though people were preparing him for the day he'd assume his rightful place. But they'd obviously underestimated the present earl.

"I must admit to being confused by your confessions. They don't paint you in a very favorable light, and I can't help but wonder if you're telling me these things because you don't want me to like you."

"I don't know why I tell you these things. Perhaps because only a soul as dark as mine could ask of me what you have."

"I am nothing like you, my lord."

"Are you not? My hand shall do the deed, but it does it at your bidding. You will share the guilt, Lady Catherine. Be certain your conscience can stand the weight of it."

"It can." At least she thought it could. She hoped it could. She hated that she doubted. But she didn't see that any other recourse was available to her. "While your pretending to be the earl's grandson saved your neck, it also came at a very costly price. Because now, as a lord, you've having difficulty acquiring what you want: Frannie."

"I'm impressed by your astuteness, Lady Catherine. I've never been overly impressed with ladies of the nobility."

"How many do you know well?"

"Obviously not nearly enough. Are you telling me that they're all as intriguing as you?"

Her heart gave a strange stutter, and she wondered if a woman could die from a man's attentions. It irritated her that she was pleased that he found her intriguing.

"I believe women are vastly underestimated.

After all, we've been known, on more than one occasion, to rule an empire."

"You seem to think very highly of your gender."

"Indeed I do."

"Shouldn't you be married by now?"

It seemed an odd change in topic. Why was everyone so concerned with her marital status? "There is no law as to when one must marry."

"Why have you not?"

"Obviously I've not yet found any man worthy of me."

He chuckled. "Heaven help the man who does think he's worthy."

"I am not as bad as all that."

"I think as a wife you will be a challenge to any man."

"You don't think Frannie will be a challenge?"

"Of course not. Not once we overcome this obstacle."

"Is that truly what you want? Someone who never offers you a challenge? I think it would be rather boring."

"I've had enough challenges in my life, Lady Catherine. I welcome a marriage without them."

"Of course. Forgive me. It is not for me to judge what you seek in marriage."

Yet, she couldn't help but think about the reason Frannie had given her for not wanting to marry Claybourne.

"I owe him everything, and he owes me nothing. I'm accustomed to dealing with numbers and keeping everything balanced. It seems to me that our marriage would be incredibly lopsided. It doesn't seem like a pleasant way to live, and in time, I fear we would regret it and eventually lose whatever affection we hold for each other."

I owe him everything.

I'm not doing for her anything I've not done for her before.

Catherine couldn't help but think that the man Claybourne had killed was somehow tied in with Frannie. Would she ever know the whole story? Did she wish to know it? If his actions were truly justified, would she begin to see him in a favorable light? Would she begin to question her own plans involving him?

He was a man that at least one person felt she owed *everything*. Frannie hadn't used the word lightly. She truly felt she owed Claybourne everything. Catherine couldn't imagine being that much in debt to anyone. Oddly, she wanted to reach across the short distance separating Claybourne from her, take his hand in hers, and plead with him to tell her every sordid detail of his past.

Why was it the more time she spent in his company, the more he intrigued her?

Thankfully the coach came to a halt before she could carry through on what she was certain would be a rash decision. Did she truly want to know his past? Wouldn't the arrangement be better served if they kept their distance, were more strangers than friends?

The door opened, and she made a move toward it.

"Allow me to go first," Claybourne said.

"There's no need for you to escort me."

"I insist."

He stepped out, then assisted her in alighting from the coach. He walked with her until they reached the gate that led to the garden and the path used by those delivering goods to the residence.

She placed her hand on the latch. "Good night, my lord. I'll see you tomorrow at midnight."

"Catherine?"

She froze. His voice held a roughness, a seriousness that almost terrified her, and an informality that was equally frightening. She thought she should look at him, but she was afraid of what she might see, what he might say. So she waited, barely breathing.

"This person you want dispensed with, is it because he . . . did he force his attentions—his body—on you?"

She dared to look over her shoulder at him. Dark and formidable, he stood there in the shadows.

"You don't have to tell me the details, but if he took your virtue against your will, you have but to give me his name now, tonight, and your portion of our arrangement will be concluded, and I shall immediately see to mine."

Her throat tightened painfully with the realization of what he was asking and what he was offering. Surely he was not as noble as all that. "Are you saying you'd not require me to teach Frannie before you took care of the matter?"

"I am."

How easy it would be to just say yes. To have the matter taken care of expeditiously and quickly. She would never see him again. And if she'd not witnessed his odd honesty, if she'd not begun to question her opinion of him, if she'd not begun to realize that he possessed a moral code that was to be admired, she might have taken advantage of his offer. But the truth was that she selfishly didn't want this moment to be the last she ever saw of him.

Earlier he'd spoken about wanting something so desperately as to be willing to do, to believe, anything in order to obtain it. He felt that way about Frannie. She was his deepest desire, marriage to her the dream he wanted realized. And he was willing to give it up, for Catherine—who meant nothing to him—if she'd been wronged.

Claybourne quite simply fascinated her. She'd never known a man who seemed quite so complex, a man who seemed to have so many varying facets to him. He was not all evil. Nor was he all good. It was an immensely captivating combination.

"My virtue remains intact."

He seemed to wilt just a bit as though he'd been preparing himself for the blow of learning that she'd been harmed.

"I'll see you tomorrow, my lord."

He bowed slightly. "Tomorrow."

She went in through the gate and closed it quietly behind her. She didn't wish to acknowledge how his concern had touched her.

Claybourne was far more dangerous than she realized. Whether a sinner or a saint, he held her interest as no other man ever had.

Chapter 6

Frannie Darling stepped out of Dodger's Drawing Room—the elegant name she'd suggested for something rather inelegant at its core, as though pretty words could make sin acceptable—and walked toward the stairs that led to the small flat where she lived. It was still part of Dodger's, but the outside entrance at least made her feel as though she were stepping away from the dregs and into a better life.

Not that she didn't have the means to live in a fancier dwelling. She did. Feagan's lads treated her as an equal, and she shared in the profits from their ventures. She could live in a palace if she wanted, but the money she earned was never for her. Others were far more deserving.

As she made her way up the stairs, she smelled the familiar richly scented tobacco. It was a much more pleasant aroma than it had been when they were children. Jack could afford the very finest customized tobacco now.

Yet still he packed it into the long clay pipe he'd begun using when he was a lad of eight. It wasn't unusual for Feagan's lads to smoke and drink spirits at a young age. Kept them warm. The pipe was part of Jack's past, a reminder of what he'd been before Luke's grandfather had offered them a chance at a better life. They'd all brought something with them.

Jack had stayed in the residence in St. James's only long enough to learn what he needed in order to gain what he wanted. He'd never been happy living with the Earl of Claybourne. But then as far as Frannie knew, he'd never been truly happy anywhere—except for the slight contentment he seemed to have with Feagan. Jack had been the most skilled of their little band, always bringing in the most coins and handkerchiefs, always sitting by the fire with Feagan—Feagan drinking his gin, Jack drinking gin and smoking his pipe—both of them whispering late into the night. As far as Frannie knew, Jack's was the only opinion Feagan ever sought.

"'Ello, Frannie," he said as she reached the landing. Outside the gaming hell, he was never the businessman he was indoors. Still, he was astute. Always looking for the angle that would give him more than he held.

"Dodger." In their youth, he'd been Dodger more often than Jack. He'd been skilled at dodging the hands that wanted to grab him when the target realized his pockets were being picked. It was usually the other thief who clumsily tipped off their intended prey. They'd all scatter when that happened.

Only once had Jack gone back to try to help a thief who wasn't quite as nimble. He'd gone back for Luke. It had been the only time Jack had ever been caught.

"Lovely evening tonight," she said.

"Oh, yeah, the fog is bloody luvely. Think there's anywhere in England where they don't have fog?"

"Would you move if there was?"

"Not likely. I doubt there's a city anywhere where I can make more money."

"There's more to life than coin."

"Not for me there's not."

Sighing, she looked out at the fog. It was like life, preventing her from seeing what was beyond reach. She wasn't unhappy. She simply felt that something important was missing from her life.

Jack puffed on his pipe, and they stood in silence for a while. She always enjoyed Jack's company even if they weren't talking. As a matter of fact, she usually enjoyed it most when they weren't. He had the uncanny knack of knowing what she was thinking.

"Why didn't you tell him the truth, Frannie, instead of making up all those silly excuses?" he asked after a while, his voice low as though he thought Luke might be waiting around a corner listening.

"I couldn't, Jack. I didn't want to hurt him. Not after all he's done for me."

"Not hurt him? All you've done is prolong the matter. And now he's brought a bloody stranger into our midst to teach you what you already know."

Her chest tightened painfully. "I know I've made a mess of things. I do love him, but I don't want to marry him. I don't want to be a countess. I just want to do what I want to do."

"He won't stop you from doing that."

"Oh, I know that well enough, but it won't be the same. Oh, God, maybe I should just marry him, be done with the worry over hurting him, but I don't think he'd be really happy with me. Sometimes having the dream makes you more content than having the reality."

"That doesn't make a bloody bit of sense."

"I heard about your blasted wagers. Why did you keep encouraging him to ask me when you knew how I felt?" she asked, almost as disappointed with him as she was with herself.

"Because he needs to know the truth, and it needs to come from you. He won't believe it from anyone else."

He puffed, she sulked.

"He likes her," Jack said, his voice low.

Frannie felt an unfamiliar prick of . . . what? Jealousy?

"Who? Lady Catherine?"

Nodding, he puffed on his pipe again. "Warned me to stay clear of her. It wasn't an idle threat either. Damned near had me trembling in my shoes the way he came after me."

She wasn't quite certain how she felt about that. She should be relieved, but a part of her mourned the prospect of losing a portion of Luke's heart. She'd held it all for so long, and yet she knew she couldn't hold it forever. It wasn't fair to him. As much as she cared for him, what she felt was the love of a sister for a brother, not a woman for a man.

"Maybe he feels responsible, bringing her into our den of criminals, thinks you'll corrupt or ruin her. You may no longer live with Feagan, but you're still recruiting people, enticing them to the dark side of London."

He grinned around his pipe. "Where's the harm? We're all going to hell anyway. Might as well have a bit of fun along the way, and the more the merrier and all that."

"You're so like Feagan. You know, I used to pretend he was my father. We both had red hair that was so irritatingly curly." She shrugged. "It seemed likely he could be."

She waited, hoping Jack would laugh at her silly confession. He'd been with Feagan the longest, knew everything. But Jack simply tapped his pipe against the landing railing, sending the ash into the darkness below.

"Good night, Frannie. Sleep well."

He jaunted down the steps. He had rooms next to hers, but she knew it would be dawn before he retired to them. She knew a good deal about Jack Dodger.

But not everything. None of them knew everything. They all had their secrets, but she suspected Jack's were the worst of the lot.

Luke strode into his library, crossed over to the table, poured a generous amount of whiskey into a glass, and immediately tossed it down, relishing the burning sensation. Whatever had possessed him to tell Catherine the things he told her?

He began filling the glass again. Tomorrow night

he'd shove his neckcloth into his mouth so he'd be unable to blurt all the irritating nonsense—

"I'll have one of those if you don't mind."

Luke swung around, knocking bottles to the floor where they shattered. He was crouched, ready to spring—

"Sorry," Jim said, holding up his hands. "It's just me."

Mortified by his reaction and his thudding heart, Luke straightened. He'd become too complacent. "No one informed me that you were here."

"I assumed you wouldn't want them to know. I slipped in on my own." Jim took a step nearer. "Are you all right? I've never been able to sneak up on you. You've always been too astute, too aware—"

"I was occupied with my thoughts." Turning, Luke snatched up a bottle. "We're in luck. One didn't fall." He began filling two glasses. "I take it you have something to report."

"Not really. She's rather boring."

"Boring? Catherine Mabry? She's anything but boring. Are you certain you're following the right woman?"

Jim chuckled. "I can't believe you asked me that. I'm the very best at what I do, and well you know it."

Jim wasn't boasting. He was simply stating fact. Luke handed him a glass and indicated a chair. After they were seated, he said, "What did she do today?"

"Not much. She called on the Countess of Chesney for perhaps ten minutes and then the

Duchess of Avendale. She went to the milliner for a new hat, which is being made, and she went to order a new gown. Apparently she plans to attend some ball. I'm working on acquiring the details. She returned home around two and was there until you picked her up this evening."

Luke pondered the information while Jim sipped his whiskey.

"You do realize her father is infirmed and her brother traveling the world?" Jim inquired.

Luke nodded. "I'd heard something about that."

"I think there's something there."

"What do you mean?"

"Her father is too ill to properly see after his estates, and his son is off seeing to his own pleasures? I think I need to investigate that."

"I don't care about her father or her brother. Concentrate on the girl. She's all I care about."

He realized what he'd said, considered rewording it, then decided against it. Making an issue of it would only serve to give his words credence they didn't deserve. He took a long swallow of the whiskey. It was tempting, but he couldn't afford to overindulge in spirits tonight.

"What if the answer concerns her father or brother?"

Luke sighed. "Do what you think best. Just find out who she wants me to kill and why."

"What if she's the only one who knows?"

"She has to have told someone."

"You didn't. Not until the deed was done."

"Not true. I told someone." Jack. His confessor in all things. And more often than not, his conspirator.

"Jack. You told Jack. You always trusted him more than you trusted the rest of us."

"He's the one who found me, shivering, starving, wretchedly afraid. I daresay I'd have died if he'd not taken care of me, taken me to Feagan."

"You know as well as I that Feagan paid us for recruitments. You were merely threepence in Jack's pocket."

"Are you jealous of my friendship with Jack?"

"Don't be absurd. But you speak as though his motives in rescuing you were pure. Nothing about Jack is pure."

"He saved your arse on more than one occasion."

"And I like him, but I don't trust him, not completely."

"With our upbringing, with what we learned about the world, do you think any of us completely trusts anyone?"

"I trust you. I'd follow you into hell without questioning why we were going."

"You've just made my point, because I'm the least trustworthy of us all. No one can be completely trusted. No one's motives are pure. Which brings us back to Catherine Mabry. Find out all you can about her."

Because Luke had a feeling she was leading *him* straight into hell, but unlike Jim, Luke wanted to know why.

Luke downed his whiskey and got up to pour himself another glass.

"How did the lesson go?" Jim asked as he walked over and held out his glass.

Luke splashed some whiskey into it. "Catherine won't speak of it. She said I'll see the results when I see the results. She vexes me as I've never been vexed. Do you know she actually had the audacity to question my selection of a wife? She's impertinent. I've never known a woman such as her." He rubbed his brow. "She makes my head hurt."

"You've always been troubled with head pains."

"It's been awhile. I've some powder to relieve it. Not to worry."

Jim set down his glass. "I'll be off then. Perhaps tomorrow I'll have more luck."

"Perhaps we both will."

Chapter 7

"I have it on good authority that Mr. Marcus Langdon has filed a bill in the Court of Chancery in order to reclaim his English estates. It is a start toward reclaiming his rightful title," Lady Charlotte said.

Catherine and Winnie, along with the Countess of Chesney, were having afternoon tea in Lady Charlotte's garden. While she'd only recently had her coming out, her father, the Earl of Millbank, was most anxious for her to marry. Who could blame him? She was the first of four gossipy daughters, which was one of the reasons she had frequent visitors. She seemed to know things before most people did.

"Then you mustn't do anything to discourage his interest," the Countess of Chesney said.

Lady Charlotte smiled knowingly. Obviously her good authority was Mr. Langdon himself. Catherine had seen them dancing together at balls and walking through Hyde Park. Still, she hadn't realized Lady Charlotte's interest in the untitled gentleman was so intense.

"But the Crown has already declared Lucian Langdon as the rightful earl," Catherine felt a need to point out. She knew Mr. Langdon—he was quite social—and she liked him well enough. He was no doubt the rightful earl. Lucian Langdon had not denied the truth of that matter, to her at least. But still she had a difficult time imagining Marcus Langdon as earl. Or perhaps it was simply that she couldn't see Lucian Langdon as *not* being earl.

"Mr. Langdon's contention is that King William was deceived, and being quite up in years—he was seventy at the time, after all—he was taken advantage of. Queen Victoria can set the matter to rights. If Mr. Marcus Langdon can simply get the courts to recognize that the property is truly his, then he will have the weight of the courts behind him when he petitions Her Majesty."

"I daresay, he's a very brave man, your Mr. Marcus Langdon," Winnie murmured. Then all eyes came to bear on Winnie, and she seemed to wither beneath the scutiny.

Catherine hated that Avendale had transformed a once-vibrant woman into such a mouse. She reached across the table and squeezed Winnie's hand. "No doubt you're quite right about Mr. Langdon. After all, Claybourne is not called the Devil Earl for nothing. I don't expect he'll go quietly into the night."

No indeed. He would fight this latest attempt to usurp his position. He was a man who wore power like a comfortable old cloak. He'd not give it up easily.

"I'm always amazed by how eloquent Claybourne is," Lady Chesney said.

Catherine felt her heart lurch. "You've spoken with him?"

Lady Chesney pressed her hand to her ample bosom, and judging by the shock on her face, Catherine might as well have asked if she'd lain in bed with him. "Of course not. Just the thought of conversing with the man sends my heart into palpitations. I daresay, if he ever addressed me, I would expire on the spot. No, no, no. I'm referring to the letters he's had published in the *Times*."

Catherine's stomach dropped to her toes. "What letters?"

"He maintains that it's unfair for children older than seven to be judged according to the law of the land."

"Well, of course, he'd think it unfair," Lady Charlotte said. "After all, he spent time in prison—even before he murdered dear Mr. Langdon's father. Can you imagine growing into adulthood knowing that your father was murdered—and that your grandfather not only welcomed the murderer into his home, but treated him as a son? Or a grandson as it were. It's absolutely shameful. Can anyone blame Mr. Marcus Langdon for striving to acquire what he knows in his heart is his?"

"Of course no one can blame him," Lady Chesney said. "I think it's frightfully disgraceful that among the aristocracy we have a lord who bears a prison brand upon his hand."

"Have you seen it?" Lady Charlotte asked, clearly horrified by the thought.

"I should say not! My dear Chesney has seen it, though, at the club when Claybourne is not wearing gloves. It fairly turns his stomach, and my Chesney is not one whose stomach turns easily."

"I think if I bore the mark of sin, I'd always hide it," Lady Charlotte said.

Catherine thought of the scar she'd seen on Claybourne's hand the night she'd gone to visit him, the burn scar on Jack Dodger's thumb. Why did Claybourne's look so different, so awful? She couldn't imagine someone intentionally pressing hot iron against a child's small hand. "Do you know how old he was when he was in prison?"

"Not offhand, no. It was years ago, I believe, when he was a child. From what I understand, he was caught stealing."

"He should have gone to prison for killing Mr. Langdon's father," Lady Charlotte said, with righteous indignation.

"Dear girl, he should have been hanged," Lady Chesney said, "but as he was never actually put on trial, he avoided both consequences. He was in a gaol for a bit, awaiting trial, but gaol hardly suffices as prison."

"Should we be speaking of Claybourne?" Winnie asked, glancing around as though she expected him to jump out from behind the rosebushes. "If we're not careful he'll be making appearances at our affairs."

"You're quite right, Duchess. He is a horrible man. I shall pray diligently day and night for the court and the Crown to bestow upon Mr. Marcus

Langdon what is rightfully his," Lady Charlotte said.

Catherine had an unkind thought that Lady Charlotte was praying so hard because she wanted to be a countess. What a selfish use of prayer that was. Would it not be better to pray for the children?

For three nights now, in between teaching Frannie proper etiquette, Catherine heard about the children's home that Frannie was building on land that Claybourne had purchased for her. It was located just outside of London. She intended it to be a place where children could, in Frannie's words, be children.

Catherine had done good works. She donated clothing to the poor. She gave coins to begging children. But she didn't wrap her arms around them as she suspected Frannie did. And now to hear that even Claybourne was taking a public stand against what he considered an unfair practice . . . she felt quite humbled.

"I don't think he's as bad as all that," Catherine muttered later as the open carriage rattled over the street, taking her and Winnie to Winnie's residence.

"Who?" Winnie asked.

"Claybourne."

"Oh, please, I really don't want to speak of him. We should be discussing the ball we'll be hosting at the end of the month. That's a much more pleasant conversation. Have you managed to acquire an orchestra for us?"

Catherine smiled. "Yes, I have. And the invitations should be ready tomorrow. I'll pick them up at the stationers, and then we can spend a terribly exciting afternoon addressing them."

Winnie laughed lightly. It always made Catherine feel better to hear her friend laugh. "You don't like addressing invitations," Winnie said.

"No, I must confess that I don't. I enjoy arranging for a ball, but the tedious tasks bore me to no end."

"I shall address them all. I don't mind. I rather like having a precise goal that can be easily met."

"But it seems like such a small goal."

Winnie stopped smiling. *Drat it!* Catherine had hurt her feelings. She was so easily hurt these days, and who could blame her? Her confidence was shattered. Reaching across, Catherine squeezed her hand. "I'm sorry, but I'm feeling a bit trite of late. Hearing that a man such as Claybourne, a known scoundrel, is taking time to speak out on behalf of children makes me feel as though I should be doing more."

"You have your father to look after."

"Yes, but he has nurses."

"And you have the estates to oversee."

"That is true, I suppose, although even then it's simply a matter of approving decisions that the estates' managers have already given considerable thought to."

"When do you think your brother will return home?"

"I don't know."

"When did you last hear from him?"

Catherine glanced about at the shops they passed. She'd been shopping too much of late, to take her mind off the bargain she'd struck with Claybourne. It was almost as though she wanted to run from her decision, even though she truly believed it was the only way to save Winnie. Threatening Avendale would only anger him further, and he would take his fury out on her friend and possibly on Catherine as well. Yes, killing him was the only permanent answer that guaranteed no harm to Winnie.

"It's been nearly a year," Catherine said quietly.

"You don't suppose something horrendous has happened to him."

"No, he's never been one for writing. He's rather selfish in that regard. He cares only about his own pleasures."

"That will all change when he returns home."

"Perhaps." She hoped so. Although she didn't think she was doing too terrible a job at managing things. She rather liked it actually.

"We really need to find you a husband," Winnie said. "Isn't there anyone who's caught your fancy?"

Catherine thought of silver eyes, the way they warmed when Claybourne looked at Frannie, the way they'd heated when he'd kissed Catherine. He was so solicitous where Frannie was concerned. How could Frannie not want what Claybourne had to offer?

When he'd first told Catherine that he wanted to marry a woman who had misgivings about marrying him, she'd thought she'd understood the misgivings. But the more time she spent in Claybourne's company the more she discovered a man of such depth that she thought a lifetime spent with him would not reveal all the layers. But what an intriguing lifetime it would be. But he was not for her, and well she knew it.

"Not really," Catherine said.

"I can hardly believe that Lady Charlotte has taken a fancy to Mr. Marcus Langdon. He's nice enough, I suppose, but I think her interest may wane if his pursuit in reclaiming the title isn't successful."

"I don't think Claybourne will give it up easily." Quite honestly, she didn't think he'd give it up at all, and while a part of her recognized that he'd stolen it, she couldn't quite see him as anything other than a lord. There was simply something about the way he held himself that seemed to indicate he'd been born into the role.

"Sometimes, like the way you sounded today when you spoke his name, it's almost as though you *know* him."

"He is so mysterious, Winnie. Maybe we should invite him to our ball."

"I daresay his appearance would certainly make it the talk of London."

Yes, Catherine thought, *it would.*

The carriage came to a halt outside Winnie's residence.

"Would you like to come in for a moment?" Winnie asked.

"Yes, I'd love to see Whit."

"That, my dear friend, is the very reason you should marry. You so enjoy children."

"I think it important to enjoy their father."

Winnie blanched. Catherine reached out and

touched Winnie's arm. "I didn't mean anything by that, Winnie."

"I know."

"For myself, I just need there to be something special between me and the man I might marry."

"I hope you find it."

In Winnie's voice, Catherine heard the despair of a woman who had not found happiness.

The footman assisted them in leaving the carriage. They walked up the steps and entered the house.

"Where have you been?"

The voice was harsh, demanding. Winnie squeaked and jumped aside, knocking into Catherine, and they both did a strange little stepping dance to keep from losing their balance.

Avendale laughed in a mean sort of way. "I didn't mean to startle you."

Catherine didn't believe that. He moved from near the window where he'd obviously been watching them.

"Answer me, Duchess."

So formal. Winnie was his wife for goodness' sakes. Catherine heard her swallow.

"We were spending the afternoon visiting with Lady Charlotte," Winnie said.

"She's naught but a gossip. Why would you spend time with her?"

"We spend time calling on many of the ladies. It's what we do," Winnie said.

He narrowed his dark eyes. His hair was almost black. Claybourne's was darker, and yet it didn't make him seem as sinister. Avendale wasn't nearly as tall as Claybourne but what he lacked in height, he made up for in width. Still, Catherine thought Claybourne could take him easily enough.

Avendale shifted his attention to Catherine, and unlike Winnie, she didn't cower. "Shouldn't you be seeing after your father?"

She wanted to tell him it was none of his business. Instead she said, "He has nurses. It would weigh on him if I spent all of my time with him."

"Where did you say you spent the afternoon?"

Why in the world did he sound so suspicious? "With Lady Charlotte."

"Where?"

"In her garden."

"For how long?"

"About twenty minutes or so."

"And before that?"

Catherine looked at Winnie who was studying the tips of her shoes. Did she always go through this inquisition?

"We stopped by to visit with the Countess of Chesney. After our visit, she invited us to join her at Lady Charlotte's."

"And before that?" he asked again.

"Would you like me to provide you with a written schedule?"

He grinned, more like one who was irritated than amused. "No need. You don't like being challenged, do you?"

"No, Your Grace, I do not, but then name me one person who does."

"I'm afraid I can't."

Winnie cleared her throat. "Did you have a need of me?"

He slid his gaze back to her and Catherine was aware of her shrinking.

"Yes, as a matter of fact. My boots were not polished to my satisfaction. I took a strap to the lad. I think he'll do a much better job in the morning, but will you please inspect them before I have need of them?"

"Yes, of course."

"You took a strap to the boy who polishes your boots because they weren't shiny enough?" Catherine asked.

"Are you questioning me in my home, Lady Catherine?"

"Yes, I rather think I am."

He snorted. "You need a man to put you in your place."

She felt fingers digging into her arm. She knew Winnie was warning her. Do not poke a stick at a tiger. Oh, but it was tempting, so very tempting.

"It's rather late, my father's expecting me. I should go"— *without seeing Whit.* But she knew she was in danger of saying something she shouldn't.

"I'll see you out," Avendale said.

He followed her out to where her carriage waited. Catherine forced herself to place her hand in his when he offered to assist her. His fingers closed painfully around hers.

"I believe you're a rather bad influence on my wife," he said in a low voice.

Catherine's heart thudded against her chest. "Are you threatening me?"

"Of course not, but I'm not certain you understand a wife's place in the world."

She met and held his gaze. "On the contrary, Your Grace, I fear it is you who doesn't understand a woman's place."

Before he could say anything further, she stepped up and into the carriage. She tugged her hand free of his.

"Take care, Lady Catherine. You never know what dangers are about."

Oh, she had a very good idea about the dangers. The carriage moved forward and Catherine took several deep breaths to calm the erratic beating of her heart. Just before the carriage turned onto the street, she glanced over her shoulder.

Avendale was still there, watching her.

Chapter 8

Traveling in his coach, Luke couldn't help but be irritated by the amount of time he was spending preparing himself for his nightly visits to Dodger's. He'd never before been on a schedule. Now he was on one every night—not only for when he went to Dodger's but for when he left. Catherine insisted. Three at the latest.

After all, she needed her beauty rest.

Not that he attributed her beauty to the amount of sleep she indulged in. He had a feeling she could go a week without sleep and still be ravishing. It was more than the alabaster of her skin or the honey of her hair. It was the confidence that she exuded—as though she somehow demanded that when a man looked at her, he would see naught but her perfection.

He'd known a good many beautiful women, but he'd never given much thought to exactly why they were beautiful. Catherine in particular puzzled him. She wasn't striking, and yet he was hard pressed to think of anyone he found more attractive.

Not even Frannie could compare, and yet, he saw more perfection in her features, and so it stood to reason that she should be the more beautiful of the two. Certainly, gazing at her had always brought him pleasure, but he saw something else there when he looked at Catherine. Something he couldn't identify, something he couldn't understand.

But it wasn't for Catherine that he'd taken to properly preparing himself for his late-night outings. It was for Frannie. He was taking an inordinate amount of time each evening because of Frannie.

Before he'd asked Frannie to marry him, he'd simply gone to Dodger's whenever he wanted, and while he never dressed as a beggar, he'd certainly never taken the time to shave, bathe, and change into fresh clothing. He brushed his hair, he applied sandalwood cologne. He was always properly decked out.

For several nights now, he'd gone to all this trouble, all this bother. It wasn't as though Frannie had an opportunity to notice. As soon as he led Catherine through the back doorway into the private hallway where customers were forbidden, she disappeared into Frannie's office, closed the door, and they were secreted away until Catherine came out, prepared to go home.

Frannie would give him a sweet smile, but by then his breath was tainted with whiskey, his hair was furrowed from the numerous times that he'd combed his fingers through it, and he was no longer in an agreeable mood because for the first time in his life he was losing at the gaming tables. He was distracted, not concentrating on the gents at the table. He wanted to know what was going on behind that blasted closed door.

To further add to his irritation, Jim's reports were of little use. Today Catherine had again visited with the Duchess of Avendale—apparently she was helping the duchess with a party that she was giving—bought a new fan and a new parasol, gone into a bookshop and come out with a purchase, which Jim, with a few well-placed coins, had learned was *David Copperfield*. According to the shop owner, Lady Catherine Mabry had a fondness for Dickens.

She'd also stopped by Frannie's orphanage. Had simply stood on the street and looked at it. What was that about? How did she even know the orphanage existed?

Now they were heading home and he knew no more at that precise moment than he had when he'd picked her up several hours earlier.

"So when will I see some progress?" he asked curtly.

"When we're ready."

"Surely by now you've taught her something."

"I've taught her a great deal."

"Give me an example."

"I'm not going to list out our accomplishments. You'll see them when we're ready."

"Can you give me an estimate as to when that might be?"

"No."

"I'm most anxious to wed her."

"Yes, I know."

She said it on a sigh as though she could hardly be bothered to care.

"I thought you were equally anxious for me to see about your business," he reminded her.

"I am . . . I was . . . I . . ."

"Having second thoughts?"

"No, not really. I just—I've heard that Marcus Langdon is seeking to prove you're not the rightful heir."

What did that have to do with their arrangement? How had she heard? And how had he not? Still, he wasn't about to let on that her words had taken him by surprise.

"You sound concerned. I assure you there's no cause to fret. He's threatened to do this on numerous occasions. Usually when he wants an increase in allowance."

"You provide him with an allowance?"

"Don't be shocked. It's not uncommon for a lord to see after those entrusted to his care. The old gent requested that I see after them, and so I do."

"Out of guilt?"

"Why can it not be out of kindness?"

"Are you a kind man then?"

He laughed. "Hardly. You know what I am, Catherine. Or more importantly, what I am not. I'm not the rightful heir. I'm not the true grandson to the previous Earl of Claybourne. But he entrusted his titles and his estates to my keeping, and keep them I shall."

"Do you not worry that I'll go to the courts and speak on Mr. Langdon's behalf?"

"I don't worry in the least. We're partners in

crime now, Catherine, you and I. Seek to drag me down, and you shall fall with me. You'll have to explain when I told you. And when it comes out that you've been in my company all these many nights . . ."

He let his voice trail off into the velvety darkness, with the unspoken promise of retribution. One he'd never carry out. He was not in the habit of harming women—in any fashion. Not that she'd know that. She'd expect the worst of him. Even though there were moments when he thought she was different, he knew that deep down she saw him as everyone else did: a cad, a scoundrel, a man whose life was built on the foundation of deception—and sooner or later, the façade would crumble.

And he saw her as . . . a lady. High-born. Elegant. Her rose scent had begun to invade his clothes, take up permanent residence in his nostrils. Throughout the day, he'd discover times when he thought he could smell her. He'd find himself looking around, wondering if she were near, if she'd somehow managed to sneak up on him. When he was walking the crowded streets, he'd sometimes think he heard her voice. He wanted to keep as much distance as possible between them, and yet, she was somehow managing to weave her way into his life.

He wanted to ask her how her day was. What she'd talked to her friends about. He wanted to know which one of Dickens's works was her favorite. Who else did she read? What did she do that Jim wasn't able to spy on? What made her happiest? What made her sad?

A horse suddenly whinnied, the coach jostled then stopped.

"What the devil?"

"What's going on?" she asked.

Luke reached for the cane sword he kept beneath the seat, because he never knew when he might be required to walk through the London streets. "Stay here."

He leapt out of the coach and closed the door firmly behind him. It was so very late and the street was empty.

Save for the six ruffians who now stood before him. One man held a knife to his footman's throat, another did the same with his driver. He imagined they'd come out of the shadows, leaping onto the coach, taking both men by surprise—even though Luke had trained them better.

It was very easy to become complacent.

"Is this a robbery, gentlemen?" he asked calmly. He could see other knives, as well as wooden instruments that could be used for bludgeoning.

"It will be, m'lord, once we've sent ye to the devil."

Catherine's heart was pounding so hard that she could scarcely breathe. She moved the curtain aside only a fraction. There was more shadow than light but she could see Claybourne was surrounded. His only weapon was his walking stick.

Then in a lightning-quick movement, he pulled it apart to reveal a rather nasty-looking swordlike instrument.

"I believe, gentlemen, you'll be breaking fast with the devil this morning, not I."

He lunged toward the man who held his footman and the footman somehow managed to break free of the hold and send the ruffian to the ground.

Claybourne's move was a feint, Catherine realized, a ploy to simply distract that man so the footman would be at an advantage, because no sooner had Claybourne made a motion to go one way, he reversed direction, making a jabbing motion toward the man who held his coachman. But the coachman had already elbowed his captor and was skillfully avoiding the knife.

While both his servants were now doing their best to fend off the men attacking them, Claybourne was left to deal with the other four—who were taking unfair advantage of the situation. But then she supposed that was what these sorts of cads were accustomed to doing.

Claybourne had somehow managed to kick one of the men in the stomach. Doubled over, he'd dropped his weapon—a large wooden stick. Catherine thought if she could retrieve it, she could give him a few good whacks on the head and even the odds a bit. Before she could think it through clearly, she'd opened the door and stepped out—

Claybourne's back was to her and a man with a wicked-looking knife was coming up behind him.

"Nooo!" she screamed.

She felt the agonizing fire erupt across her palm, and only then did she realize she'd put her hand up to stop the knife from slicing Claybourne. The man wielding the weapon seemed to be in shock that he'd attacked a lady.

Catherine looked at the crimson flow invading her glove and staggered back.

"Let's go, mates!" someone yelled.

She was vaguely aware of someone grunting, the echo of pounding footsteps.

"Catherine?"

She blinked. Claybourne was kneeling beside her. What was she doing on the ground? When had she fallen? Why was it suddenly so very dark?

"He was going to kill you," she murmured. Or thought she did. The words seem to come from a great distance.

"That's no excuse to put yourself in harm's way."

The insufferable ingrate lifted her into his arms and carried her to the coach. He'd barely gotten her inside before following after her, sitting beside her. "Here," he said, and she felt him wrapping something around her hand as the coach lurched forward.

"Your servants—"

"They're fine."

"What's that?"

"My handkerchief."

"It'll be ruined."

"Good Lord, Catherine, your hand is likely ruined. I don't give a damn about a bit of cloth."

"Your language is vulgar, sir."

"I believe the occasion warrants it."

"Indeed it does."

He chuckled, a soothing sound that made her want to reach out and comb her fingers through his hair, assure herself that he was indeed unharmed.

"Who were they?" she asked.

"I don't know," he said quietly.

"They wanted to kill you."

He said nothing.

"Why?" she asked.

"I'm a man with many enemies, Catherine." He tucked her up against his side, pressed his lips to the top of her head. "But never before have I had a lovely guardian angel."

Chapter 9

"It's my hand, not my legs," Catherine said as Luke swept her into his arms as soon as she appeared in the doorway of the coach intending to step out.

Luke had instructed his driver to go to his residence straightaway, to the back, where none would witness who was coming inside.

"Yes, but the faster I get you indoors, the more quickly I can have a look."

"I'm quite capable of moving quickly."

"Stop complaining and just accept that on this matter you'll not win."

"Such a bully," she muttered, before nestling her head more securely against his shoulder.

Luke was smiling before he realized it. How was it that she managed to stir to life every emotion possible in him? First she irritated him like the devil, and then she had tried to protect him. He'd spun around in time to see her, to see the knife slashing—and his stomach had dropped to the ground. Fury had almost blinded him. At that precise moment, he'd thought he could have killed all six ruffians without breaking a sweat. They must have realized their mistake in turning on her, must have seen the murder glittering in his eyes—to have run off as they had. Luke couldn't bear the thought of losing her, and even as he thought that, he realized she wasn't his to lose.

They were merely partners. He should have felt a detachment where she was concerned, but what he was beginning to feel toward her was an appreciation. It bothered him that he was coming to care for her, that he thought of her far more than he should.

The footman darted ahead and opened the door that led into the kitchen. Luke shouldered his way through. "Go fetch my physician. Quickly now."

"Yes, m'lord."

Catherine stiffened in his arms. "No, no, we can't have anyone else aware that I'm here."

"It's all right. He's very discreet."

Gingerly he set her in the chair. Reaching out, he turned up the flame in the lamp that Cook left on the table every night. He liked the rooms in his house lit. He'd had too many nights in utter darkness.

Turning from her, he grabbed a knife. Then he pulled out a chair, settled it in front of her, sat down, and placed the knife on the table.

"What are you going to do with that? My hand is already sliced."

If she weren't so pale with a fine sheen of sweat across her brow, if she hadn't been so damned brave, he might have lashed out at her. Instead he just asked quietly, "Do you not trust me at all?"

She nodded, and he wasn't certain if she was nodding yes, she didn't trust him or yes, she did. It suddenly occurred to him that it really didn't matter. All that mattered was that he trusted her.

Very gently he took her hand. He could feel the small tremors traveling through it. "This is likely to hurt," he said as he began to remove the handkerchief.

"You say that as though it's not hurting now."

"Is it hurting very badly?"

Catherine tried not to look, tried so hard not to look, but there was so much blood, it was as though each drop were a magnet for her eyes. "It hurts like the very devil."

He chuckled low. "You're such a brave girl."

She didn't know why his words warmed her, why she cared that he had a good opinion of her. "There's so much blood."

"Yes," he said quietly, removing the last of the cloth, revealing the ghastly parted flesh with the river of crimson running through it. She wondered how much worse it might have been if the knife hadn't had to first slice through her glove.

"Oh, dear God." She turned her head away as though closing her eyes wasn't enough.

His hold on her hand tightened. "Don't swoon on me."

"I'm not going to swoon." She didn't bother to keep the irritation from her voice. "I hate that you think I'm such a ninny."

"I assure you, Catherine, that particular thought regarding you has never once crossed my mind."

She heard a scrape of metal over wood and opened her eyes in time to see him lifting the knife. Very gingerly, he used it to slice her glove further, to the end. Then he very carefully parted the cloth and slowly peeled back the material, gently tugging it off each finger. She was suddenly having a very difficult time drawing in a breath, the room had grown incredibly hot, and she feared she *might* be in danger of swooning—even though she'd assured him she wouldn't.

She imagined him in a bedroom, removing clothes from a woman—from her—with the same care. Revealing every inch of her flesh for his perusal. He was studying her hand as though he'd never before seen bare fingers. He slowly trailed his finger along the outline of her hand.

"I don't think it's too bad," he said quietly.

Swallowing, she nodded.

"If you ever put yourself in harm's way like that again, I'll put you over my knee."

"And do what?" she asked indignantly.

He lifted his gaze to hers, and she saw the worry in his eyes, before he smiled. "Kiss your bare bottom."

Her face must have shown shock at his words—she could only hope it revealed shock and not desire—because he shook his head. "My apologies. That was entirely inappropriate. I forget who you are."

"And who is that?"

"Not one of Jack's doxies."

She didn't want to contemplate him kissing a woman's bare bottom, kissing anything for that matter.

He held her gaze, held her hand. Looking into his eyes was so much more welcoming than looking at her raggedly torn palm. They drew her in, made her forget that he'd almost been killed. She reached up with her unwounded hand and brushed the hair back from his brow. She should ask him to slice off that glove as well so she could feel his skin against her fingertips. His eyes darkened, his gaze became more intense, grew closer as he leaned in—

The door opened and they both jumped.

"What trouble have you gotten yourself into now, Luke?" the man asked, closing the door behind him. He reminded Catherine of an angel, with a halo of blond curls around his head. His eyes, as blue as the sky, widened. "What have we here?"

"A bit of a mishap," Claybourne said as he rose from the chair.

The man set his black bag on the table and took the chair Claybourne had vacated. "*Who* have we here?"

"You don't need to know," Claybourne said.

The man smiled. "I treat far too many to remember all their names. I'm William Graves."

"You're a physician?" Catherine asked.

"Quite right." He placed his hand beneath hers with extreme gentleness, but she didn't grow warm, her breath didn't catch, and she didn't feel in danger of swooning.

"I'm Catherine," she felt compelled to say.

"Are you one of his rescued lambs?" he asked as he studied her wound.

"No, she is not," Claybourne snapped. He dragged a chair over and sat beside her. "You're not here for gossip. How badly is she hurt?"

"It's rather nasty, but it could have been worse." He lifted his gaze to hers. "I want to stitch it up. It won't be pleasant, but it'll heal better, more quickly."

He seemed to be asking for her permission, so she nodded.

"Very good." He pressed a cloth to her palm. "Hold this in place while I prepare things. Luke, go fetch some whiskey."

He took objects out of his bag and laid them out on the table. Then making himself quite at home, he began moving around the kitchen, setting a kettle of water on the stove.

"You shouldn't bother with tea," Catherine said. "I really don't think I could drink it."

He smiled at her. "You'll be drinking the whiskey. The water is so I can keep things clean. I've noticed that those I treat in squalor tend to die of infection more so than those I treat in tidy houses."

Claybourne walked back in, holding a bottle and a glass filled to the brim. "Here, drink this."

Taking a sip of the bitter brew, she grimaced.

"All of it," he ordered.

"I don't know if I can."

"The more you drink, the better it tastes."

She took another sip. It didn't taste any better.

"It's not tea, gulp it," he ordered impatiently.

"Don't be tart with me. I saved your life."

Setting the bottle on the table, he sat again in the chair beside her. "Yes, you did."

He trailed his fingers tenderly along her cheek. It was all she could do not to turn her lips into his palm. She moved her head beyond his reach and concentrated on taking several gulps of the whiskey. It did seem the more she drank, the better it tasted. She was becoming light-headed, which made her want to curl up in Claybourne's lap and sleep, safe and secure.

Dr. Graves came to stand in front of her, took her wounded hand, and placed it on the table. "Close your eyes and think about something else."

She closed her eyes and started to think about—

She took a sharp intake of breath and her eyes flew open as liquid fire poured over her palm. "Oh, dear God, what was that?"

"The whiskey," Dr. Graves said.

"You poured—"

"I think it kills germs. Try to relax. You're going to feel a stab—"

"Catherine?"

A warm hand cradled her cheek, turned her head. She gazed into eyes so silver, so filled with concern. "Think about something else," Claybourne ordered.

She shook her head, trying. To her mortification, she flinched and released a tiny squeak when she felt something sharp being jabbed into her flesh.

Claybourne leaned near and then his mouth was blanketing hers, skillfully plying her lips apart. Oh, the fool, did he not fear that she might bite down—

He tasted of the whiskey that he'd ordered her to drink, and she wondered if he'd needed some to fortify himself for what she was about to endure. She didn't know if it was his whiskey mingling with hers or his mouth plundering hers that was such a distraction, but she was suddenly only vaguely aware of something happening with her palm and incredibly aware of the taste, feel, and tangy scent of Claybourne. His hands were rough in her hair. She heard a hairpin drop to the floor. She was surprised they didn't all tumble out.

Deepening the kiss, he swirled his tongue over hers, and she thought if she were standing that her knees would have been too weak to support her. She knew she should pull back, should slap him with her one good hand, but he was so incredibly delicious. And while she knew it wasn't desire for her that prompted his actions, but simply desire to distract her, still she was grateful for the moment, grateful to have one more opportunity to experience his kiss. She'd been haunted ever since he'd kissed her in the library. The kiss hadn't been nearly long enough then, and she knew that no matter when this kiss ended, it wouldn't be long enough either.

The kiss seemed to encompass more than her mouth. It seemed to reach into the very core of her womanhood and awaken yearnings she'd never before known. Desire rushed forward, dulling everything else. She knew she was wanton, loose, shameful to harbor this intense craving for him to come nearer, for him to press more than his lips against hers. She thought of all the warnings he'd given her that first night. She risked more than her reputation with him; she risked her heart.

"Luke? Luke, I'm finished."

Claybourne broke free of the kiss and drew back; he seemed as dazed as she.

"Not sure I've ever seen quite so inventive a distraction," the doctor said.

"Yes, well, it worked didn't it?" Claybourne got to his feet, snatched up the glass of whiskey she'd set aside earlier, and downed the contents in one long swallow.

Oh, yes, it had worked. Her hand was not only stitched but it was wrapped in a white bandage.

"It's common to feel dizzy after such an ordeal," Dr. Graves said. "Give yourself a few moments."

She nodded. "Thank you, thank you for your attentions. I assume Claybourne will pay you for your services."

"He paid me long ago."

"You're another one of Feagan's children, aren't you?"

He gave her a wry smile, before coming to his feet and beginning to put the tools of his trade back into his bag. "In about a week, anyone should be able to remove the stitches for you. But if you'd rather I do it, just have Luke send word."

"Thank you," she said again.

"It was my honor to be of service." He snapped his bag closed, stopped to whisper something to Claybourne, and then made his way out the door, leaving her alone in the room with Claybourne. She dearly wanted him to move nearer, to touch her, to kiss her. The whiskey was influencing her thoughts. Or perhaps it was simply the ordeal of the night. Their surviving had created a bond between them that hadn't existed before.

"How will you explain it?" Claybourne asked.

"Pardon?" She felt as though her thoughts were moving through honey, especially those that concerned him. How would she explain wanting him to kiss her again?

"The hand?"

"Oh." She looked at it, turning it one way and another. It was aching. Perhaps she should drink more whiskey before she left. "I'll just say I cut it on a piece of glass or something. There's really no one to challenge me. One of the advantages to my brother traipsing all over the world."

"I should get you home now."

"Oh, yes, indeed."

To her surprise, in the coach, he didn't sit opposite her as a gentleman should, but he sat beside her, his arm around her, holding her as close as a dear friend—or dare she think it, *as a lover?*

"I'm sorry this happened," he said, his voice low and intimate within the confines of the coach.

She was incredibly exhausted. All she wanted to do was sleep. "Not to worry."

"About the kiss—"

"Don't be concerned. I shan't mention it to Frannie. I know it was the only recourse you had to distract me."

"I know some coin tricks, but I didn't think they'd be as effective."

"I'm certain they wouldn't have been." She sighed. "Are you attacked often?"

"From time to time, there have been dangers."

"Do you think it was Mr. Marcus Langdon?" She knew better than to refer to him as a cousin.

"My death would certainly expedite things for him, but unlike you and I, he's not of a bloodthirsty nature."

She brought her head up quickly, was immediately hit with a spinning world, and dropped her head back against his shoulder. "You think me bloodthirsty?"

"You want me to kill someone."

"Oh, yes. Quite." She'd almost forgotten what had brought her to his door. It was sometimes easy to forget—when Winnie wasn't bruised. When she seemed happy.

Was Catherine's solution a rash one?

As often as she'd lain awake at night pondering solutions before she'd approached Claybourne, she didn't see any other way. And yet sometimes her decision seemed extreme. If only two of Avendale's wives hadn't died mysteriously. If only he didn't take his fists to Winnie.

"Tell me about the rescued lambs," she said, needing a distraction from the discomfort of her thoughts and aching hand.

He groaned low as though irritated—or maybe embarrassed—by the question and she thought he would leave it at that. Finally his low voice filled the coach, lulling her with its purring resonance.

"Each of us has our weakness. For Frannie, it's children. For me, it's unmarried mothers. It began innocently enough. One of my servants had a friend who found herself with child, and she was let go. I suspect the babe's father was the lord of the manor, but he wouldn't claim it. So I sent her to one of my lesser estates. I wasn't using it. I've sent *rescued lambs* there ever since."

He made it seem so unimportant.

"Your good works must cost you a fortune."

"You say that as though you find me generous. If you'll not consider me a braggart, I'll confess that I'm in possession of a fortune, a very nice fortune. What I give is nothing. The truly generous man is the one who gives away his last ha'penny when he can ill afford to do so."

Or one who gives away the last of his soul, she thought desolately, *when it's all that remains to him.* Was she asking too much?

When they arrived at Catherine's residence, the coach came to a halt in the alleyway. Claybourne didn't stop at the gate, but escorted her all the way to the servants' entrance, his hand sturdy beneath her elbow as though she needed the support. Perhaps she did. Sometimes she felt like she was floating, that everything was at a great distance—and then suddenly it would be before her.

"Will you be all right?" he asked.

She nodded. "I'll see you at midnight tonight. Or is it tomorrow? I'm never quite sure how to refer to the upcoming night when dawn has not yet taken this one away."

Cradling her chin, he rubbed his thumb over her lips. It was so dark and foggy that she couldn't determine what he was thinking.

"Do you think you'll be up to teaching Frannie?" he asked.

His question surprised her. She'd expected something a bit more intimate after all they'd shared tonight.

"Yes." She sounded breathless. It irritated her that he had such power over her.

"Good. Tonight then."

He quickly disappeared into the fog, like a phantom. Opening the door, she slipped inside, then pressed her back to the wood. She'd not expected to like Claybourne. She'd wanted only to use him, then forget him.

But she knew now that no matter what the outcome of their arrangement, she would never forget him. Never.

Luke listened to the sounds of the city coming to life as his coach traveled toward its destination. He'd always enjoyed the hustle and bustle of London, but particularly in the early hours of the morning. As a lad, he'd always felt that it offered the promise of opportunity: pockets to be picked, food to be stolen, tricks to be played on the unsuspecting. And always there was Frannie.

From the first night that Jack had taken him to Feagan's, the first night when he had spotted the little girl sitting by the fire, the first night when she had crawled onto the mound of blankets, tucked her small hand in his, and told him not to be afraid, he had loved her.

He remembered nothing of his life before Jack found him. Marcus Langdon and his attempt to claim the title had Luke trying to remember what he could of his past. But there was nothing there. All his memories were of the streets.

Perhaps he should return to them, return to them with Frannie. Let Langdon have the title. Luke certainly didn't need the income. Because of his partnership with Jack, he was a man of wealth in his own right. But he couldn't quite bring himself to give up the title that the old gent had assured him belonged to him. He'd grown to care for the old gent, in his own way, and a part of him thought it would be a betrayal to the one who had saved him from the gallows and looked after him so well.

The coach came to a halt in front of a house that Luke seldom visited. He stepped out onto the cobblestone drive and strode up the steps. He didn't knock or wait for admittance, but simply opened the door and went inside.

A maid, dusting the banister on the nearby stairs, released a tiny screech, then recognizing who he was, curtsied.

"Where are they?" he asked.

"In the breakfast dining room, my lord."

That surprised him. He'd expected to find them still abed, had relished the notion of rousing them from slumber. But perhaps he shouldn't have been surprised. A guilty conscience made it difficult to sleep late, made it difficult to sleep at all. Without hesitation, he made his way through the residence. He wore neither hat nor gloves, because he'd not thought the formality was required when taking Catherine home. It was only on his way back to his residence that he'd changed his mind and decided to stop by here first. His clothes were unkempt, but then he'd never been interested in impressing them.

He strode into the breakfast dining room as though he owned it. His determined footsteps no doubt alerted the occupants to his arrival. Scraping back his chair, Marcus Langdon came to his feet with such swiftness that he nearly lost his balance. His mother gasped, her fleshy face quivering as she struggled to rise.

"You have no right to be here, sir!" she exclaimed, spittle flying over her plate, a plate heaped with enough food to feed a family of four.

"On the contrary, madam, I pay the lease on the residence." He walked to the sideboard, took a plate, and began selecting items of interest. They certainly didn't skimp when it came to their palate. "I daresay I purchased the goods that provided this lovely breakfast as well as the servants who prepared it." He raised an eyebrow at the footman standing nearby. "See that I have some coffee."

"Yes, my lord." He immediately headed for the doorway that would lead to the kitchen.

Luke carried his plate to the table, took the chair opposite Langdon's mother—he had no doubt she was the more dangerous of the two—and smiled as though all was right with the world. "Please, don't let me interrupt your meal."

Langdon sat down cautiously, his mother less graciously.

"Good God, is that blood on your shirt?" Langdon asked.

Catherine's blood. Luke hadn't given any thought to the fact that she'd bled on his clothing. Thinking about how close he'd come to losing her, he had a strange sensation, as though he might be ill, but he couldn't dwell on that now or afford to be distracted. He had these two to deal with first.

As though Langdon's question were of no consequence, Luke began slicing off a bit of ham. "Yes, as a matter of fact. You'll no doubt find this interesting. A strange thing happened on my way home from Dodger's in the early hours of the morning. My coach was stopped and some footpads threatened my life. Can you imagine?"

Langdon paled. His mother turned a ghastly, blotchy red. Luke suspected that before bitterness had hardened her features she'd been a lovely woman.

"Were you hurt?" Langdon asked.

Luke wasn't surprised by the true concern echoed in the man's voice. Marcus Langdon was two years Luke's senior. He had the famous Claybourne silver eyes, as well as the dark hair. He was a handsome fellow. Luke suspected that if not for Langdon's mother's resentment of Luke that the two men might have even been friends. But Langdon's loyalty rested with his mother, not with the man who had usurped his right to the title.

"Barely at all," Luke assured him. "As you can imagine, growing up on the London streets as I did, I'm quite adept at dealing with those who crawl up out of its underbelly. Any notion who might want me dead these days?"

Langdon shifted his gaze to his mother, then back to Luke. "No."

"Most of London, I suspect," Mrs. Langdon said. "You're not a popular sort, but then thieves never are."

Luke gave her an indulgent smile. "Are we back to that? I've heard that you've filed with the courts."

Langdon cast another quick glance at his mother, who'd squared her shoulders in defiance.

"How'd you hear of that?" Langdon asked.

"I have my ways."

"The title rightfully belongs to *my* son," Langdon's mother said.

"The old gent didn't agree."

"You never call him your grandfather. Marcus did."

Luke fought not to show how the force of her words struck him. "I'm well aware of that, madam, but you'll not wrest the title from me. I enjoy too much the benefits that come with it." He came to his feet and looked at the man who no one in the room believed was truly his cousin. "If you've ever a desire to earn decent pay for an honest day's work, let me know."

"Honest? At Dodger's?"

"I have other business interests. They don't pay as well, but they're more respectable. I could use a good man to help me manage them."

Langdon scoffed. "You don't understand what it is to be a gentleman. You've never understood. We don't *work*."

"Tell me, Langdon, if I cut off your allowance, how would you pay for the solicitor you've hired to represent you in court?"

The man remained silent. Luke knew he was pushing him—and that he was unwise to do so. Yet he seemed unable to stop himself. "The next time I meet with my man of business, perhaps you should come with me, so you'll see exactly what you will inherit if you meet with success in the courts. I assure you that the income you'll derive from your estates will not be nearly as generous as I am. Consider that."

He gave them each a mocking bow before seeing himself out. He'd barely made it into his coach before the pain tore through his head. The head pains came whenever he confronted them, no doubt a result of guilt because he knew they were right and he was wrong. He was holding on to that which didn't belong to him. God knew why he refused to give it up. Perhaps because he thought some good could come from his being considered a peer.

Or perhaps it was simply because the old gent had believed so fervently that Luke belonged here, and for some reason that Luke failed to grasp, he didn't want to disappoint him.

"You tried to have him killed?" Marcus Langdon asked as he paced in front of the fireplace.

"It seemed the most efficient way to achieve my ends."

"But as I explained, I wanted to go through the courts. I want everything legal."

"That could take years."

"I want there to be no doubt that I am the true Earl of Claybourne."

"There's no doubt now. All of London knows he's an imposter."

Marcus despised the calm voice, the absolute absence of emotion.

"I don't want to be party to this—"

"It's far too late to have misgivings now."

Marcus shook his head.

"Why do you have such qualms? He murdered your father."

"That was never proven."

"He's never denied it."

"Quite honestly, he doesn't seem like a killer."

Dark laughter echoed through the room. "But then, neither do I."

Marcus had always thought of hatred as a heated emotion, but looking into the dark eyes of the person standing opposite him, he realized it was cold, very cold—and very, very dangerous.

Chapter 10

Not tonight.
—C

Catherine studied the missive that had been delivered earlier in the evening. Then she compared it to the one she should have burned. It was incomprehensible that they were written by the same hand. The latest was more scribble than anything else, looking like something her father in his infirmity would have written.

Not something that the bold, strong, and daring Lord Claybourne would write.

Unexpected dread filled her. He'd been fighting the ruffians long before she'd stepped out of the coach. He'd disappeared into shadows, only to re-emerge. She'd assumed he was unscathed, but her assumption could be wrong. He could have been wounded. Seriously. And it would be just like him to worry over her wound and allow his own to go untended—to strive to be so amazingly brave and sacrificing.

This very moment, he could be fighting an infection, shivering with a fever, writhing in pain.

His handwriting certainly indicated that something was amiss. And his missive was so blunt, so curt. After all they'd shared, she was owed an explanation. One way or another, she intended to get it—on her schedule not his.

She waited until later, until most decent people wouldn't be about. Then she called for the carriage. Just as she had the first night she'd visited Claybourne, she had the driver drop her off at St. James's Park.

"No need to wait," she said.

"My lady—"

"I'll be fine." And then she walked away before he could argue further.

She slipped through alleyways, hid behind trees, and made her way cautiously to the servants' door. She knocked briskly.

A plump woman who wore her apron over her nightgown opened the door. The cook, no doubt, always ready to prepare a meal at a moment's notice.

"I need to see his lordship," Catherine said.

"He's not receiving guests."

"Is he home?"

The woman hesitated.

"It's important that I see him." Catherine brushed past the woman, ignoring her protests.

"Mr. Fitzsimmons! Mr. Fitzsimmons!" the cook screeched.

Catherine would never tolerate such caterwauling in her household. Claybourne needed a wife, and before the thought had reached its end, she remembered that his acquisition of a wife was uppermost in his mind. Otherwise, they'd not now be in partnership.

The butler walked into the kitchen, his eyes widening in surprise when he spotted Catherine.

"I need to see Claybourne," Catherine announced without preamble.

"He's abed, madam."

"Is he ill?"

"I do not discuss my lordship's business."

"I must see him. It's a matter of life and death. I daresay, you'll be sacked if he learns I was here and was not taken to him immediately."

He studied her for a long moment as though he might have the audacity to argue, then he bowed slightly. "If you'll be so good as to come with me."

She followed him out of the kitchen and into the hallway.

"Madam—"

"No one knows I'm here," she interrupted, certain that he had plans to distract her from her purpose. Also very much aware by the way he addressed her that he hadn't a clue to her proper station in society, which was to her advantage.

He sighed as though she were a burden too great to bear. As he escorted her up the stairs, Catherine thought to ask, "He is alone, isn't he?"

"Yes, ma'am."

Catherine suddenly wondered what in the world she thought she was doing here. Other than being reckless. Their relationship was one of master and servant with her being the master. No, it wasn't. It was a partnership. And she needed him in good health to carry out his part of the bargain. So she would check on him, determine what he needed, and see that he acquired it.

After they reached the top of the stairs, the butler walked down the hallway to a closed door. Catherine grabbed a lamp from a nearby table.

"If you'll wait here—" he began as he opened the door.

But Catherine had no plans to wait, to risk having Claybourne insist his servant remove her from the premises. Before the butler could announce her or discuss her with Claybourne, she brushed past him saying, "Your services are no longer required."

She closed the door on his stunned expression, then quickly turned to face the person lying on the large four-poster bed.

Claybourne flicked the sheet over his hips, but not before she caught sight of an incredible expanse of bare leg, firm thigh, and rounded buttock. He wasn't wearing a nightshirt. Apparently he wasn't wearing anything at all.

"What are you doing here?" he ground out, pressing the heel of his hand against his forehead. "I sent . . . a missive."

"You're in pain."

"I am well aware of that."

"Did you get conked last night?"

"Don't be absurd. Just go."

She remembered how her father had suffered terrible head pains, and then one night—

"You should send for your physician—Dr. Graves."

"He's already been here. It's only my head. I'll be fine by tomorrow. Just leave me to it."

"You say that as though you've encountered this before."

She took a step nearer. It didn't smell like a sick-room, didn't smell like her father's room. It carried the strong, tart fragrance of male. For some strange reason, the scent appealed to her, more than the fragrance of flowers in a garden.

"You weren't wounded last night?" she asked again.

"No." He was breathing heavily, laboriously.

She placed the lamp on the bedside table, removed her cloak, and draped it over a nearby chair. She sat on the edge of the bed.

"This isn't prop—" he began.

"Shh! Since when do you care about what's proper? Just lie still."

Leaning forward, she placed her hands on either side of his head and, with her fingers, began to gently massage his temples. His brow was deeply furrowed, his jaw clenched. She could see the pain etched in the silver of his eyes as he held her gaze.

"You're playing a dangerous game, Catherine."

"No one knows I'm here. I took precautions and was very careful. Even the man who's been following me wasn't about."

"What?" He shot up in bed, groaned, grabbed his head, and fell back down.

"Damn, damn, damn," he muttered, breathing with short, quick gasps.

"Is swearing thrice more effective than swearing once?" she asked.

He chuckled low in his throat. "Hardly. But it brings me some satisfaction. Now, tell me . . . about this man who's following you."

"Only if you'll close your eyes and allow me to do what I can to ease your pain. My father suffered horrendous headaches. Applying pressure at his temples helped."

She was near enough to see that Claybourne was no stranger to hurt—his body bore the evidence with small scars here and there on what was otherwise an immensely attractive chest. She hated the thought of him enduring any sort of discomfort. What had he ever done to deserve such a harsh life? That even now, when he had almost everything, he still suffered.

"Close your eyes," she ordered.

To her immense surprise, he complied without arguing.

"Shouldn't—"

"Shh," she interrupted. "Just relax. Shh. I'm going to turn down the lamp just a bit."

She moved away to turn down the flame in the lamp on the table beside his bed. He groaned as though the pain had spiked. Returning her hands to his face, she began circling her fingers over his temples.

"Your hand."

"It's not bothering me," she lied, not certain why she felt this great need to ease his suffering even at the expense of her own comfort. Perhaps the scuffle last night had formed a bond between them. They'd fought the same battle and survived. "Did you send a missive to Frannie?"

He moved his head slightly from side to side. "They'll know."

Then this was something he'd suffered before, no doubt suffered alone. Why wasn't Frannie here to ease his hurt?

"What did Dr. Graves recommend?"

"He gave me a powder. Didn't help."

His breathing became less labored. "Now, tell me about this man."

Even now when he was in pain, he was concerned about her. And even though she was alone in his bedchamber—in his bed for that matter—he was being a perfect gentleman. She'd always thought of Lucian Langdon as a rogue, a scamp, and far more unflattering terms, but she was discovering the legend of Lucian Langdon was far removed from the reality. The legend was a man to be despised; the reality was one that she thought she could very easily come to care for a great deal. She wanted to end his discomfort and bring him what comfort she could.

"I don't know. I'm probably being silly, but I keep seeing a gentleman. I think it's the same gentleman. It's difficult to tell, because I've only been able to catch glimpses of his face. He always turns away, and it would be entirely improper for me to approach him."

"Then perhaps it's nothing."

"That's what I tried to tell myself, but it's his not trying to garner attention that captures my attention. Yesterday I went into various shops, made unnecessary purchases, and he always seemed to be waiting when I came out. When I looked away to see if anyone else was about, and then looked back to where he'd been, he'd disappeared."

"Perhaps he's one of your many admirers."

She scoffed. "I have no admirers."

"I find that difficult to believe."

He sounded as though he was on the verge of drifting into sleep, and she couldn't help but believe her ministrations were causing his pain to recede. She tried to squelch the spark of envy that flared with the thought of Frannie being here and ministering to his needs. She liked Frannie. She truly did. She was sweet, and kind, and so unpretentious. Catherine understood why the young woman feared moving about in aristocratic circles, where ladies were so much more confident.

"This fellow . . . is there a reason for him to follow you," Claybourne asked.

"None that I can think of. You don't suppose he's responsible for last night's attack, do you?"

His eyes flew open, concern furrowed his brow. "Why would you think that?"

"It just seems too coincidental. I can't think of a reason for anyone to follow me."

"I'm certain the attack last night had more to do with me than you. A description of the fellow would be helpful."

"Helpful for what?"

"For determining who he is."

"Oh, you know all the ruffians in London, do you?"

"I know a good many. So what does he look like?"

"He wears a large floppy hat pulled low so I'm

not certain of his hair color. Dark I think. His features are very rough-looking, difficult to describe because there's nothing distinctive about them."

"Would you recognize him if you saw him again?"

"Possibly, but you shouldn't worry about it right now," she said softly. "You need your pains to go away."

He barely nodded before closing his eyes again.

"Keep talking," he ordered, so gently that it was more of a plea.

"About what?"

"Tell me . . . how it goes with Frannie."

She sighed. She should have expected that he'd want to speak of his love.

"It goes very well. She is bright as you said. But I think we need to expand the lessons beyond her workplace. I think it might be better to have them here. For example, there is no tea service at Dodger's. No drawing room. It is not a lady's world."

"Here . . . is not a lady's world."

"But it will be, once you marry. We'll discuss it when you're better."

A corner of his mouth quirked up. "You don't like losing arguments."

"I didn't realize we were arguing, but honestly, does anyone want to lose?" She leaned up and whispered near his ear, "Go to sleep now. You'll awaken to no pain."

Her arms were growing tired. She moved up so she could rest her elbows on the bed. She'd hardly given any thought to the notion that her change in position would place her breasts against his chest. But he was too far gone to notice, while she was acutely aware of her nipples tightening. Almost painfully so. Perhaps they'd both be in pain before the night was done.

Yet she couldn't deny she was content to remain where she was.

She continued to rub his temples. With her thumbs she began to stroke his cheeks.

All the while taking note of the fine lines etched in his face. He was not much older than thirty, and yet strife had chiseled at his features. That first night in the library, she'd studied the portrait of the man who should have been earl before him. It wasn't difficult to see the similarities. Even though Claybourne claimed she'd find none, she almost imagined that she had. How different the portrait might have looked if the man had lived a life as rough as the man she now comforted.

She didn't like acknowledging how worried she'd been, how much she was coming to care for him. As a friend. One friend for another. There would never be anything more between them than that.

He was in love with Frannie, and Catherine, well, Catherine had yet to meet anyone who could claim her heart. Although she couldn't deny that something about Claybourne did stir her. His odd honesty. His willingness to defend her. The depth of love he held for another woman and the lengths he would go to in order to have her in his life.

Catherine couldn't imagine having a man's devotion to that extent. Having met Claybourne, she didn't know if she could settle for less in her own husband—if she were ever to meet a man she thought she could be content to marry.

She felt the tension slowly easing out of Claybourne, was aware of him drifting off to sleep. She could probably leave now, and yet she had no desire to go. Against her better judgment she laid her head on his chest, listened to the steady pounding of his heart.

He'd been in intense agony and yet he'd still been considerate enough to send her a missive.

Considerate. She'd not expected that of him.

Kind. Honest. Courageous. Gentle. Caring.

She'd thought she'd be dealing with the devil. And he was very slowly, in her eyes at least, beginning to resemble an angel.

A dark angel, to be sure, but an angel nonetheless.

"Mummy!"

"Shh, darling, shh, we have to be quiet. We're playing a game. We're going to hide from Papa."

"Scared."

"Shh. Don't be frightened, darling. Shh. Mummy will never let anything bad happen—"

Luke awoke with a start, a weight pressing down on his chest. The dream was bringing back the headache that he'd been fighting all day, ever since leaving Marcus Langdon's. But it wasn't Langdon he kept thinking about. It was being in the alley—the knives, the clubs, the viciousness of the attack. Luke kept seeing Catherine, as he had last night, out of the corner of his eye, defending him, raising her arm to take the blow meant for him.

He usually had his coachman take a circuitous route home, because on more than one occasion they'd been set upon. But ever since he'd begun his association with Catherine, he'd become reckless. He wanted to get her home as quickly as possible. He didn't want to spend any more time than necessary in the coach inhaling her sweet fragrance, carrying on conversations, coming to know her, to see her as more than the spoiled daughter of a duke.

He'd avoided the aristocracy because he didn't want to see the similarities. He didn't want to see them as people he could respect. Through Catherine, he was beginning to understand that they had fears, dreams, hopes, and burdens. They had troubles like everyone else and they faced them head on—like everyone else.

If he saw them as they truly were, the actions he'd taken to become one of them would shame him more than they already did. He'd been brought up to take what wasn't rightfully his in order to survive. If he declared that he wasn't the Earl of Claybourne, would they forgive him his sins? Or would he find himself dancing in the wind?

When he'd rather dance with Catherine.

He jerked out of the lethargic place where he'd been drifting. Why was he thinking of Catherine, dreaming of Catherine . . . why was her scent so strong?

Opening his eyes, he looked at the weight upon his chest.

Catherine. What is she doing—

Then he remembered: her arrival, rubbing his

temples, and sending him into a deep slumber. Had he ever slept that soundly?

Until his dream. When he tried to recall it, his head began to pound unmercifully, so he let it go. The headaches weren't nearly as frequent in London, but when he was at his country residence, they were an almost daily occurrence. Something in the air there was disagreeable to him. He was almost certain of it.

He turned his head slightly and saw Catherine's bandaged hand, marred with blood, resting on his pillow where it had no doubt fallen after she'd succumbed to sleep. It *had* hurt her to rub his temples, and he should chastise her for it.

But it had felt so comforting not to be alone with his pain. He could think of a thousand reasons why she shouldn't be here. The worst of which was that she tempted him as he'd not been tempted in a good long while.

It was because he'd been so long without a woman. He told himself that. He wanted to believe that—as much as the old gent had wanted to believe that Luke was truly his grandson, Luke wanted to believe that what he was beginning to feel for Catherine was just lust, was just his bodily needs, that she called to his desires of the flesh and nothing more.

Because a man couldn't love two women. And his heart was Frannie's. It had always belonged to her. And Catherine was just . . . brave, strong, determined. Irritating.

Even as he thought about how annoying she was, how she'd never bend to a man's will, he took several loosened strands of her hair between his thumb and forefinger, stroking gently and imagining setting it all free and feeling the silkiness cascading over his chest. How he'd like to bury his face in it. How he'd like to feel more than the silkiness of her hair. How he'd like to feel the velvetiness of her flesh. How he'd like to plunge himself deep inside her, be surrounded by her heat, her scent, her softness.

The groan of desire came unbidden.

Her eyes fluttered open and she smiled at him, innocent to the torment raging through his body.

"How's your head?" she asked, as though waking up in a man's bedchamber was as natural as sipping tea at breakfast.

"Much better."

"Good."

She eased up, and he realized with alarm that the tent in the middle of his bed was going to make it impossible for her to miss his reaction to having her so near. Any other unmarried woman might not know what it meant, but hadn't she told Jack that she fantasized about men? And if she fantasized, then she knew . . .

Reaching up, he cupped her cheek to prevent her from turning her face in a direction that would no doubt cause embarrassment for them both. "Give me a moment."

She furrowed her brow.

"To make certain the headache's not going to return."

She skimmed her fingers over the hair at his temple. "It shouldn't, at least not for a while I shouldn't think."

That wasn't helping at all. If anything it was making the tent rise higher.

"How did you know what to do?" he asked, searching for a distraction, for anything to keep her occupied and to give himself a chance to regain control of his rebellious manhood.

"I told you—my father had headaches."

"I've heard that he's ill."

Nodding, she sat up a little straighter and put her hands in her lap. "Yes, he was struck with apoplexy."

He lowered his arm, so he was no longer touching her. "I'm sorry. That's quite a burden for you to carry. Shouldn't your brother be here?"

"My brother doesn't know. He and Father had a row and Sterling left. I don't know what it was about. I heard only the shouting. I'll wager you didn't know that."

"No, I didn't."

"Everyone thinks Sterling is irresponsible, a cad. I've thought about writing to tell him, but Father gets so agitated whenever I mention it. But of late, I've been thinking about what you said about the previous earl wanting you to be his grandson so badly . . . what if it's Father's deepest desire to see his son once more before he dies, but he's just too proud to admit it? Will Sterling forgive me if I don't write him, if I don't tell him the truth of the situation? Would you do it?"

Her words took him aback, enough so his body had returned to a more normal state. *Thank God. Thank God.* "You want me to write your brother?"

She smiled sweetly. "No, of course not. But should *I*—even knowing that Father doesn't want me to? If he was your father, would you want to know?"

"I think you have to seek your own counsel on this matter. Do what your heart tells you to do."

She released a very short burst of laughter, and he sensed that she was amused with herself. Did he know any woman who was as comfortable in her skin as Catherine? When he killed for her, what inside of her would he also murder? How would his actions affect her? He thought doing anything to change her would be a worse crime, an unforgivable sin.

"Do you know, before the night I showed up in your library, I thought you were a man without a heart?"

"You thought correctly."

She shook her head slightly. "No, I don't think so. You're a very complicated man. I'm not even sure you appreciate how complicated you are." She skimmed her fingers over his shoulder. "How did you get these scars?"

His body reacted with a swift vengeance. He grabbed her hand, her injured hand. She gasped. He swore.

"I'm sorry." He brought her curled fingers to his lips and pressed as gentle a kiss to them as he could. "You just really shouldn't . . . you just shouldn't."

Her eyes widened as though she'd only just fully awakened and realized—

"Oh, good Lord, of course I shouldn't. I'm in a man's bedchamber. Oh, forgive me, whatever was I thinking. I shall leave now."

She came off the bed quickly and hurried to

the door. He rolled to the side, away from her, but twisted his head back to look at her. "Catherine?"

She stopped at the door, her hand on the knob, her face averted.

"Tell me you didn't have your carriage deliver you to my front door."

She shook her head. "To the park, but I told the driver not to wait."

"Then give me a few moments to make myself presentable, and I'll escort you home."

Nodding, she opened the door and slipped out.

He rolled onto his back and stared at the velvet canopy over his bed. He'd never had a woman in his bedchamber, in his bed, without making love to her. It seemed inconceivable that he had last night, but what was even more amazing was the immense satisfaction he felt in simply having had her here. It was enough.

Oh, he wanted more, he wanted a great deal more, but what she'd given him was enough.

He loved Frannie, he'd always loved Frannie. But of late, it seemed he was only capable of thinking of Catherine.

Chapter 11

Catherine was mortified. Quite simply and completely mortified.

She sat on a bench in the hallway and fought to quell her trembling. She'd been carrying on a conversation with a man in his bedchamber—worse than that! In his bed!—as though they were sitting in the garden sipping tea and nibbling on biscuits. With nothing except a thin sheet hiding the treasures of his body.

Oh, how she'd wanted to explore those treasures.

Falling asleep on his chest had been lovely. He had such a magnificent chest. Even the scars didn't detract from his rough beauty. She couldn't imagine that he'd gained any of them after he came to live here. No, he would have acquired them when he was a lad living on the streets. She wanted to weep for what he must have endured.

Who could blame him for turning to deceit in order to gain a better life?

She wanted to hold him close, stroke him, and take away all the bad memories that must surely haunt him. No wonder he had debilitating headaches. Who wouldn't with the horrendous memories with which he no doubt lived?

Was she adding to his burden by asking him to kill for her? When he gave up the last of his soul, would he give up the last of his humanity?

She'd not expected him to be kind. She'd not expected him to be tender.

If someone had asked her who would be the worst man in all of England to marry, who would beat his wife and terrorize his children, who would selfishly care about only his own needs, wants, and desires, who would put himself first above all others—if someone had asked her, she'd have said Claybourne without hesitating. She'd come to him because she'd believed he was worse than Avendale—and one didn't ask an angel to destroy the devil. One asked another devil.

But he was not at all as she'd envisioned him to be.

Good God, he hadn't even taken advantage of her being in his bed, and that gentlemanly behavior, to her everlasting shame, disappointed her.

His bedchamber door opened, and he stepped out. Clothed. Fully clothed. Thank the Lord for small favors, even if they did provide a measure of regret.

"I feel like such a ninny," she said. "Really there's no reason for you to escort me home. If you'll just provide the carriage—"

"You can't possibly believe after our encounter with those ruffians and your belief that you're being followed that I'm going to put you in a carriage and not ensure your safe return home."

Before she could frame her argument, his stomach made a rumbling noise, and Catherine thought he was blushing. Who would have thought the Devil Earl would be so easily embarrassed? She might have considered it precious if he weren't so masculine, so much a man. He was so very different from what she'd thought. Oh, he could be formidable when he wished to be. She'd never forget how he'd made her tremble in his library and doubt her wisdom in going to see him. But he could be equally gentle.

"My apologies," he said. "I can't eat when a headache is upon me, and now that I'm feeling better, I have an appetite." He glanced at the hallway clock. "We have a couple of hours before daylight. Will you join me for a bit of breakfast?"

She had every intention of being proper and saying no, but she heard herself say, "Yes."

Thank goodness, her mouth was wise enough to snap shut before she added that she'd enjoy it very much. As his butler didn't seem to know who she was, she thought she'd be spared from inciting gossip.

To her surprise, after he escorted her to the kitchen, he didn't wake the cook. Instead, he sat Catherine in a chair at the servant's table, found some cloths, and took her hand in his.

"I thought we were going to eat," she said, while he unwrapped the bandage.

"We will." When he'd removed the wrapping,

he studied her hand. "It doesn't look too bad. Does it hurt?"

"It aches a bit, but nothing I can't live with."

He raised his eyes to hers and she was struck by the force of his gaze, as though he had the power to peer into her heart.

"Last night you lied to me when you said it wasn't hurting."

"It wasn't that bad, truly."

"It was bad enough to bleed."

"It seems rather ungrateful to be put out with me after I worked to make your pain go away."

His mouth twitched slightly. "I suppose you make a valid argument."

Very gently, he began to wrap a clean strip of cloth around her hand.

"We'll be alike now," she said. "Both of us with a scar on our hand. Yours is from prison, isn't it?"

"Yes."

"I noticed that Mr. Dodger has one. Yours is very different."

"Mine shamed me. I tried to slice it off. Only served to make it more noticeable."

Her stomach grew queasy at the thought of him taking a knife to himself. How desperately he must have wanted to be rid of it. "Were you in prison long?"

"Three months."

"What was your offense?"

He gave her a cocky grin. "Getting caught."

He stood and she grabbed his wrist. "What did you do?"

"I stole some cheese. It's not easy to run with

a block of cheese. Lesson learned: steal smaller items."

Turning away, he said, "I'm very skilled at making a ham and cheese omelet. Interested?"

"As stealing it was your downfall, I wouldn't think you'd care much for cheese."

"I'm very fond of cheese. Why do you think I tried to steal some?"

She watched as he shrugged off his jacket and draped it over a chair. He began rolling up his sleeves.

"You're really going to cook it yourself?" she asked.

He gave her a self-deprecating smile. "I keep odd hours. I often can't sleep. It would be unfair to ask my cook to maintain the hours I prefer keeping."

"But that's the whole point in having servants. They're supposed to be at your beck and call."

"They're available when I need them. Presently, I don't." He lit the wood already stacked in the stove. "You see? My cook keeps things ready for me." He looked at her, lifted a brow. "Omelet?"

"Yes, please. What can I do to help?" She started to rise but he stilled her actions with the raising of his hand.

"You've done enough, Catherine. Now it's my turn to do something for you. Relax and enjoy the pampering."

She watched as he moved about the kitchen. He knew where everything was. Leaning forward, she put her elbows on the table and her chin in her unwounded palm.

"Is that a hint of a smile on your face?" she asked, thoughtfully. It transformed him.

"I actually enjoy cooking." He broke eggs into a bowl and whisked them around. "Brings back good memories."

"Of your home? Before you were orphaned?"

He stilled for a moment, shook his head, and went back to preparing the eggs. "No, as we got older, Frannie began to do the cooking. I took pleasure in watching her. She was like a little mother."

"When you were living with that man? Feagan was it?"

"Yes, Feagan." He added the ham and cheese, then whisked the eggs some more, before pouring the batter into the skillet that had been warming on the stove.

"Your punishment for stealing cheese seems a bit harsh," she told him.

"I thought so as well, and I was determined to never get caught again."

"What was it like, truly, growing up as you did?"

He studied the eggs cooking in the skillet. She thought he wasn't going to respond, but then he said, "Crowded, very crowded. We lived and slept in a single room, spooning around each other for warmth. But we weren't hungry. And we were made to feel welcome. The first time I walked into Feagan's was a very different experience from the first time I walked into a ballroom."

"I suspect your age had something to do with the way you were greeted. Children are always more eager for new playmates than adults."

"Perhaps."

"I've been reading *Oliver Twist* to my father. It's the story—"

"I've read it."

"Did Dickens have the right of it?"

"He painted a very accurate portrait of life in the rookeries, yes."

"It wasn't a very pleasant life."

"Who would you die for, Catherine?"

It seemed an odd question. He looked at her over his shoulder, as though he were truly expecting an answer.

"I've never given it any thought. I suppose . . . I don't really know. My father, I think. My brother. I don't know."

"The thing about the way I lived as a boy is that it gave me friends for whom I would die. So as awful as some moments were, overall, it was not such a horrible way to live. It bound us together in a way that living an easier life might not have."

He slid the omelet onto a plate. Joining her at the table, he set the plate between them, handed her a fork and knife before giving her a wry grin. "I only know how to make one at a time. We either let this one get cold while I cook another or share."

He seemed to be waiting for her to answer. Sharing seemed so intimate, but then she'd shared his bed, in a way.

"I'm perfectly fine sharing," she said.

He grinned as though he found her answer amusing. "Would you like some milk?"

"Yes, please."

He removed a bottle from the icebox, poured milk into a glass, and set the glass on the table. He rolled down his sleeves and slipped his jacket back on, before sitting at the table with her.

"Try it," he ordered.

She sliced off a bit of omelet and popped it into her mouth. She chewed and swallowed. Then she smiled at him. "It's rather good."

"Did you think it wouldn't be?"

"I've never known a lord to cook."

"But then we both know I'm more scoundrel than lord." He cut off a much larger piece and ate it.

"I was having tea with some ladies the other afternoon," Catherine began, "and one mentioned that you didn't think children should obey the law."

"Where would she get an idea like that?"

"She said from a letter you'd written in the *Times*."

"No, what I argued in my letter was that children, even if over the age of seven, should not be held accountable for understanding the law and, therefore, shouldn't be punished as though they had the reasoning power of an adult."

"But the law should apply to all people."

"Indeed it should. But a child doesn't realize he's breaking the law."

"But if he's punished, he'll learn the difference between right and wrong."

"You're assuming that he's taught what is right and what is wrong and that he is making a willful decision to do wrong. But that's not the way it is if you're a child growing up on the streets. You're told it's a game. Do you see that cart with the apples on it? You're to take an apple without being seen. And if you're seen, you must run as fast as you can and not get caught. Bring me a dozen apples and your prize will be one of the apples. And you'll not go to bed hungry. They believe the carts are there for their games. And when they're caught they're punished as though they knew better. Recently I learned about an eight-year-old girl who was sent to prison for three months for stealing peppermints, for stealing sweets, which were probably valued at no more than a penny."

The longer he spoke, the more his voice took on an edge of outrage that astounded her. She'd not have thought he'd care about children or prison reform. She'd thought he was a man who cared only for his own pleasure.

She no longer felt like eating, but he'd gone to such trouble to make it for her. "Is that how it was for you?"

He slowly shook his head. "No, I knew better. I don't know how I knew, but I did."

He sliced off more of the omelet and studied it on the end of his fork before looking at her. "You're a charming conversationalist during meals. I do hope this isn't what you're teaching Frannie."

No matter in what direction the conversation went, it always came back to Frannie. Catherine couldn't imagine having a gentleman care for her so much that she was forever on his mind. She'd never really envied anyone, and she didn't think what she felt toward Frannie was envy, but she did find herself longing for what the young woman had—what she had and was afraid to embrace.

"Have you spoken out on the matter in parliament?" she asked.

"No. I've yet to earn the acceptance of my peers, and until that happens they'll not listen to anything I say or give it any credence."

"You can hardly blame them. You don't attend balls or social functions—"

"I can't see that they serve any purpose."

"Is that the reason you ignored my invitations?"

"You sound as though you were wounded."

"No one likes to be rebuffed."

He placed his elbow on the table and leaned toward her. "*Why* did you invite me?"

She angled her chin haughtily. She wasn't about to reveal that he'd always intrigued her. "It seemed the polite thing to do."

He had the audacity to laugh, and she was struck by how joyous a sound it was. As though he were truly amused, as though he suspected she'd not told the entire truth.

"Here I thought you invited me because you possessed a touch of wickedness and wanted to play with the devil. You believe it important to be polite?" he asked.

"I do. At all times. For example, it's very rude to place your elbow on the table while we're eating. I have to question whether or not you, as well as Frannie, need lessons in manners."

"I promise you. When the situation warrants it, I have impeccable manners."

"So you say. Perhaps I need proof. Do you think

it would be possible for the three of us—you, Frannie, and me—to have dinner here one evening? Are your servants familiar with all that is necessary to serve guests?"

"I should think they are. The old gent hired only the best."

"You never refer to him as your grandfather."

"As you well know, he wasn't."

"Are you absolutely sure?"

He dropped his gaze to the table, and only then did she realize that she'd leaned forward, placing her elbows, both of them—*Drat it!*—a much worse offense, on the table. She straightened. "You're avoiding my question."

"The old gent's son and his wife had taken their six-year-old son to see a menagerie. The son and his wife were found murdered in an alley surrounded by garbage. I should think—if I was that child—I would not soon forget watching the horror of my parents being killed."

"Unless you ran off, unless you didn't see it."

He seemed to ponder that for a moment, then shook his head. "I should still remember them. I don't."

"But the names Lucian and Luke are so much alike—"

"Coincidence."

He was infuriating in his determination not to believe he was the rightful heir. For reasons she couldn't explain, she wanted him to be—desperately. She didn't want him to be a scoundrel who'd stolen what rightfully belonged to another.

"Who are your parents then?"

"I haven't a clue. In my mind, it's as though I didn't exist before Jack took me to Feagan."

"So you could be the lad."

"It's inconceivable that I could be." He pressed his fingers to his brow. "When Jack took me to him, Feagan would have recognized by my attire that I was of quality. He would have taken advantage."

"Perhaps your clothes were tattered by the time you were—"

He slammed his hand down on the table, making her jump. "Why are you determined to make me who I am not?"

"The very first Earl of Claybourne was granted his title for services to king or queen. He earned the right to pass that title on to his son. If you're not a descendant of that first earl—as much as I like you—it's a disgrace for you to hold the title."

"As you're well aware, I live for disgrace."

"No, you don't. You talk as though you do, but your actions show you to be a liar. You're much more honorable than you give yourself credit for."

He narrowed his eyes. "I suppose you think I should give the title to Marcus Langdon."

"It's not a matter of giving. It's a matter of to whom it rightfully belongs."

"The old gent believed it belonged to me. Out of respect for his wishes, I shall hold it until my dying breath."

She couldn't believe her disappointment in his words, or her relief. For all the reasons she gave for why he shouldn't be earl, she had to admit that she couldn't envision anyone else as the Earl of Claybourne.

Sighing heavily, he rubbed his temples. "How in God's name did we fall into this argument?"

"Is your head starting to hurt again?"

"A bit. It'll go away. And speaking of going away, I should get you home."

She was surprised to discover their omelet was gone, although he'd eaten the lion's share. She heard a distant bump and a thump.

"My servants are getting up," he said.

They both stood. He walked around the table, took her cloak from the chair, moved behind her, and draped it over her shoulders. His hands seemed to linger, and she almost imagined that she felt him placing a kiss against the nape of her neck. A delicious little shiver cascaded through her.

"Thank you," he said quietly, his breath wafting over the sensitive skin below her ear. "For caring."

"I need you in good health to carry out your portion of the bargain," she said succinctly, before moving away and turning to face him. "I daresay you're giving my actions too much credence."

Could he tell that she was having difficulty breathing, that his nearness caused inexplicable pleasures throughout her body?

Chuckling low, he strode past her and opened the door. She was only halfway through the doorway when he said, "So you don't want me to kiss you again?"

He was slightly behind her, so he couldn't see her face. Still she slid her eyes closed and shook her head. She felt his ungloved hand—his fingers strong and warm—cradle her chin and turn her head back. She opened her eyes to find his gaze on her mouth.

"Pity," he said quietly.

"The first time you kissed me to intimidate me. The second to distract me. What would be your excuse this time?"

"Damned if I know."

She took immense satisfaction in his answer, but she had no desire to reveal her thoughts. "A gentleman doesn't use profanity in the presence of a lady."

"But then, you and I both know I'm not a gentleman."

She licked her lips, wondering what harm there would be in having one more small taste of him.

Groaning, he released the featherlike hold he had on her and ushered her through the doorway. She could hear the city coming to life, deliveries being made. She waited while he had the coach readied.

He didn't say anything when the coach arrived or as he helped her climb inside. He held his silence as they traveled through the streets. It wasn't until they were at her gate that he finally spoke.

"You intrigue me, Catherine Mabry."

"I'm not certain that's a good thing."

"I'm sorry I'm not the man you wish I were."

"Actually, I give you a good deal more credit for your honesty than you probably deserve."

"Probably." He touched the tip of her nose. "I'll see you tonight."

She nodded. "Indeed."

Only when she'd closed the gate behind her did she hear him walking back to his coach. He was a contradiction. Was he a scoundrel? Or was he not?

She no longer knew. More disturbing than that was the fact that she no longer cared.

Chapter 12

Exhaustion claimed her the moment she walked into her bedchamber. Her bed called to her like a siren's song. It was all she could do to remain patient while Jenny helped her out of her clothing. She wanted to simply rip it off and fall into bed. Dealing with Claybourne was always tiring—and exhilarating. Which only served to make it more tiring.

She had to keep her wits about her at all times, although this morning they'd seemed to settle into a kind of companionship. Perhaps they would become friends and when he married Frannie and they moved more frequently within Catherine's circle of acquaintances, the blasted earl would at last accept her invitations. Or at least his wife would.

Catherine had been drawn to him that first night—that first ball. But what she felt now ran more deeply. She wanted to know everything about him. Once she knew everything, perhaps she'd no longer be intrigued.

She crawled into bed, yawned, and told Jenny, "Wake me at two."

She needed to pick up the invitations. And even though Winnie would be appalled, Catherine was determined to send one to Claybourne. If for no other reason than to irritate him. He wouldn't come to the ball, so what was the harm?

Winnie would never know, and it would give Catherine a sense of satisfaction.

Before she was even finished contemplating Claybourne's reaction, she was asleep. It seemed as though only seconds passed before someone was gently shaking her shoulder.

"My lady? My lady?"

She squinted. "What time is it?"

"Two o'clock."

Groaning, she threw back the covers.

"A package arrived," Jenny said. "I put it on your secretary."

"A package?"

"Yes, my lady. From Lord's."

"Lord's?" The shop specialized in the finest of accessories. But Catherine hadn't purchased anything there of late.

Her curiosity piqued, she padded in bare feet across the room to her secretary where she spied the oblong package. She unwrapped it to reveal a gorgeous hand-painted floral glove box. Inside, lying on the puffed satin, was an exquisite pair of cream colored kidskin gloves.

"Is something amiss, my lady?"

Only then did Catherine realize that tears dampened her eyes. How silly. She never wept.

"Was there no note?" she asked.

"No, my lady. The gent who delivered it said

simply that the package was for Lady Catherine Mabry."

Of course, there'd be no note, because if there was, she'd have to burn it. The gloves were from Claybourne. Her injured hand was too sore, but she couldn't resist having Jenny help her tug the glove onto her uninjured one. It was a perfect fit.

Oh, dear Lord, she wished he hadn't done this. It was so much easier to deal with him when she believed he was the devil, so much harder when she realized he was a man who could easily win her heart.

"You've lost your knack. She spied you following her around."

Luke had decided that he needed a word with Jim, before he picked Catherine up for their nightly ritual. Now he was pacing in Jim's lodging. When had it grown so small? He barely had the room to stretch his legs. Ever since Catherine had left his bed that morning, he'd felt like a ravenous beast on the prowl—with no clear understanding of what it was he was seeking.

Whatever had possessed him to ask if she wanted a kiss? For more than a year, he'd been fiercely loyal to Frannie, not taken the least bit of interest in another woman. Whatever madness had claimed him? What was he thinking to tempt himself and Catherine with the promise of a kiss? He'd been disappointed. Well, and truly, disappointed when she'd shaken her head. Then he'd gone to Lord's and purchased her new gloves like some besotted fool.

No, he chastised himself. He was simply replacing the pair that had been destroyed when they'd been attacked, replaced the one that now rested in a drawer in the bureau in his bedchamber. The one that he'd held and studied that morning after returning to his residence, thinking about how close she'd come to having her life ended with the slash of a blade.

Pain shot through his head. He had to stop thinking about that encounter in the alley. Why was it that it troubled him so? She was nothing to him except a means to an end.

"She didn't see me," Jim insisted, lounging in his chair by the fire as though nothing were amiss.

"All the running around she did earlier in the week? She did it to befuddle you, to make certain you were following her."

"If she spied someone following her, it was not me. She saw someone else."

Jim sounded so certain of himself. Not that Luke could blame him. He'd always been the best, the very best. So good in fact, that he'd managed to carry out his duties at Scotland Yard during the evening while pursuing Catherine during the day. He'd merely claimed to be following up with some witnesses to a burglary.

"Why would someone be following her?" Luke asked.

"Maybe it's the bloke she wants killed."

The thought of her being in danger caused Luke to break out in a sweat. "Did you see someone following her?"

"I wasn't looking for anyone else. I was concentrating on her and making certain she didn't spy me."

"We need to determine if it was you she saw."

"Now, that's a jolly good idea. Let's ask her shall we? And then she'll know you're having her followed. Do you think she's going to take kindly to that news?"

"I'm not as daft as all that. We need to come up with an innocent opportunity for your path to cross with hers." He walked over to the window, moved the drapery aside slightly, and peered out.

"Once she's seen me, she's more likely to notice me and become suspicious."

"If she does, we'll simply say I was worried about her safety, that you're following her is a new development."

"So how do you propose we *innocently* cross paths?"

How indeed without arousing suspicions?

"We just need a small ruse," Luke said quietly. "Something simple, easy to bring about." He considered his options, the players at his disposal. Finally he faced Jim. "Get word to Bill. We're going to play some cards tonight in Dodger's back room."

"I'm all for a bit of gaming, but how does that achieve your end?"

"We'll have Frannie bring Catherine into the room—quite innocently. Catherine's reaction to seeing you should tell us everything."

"What excuse will Frannie use to bring her into a room where gents are playing cards? It will be apparent that it's staged."

Luke waved off his concerns. "Perhaps Frannie will want to show me something that she's learned. We'll leave the reason to her. I have no doubt she can lure Catherine into the room without raising suspicions."

Feagan's children were all skilled at delivering lies so easily that they resembled truths. That talent had allowed him to convince the old gent that Luke was his grandson. What he required of Frannie tonight wasn't nearly as complicated, but in some ways, Luke feared more was to be gained or lost.

"Do you know that Luke has never kissed me?"

Catherine looked up from her feeble attempt to write. While Frannie was writing out a menu that Claybourne could deliver to his cook for the dinner party that the three of them would have at his residence tomorrow night, Catherine was using her time to test her ability to write, scribbling nothing of importance. With her wounded hand, she was having difficult properly holding a writing instrument. How was she going to help Winnie address the invitations to their ball? Although that concern slipped to the back of her mind with Frannie's announcement.

She felt her cheeks warm and wondered if Frannie had some sort of inkling that Claybourne had kissed her. Did her lips now carry a brand as visible as that upon his thumb?

Catherine swallowed. "Because he respects you."

"I suppose. It has just always seemed to me that if a man is attracted to you that he shouldn't be able to resist, that you should have to scold him and make him behave."

"But a gentleman doesn't kiss a lady until they're betrothed, so perhaps since you haven't accepted his offer of marriage—you haven't, have you?"

"No. He hasn't asked again, thank goodness. I'm not ready to say yes." She set her elbow on the desk, her chin in her hand. "I felt so badly that night. He'd taken me out in his coach. It was filled with flowers. Terribly romantic."

"Indeed." Something else about Claybourne that she'd never expected. "How fortunate you are to hold his affections."

"Fortunate?" Frannie straightened. "I work all evening and then I have to take lessons, while Luke is off playing. His affections have added to my burdens."

Her attitude surprised Catherine. She'd never consider Claybourne's affections as a burden. For an unkind moment she wasn't certain Frannie deserved him. But it was not her place to judge, to decide whom he should love and who should love him.

"I thought he was here," Catherine said. She'd never questioned what he was doing while she was showing Frannie various things.

"He is, but he's in a room farther in the back, playing cards with Jack and the others."

"The others?"

"Friends. Old acquaintances. Lads we grew up with. If I didn't have to take my lessons, then I could play with them. I'd much rather be playing than taking lessons."

"Is it so difficult to design a menu?"

"So many different dishes need to be served. How can one person eat them all?"

"They're very small portions. I know you're nervous, but it's really not as bad as all that."

"Still, it doesn't seem fair that we have to work while they play. And it's also not fair that you have to teach me etiquette, while I'm teaching you nothing."

She was teaching more than she knew, teaching Catherine about Claybourne. Did he kiss Catherine because he had absolutely no respect for her? Or could it be as Frannie surmised—he was unable to resist because he was attracted to her? No, it had to be the former. He never left any doubt that Frannie held his heart. His reasons for kissing Catherine were either to unsettle or tease her or distract her. They were not the result of passion, although they'd certainly felt as though they were.

"You don't have to teach me anything," Catherine said. "My arrangement is with Claybourne, and I'm quite satisfied with it."

"But wouldn't it be fun to play a little trick on Luke?"

Catherine hardly thought him the type to enjoy having pranks played on him. Yet she was intrigued by the notion. "What sort of trick?"

Frannie opened a drawer, took out a deck of cards, and placed it on the desk between them. And then she smiled, rather cockily—the first truly confident smile Catherine had received from her—as though she were finally in her element. Catherine realized it transformed her, and for the first time, she thought she could see what it was about the woman that appealed to Claybourne.

"How about I teach you how to beat a man at his own game?"

Luke glanced at his watch, the watch he'd inherited from the old gent, then stuffed it back into his waistcoat pocket. It was coming close to the time for him to take Catherine home. Why hadn't Frannie brought her in here?

"Are you going to pass?" Jack asked.

Luke looked at his cards, looked at the door. "They should have been in here by now."

"Based on Lady Catherine's stubbornness, I expect Frannie is finding it more difficult than she imagined it would be to lure her in here."

Luke glared at Jack. "What do you know of Catherine's stubbornness?"

"I've met the woman. 'Tis enough."

"I thought she was most pleasant," Bill said.

On the journey here, Jim had explained to Bill exactly who Catherine was and Luke's arrangement with her.

"Boring is what she is," Jim said.

"She's not boring. How many times must I tell you that? I swear to God, I'm not convinced you're following the correct woman," Luke said.

"She shops." Jim cast a quick look at his friends. "She shops. She visits. Where is the excitement in that, I ask you? The only thing she does of any note is meeting you at night."

"And getting her hand sliced to ribbons," Bill said quietly.

A result about which Luke continued to feel guilty. Once they'd settled into the coach earlier, she'd thanked him for the gloves. Told him they weren't necessary. Had made him feel rather silly for taking such pleasure in purchasing them for her.

"It'll heal," Luke said brusquely.

"It's going to leave a nasty scar," Bill said.

Add that burden to his guilt.

"She shouldn't have gotten out of the coach to begin with," Luke said.

"She doesn't strike me as a woman who obeys," Jack murmured.

"You think you know her so well. You know nothing at all about her."

Jack leaned forward, placing his elbows on the table and his hard-edged glare on Luke. "Enlighten me."

What could he say? That she was bold, courageous, kind, caring . . . that her scent still lingered in his bedchamber. He wasn't certain he'd be able to sleep with it there. He would wake up searching for her. How was it that she was managing to work her way into every facet of his life?

Before he could form a comprehensible answer, the door opened. *Thank goodness!* Luke had situated himself so he was facing the door, giving him a clear view of her face, her features, and her expression as she took stock of her surroundings. All four gentlemen came to their feet.

"Gentlemen," Frannie said, sweetly. "Lady Catherine gave me permission to take a small respite from my studies, and I thought we would stop by and say hello."

That was it? That was the best she'd been able to come up with? The elaborate ruse?

Then Catherine smiled beautifully. "Dr. Graves, I didn't know you were here. It's so lovely to see you again."

She extended her hand, and he took it gently, placing a kiss on her fingertips. Luke didn't understand his reaction. His body stiffened and he wanted to smash his fist into Bill's face, wanted to pull Catherine away from the man who was now turning her bandaged hand over and looking at her covered palm.

"How is it doing?" he asked.

"It's a bit sore, and I'm having a devil of a time writing, but other than that, I can't complain."

She turned her attention to Jack, who was standing to Luke's left. "Mr. Dodger."

"Lady Catherine."

"I don't mean to be pious, but I thought gambling was outlawed."

He gave her his devil-may-care grin. "Not in private clubs. And this, my lady, is a very private club. Exclusive, in fact."

"Are you winning?"

"I always win."

"I would have thought that honor would fall to Claybourne."

Luke's heart gave a little stutter. "Why would you think that?"

"Perhaps I simply have faith in your ability to succeed."

Was she mocking him? Would it be worse if she weren't? If she truly did have faith in him? Had anyone of the aristocracy—other than the old gent—ever even considered that Luke was worthy of having faith placed in him?

He cleared his throat, studied her more closely. "I don't believe you've met Mr. Swindler."

Jim was standing to Luke's right, out of his field of vision, but he knew the man well enough to know that he'd not give anything away with his expressions.

"It's a pleasure to meet you, sir." She did nothing but present a welcoming smile.

"The pleasure is mine, my lady."

Her brow furrowed. There! Luke thought. She's recognized him!

"I daresay, it's a rather unfortunate name you have, though, isn't it?"

Or perhaps not.

Jim chuckled. "When I was young and in search of a name, it seemed appropriate. As I've grown older, I recognize the foolishness of my youth."

"You're another one of Feagan's children."

He tilted his head slightly. "I am."

"I shan't hold your choice of name against you. I expect if we were all honest, we'd discover we've all been foolish at one time or another."

"You're very kind."

What the bloody hell was she doing? She was charming them. Charming them all. As though they were equals, as though they had something in common. All three of his mates were looking at her like besotted fools.

Her gaze darted around the table. "What have you here? What game are you playing?"

"Brag," Luke said.

"Oh?" She looked at him with interest, a smile

upon those red lips—lips he knew the feel and taste of—and arched a brow. "How is it played? The one with the best card brags on his exploits?"

He scowled, growled, and was fairly losing patience. "One wagers on the outcome. The gent with the best set of cards wins—or bluffs the others into believing he has the best set of cards."

"And what if a lady has the best set of cards?"

The little chit! With the set of her chin, the challenge in her eyes, she was daring him to let her play.

"Then the lady would win. But I've never known that to happen. Frannie has tried on many occasions, but she's never met with success."

"So it's a gentleman's game?"

"Quite."

She gave him a sweet smile. "May I try?"

"Have you any idea how to play?"

"I have an inkling. After all, I have a brother, and he's a rather notorious rake."

"So you've played before."

"I've watched." She gave him an impish smile. "I was teasing earlier. I know what brag is. So may I play?"

"By all means. Jack, give her your chair."

"I'm not sitting this one out," Jack said, grinning. He did offer his chair to Catherine, before securing another for himself and bringing it to the table.

"Did you want to play, Frannie?" Luke asked.

"No, as you so kindly pointed out, I have no skill when it comes to cards."

Damnation! Had he hurt her feelings?

"I meant no offense," he said.

"None was taken. I will, however, front Lady Catherine two hundred pounds."

Luke narrowed his eyes. Something was afoot. "What were you studying tonight?"

"How to determine the menu for dinner. Rather boring actually." Frannie pulled up a chair and sat between Jack and Catherine, slightly behind Catherine. "But I shall gladly watch. Perhaps I'll learn something."

"You're going to learn how to lose two hundred pounds, right fast," Jim said.

Frannie did little more than offer him a mischievous smile.

Luke gathered up the cards and began to shuffle. "I'll deal. Minimum bet is five pounds, maximum is twenty-five."

He watched as Jack slid the chips over to Catherine. "Each of these is worth five. And the first thing we do is ante up." He tossed a chip into the center of the table. Catherine followed suit. Everyone else tossed in his ante.

"The game is five-card brag," Luke said. "The rules are these: Never show your cards to anyone—not even to Frannie. Never say anything about your hand. And *never* fold out of turn."

"Oh, I shan't fold at all. I'll have no chance of winning if I fold." She leaned toward the table, peered around, and whispered. "My brother always gave up so easily. The other gents took his money. I don't think he understood the strategy."

Luke met Jack's gaze and knew he was thinking the same thing: it was going to be like pilfering the pockets of an old man. Far, far too easy.

She picked up her cards and studied them. Her brow furrowed. She scowled. Then she set them in her lap.

"You must keep them on the table," Luke told her.

Laughing, she set the cards on the table. "Oh, you think I'm cheating?"

"No, but it's the rules."

She nodded. "Very well. I bet first?"

Luke nodded.

Gnawing her lip, she looked at each set of cards—even though she could only see the back of them. "I'll wager five." She tossed her chip into the center.

"Ten," Jack said.

"Oh, Jack," Frannie scolded, slapping his arm. "Don't take all her money the first round."

"Come on, Frannie, it's always more fun when there's more at risk."

"I'm probably going to regret this," Bill said, "but I fold."

"I'll match the bet," Jim said, and tossed in his ten chips.

"Shouldn't it be fifteen?" Catherine asked.

"No, you only match the last bet made." Luke matched the ten. "Now you match the ten."

"Or I can wager more?"

"You can, but—"

"I'll wager twenty."

"Twenty-five," Jack said.

Catherine looked at him and smiled. "You must have a jolly good hand."

Jack grinned. Luke knew that grin. The blighter had nothing.

Jim shook his head, tossed down his cards. "Fold."

Luke bet his twenty-five. Catherine bet hers.

Jack studied Luke. Studied Catherine. "I fold."

Catherine looked so incredibly pleased.

Luke matched the bet. Catherine placed fifty pounds worth of chips in the center. "See you."

Luke sighed deeply. "Catherine, the maximum is twenty-five, and the only way to win at this game is not to let people know what you're thinking."

"And you know what I'm thinking?"

"I do."

"Then I shall lose."

"Indeed."

"I should not have placed the wager."

"You shouldn't have placed any of them. At least take the last one back and fold."

"But once a wager has been made, it can't be withdrawn."

"We shall make an exception."

"I don't wish to have an exception made. I'm of the belief that a person learns more from his mistakes than his successes, and I'm quite willing to put that belief to the test."

He sighed again and waved his hand over the chips. "Gentlemen. I'll allow the lady to learn from her mistake."

He turned over three kings.

Catherine turned her cards over. Luke stared at the three threes. There was no better hand in brag.

"If I remember the rank of better cards, while it would seem that three kings are better, actually my hand is, and so it appears that all this lovely money comes to me."

"But—"

"I would venture to guess, my lord, that you did *not* know what I was thinking." She stood. "I believe, I've made my point. It's getting rather late and we should be leaving soon."

Frannie helped her gather up all her chips. Catherine walked out as though she'd just been crowned.

Luke couldn't help it. He burst out laughing. "Damn, but I do enjoy her."

His outburst was met with silence, and he was suddenly very much aware of what he'd said. Coming to his feet, Luke gave Jim a hard look. "She didn't seem to find you familiar."

"I told you she wouldn't."

"Find out who is following her and the reason for it."

He was smiling when he came to get her. Truly smiling. Not one of his sardonic twists of the mouth. Not one of his mocking smiles. Not a sneer or an insolent pout.

Catherine had not expected this reaction. Hadn't even thought him capable of it. She'd expected him to be miffed that she'd taken his money, expected to find him in a foul mood. But his eyes were lighter than she'd ever seen them, as though there was suddenly a brightness inside him.

He led her through the now-familiar dark corridor to the back door, where his coach waited on the other side. For the first time since they'd begun their nightly ritual, he kept the coach lantern lit inside. The curtains were in place, preventing anyone from peering in. He settled back in the corner, and while she knew she should be embarrassed by his perusal, she wasn't. On the contrary, she rather liked it. And she was feeling a trifle smug that she'd duped him.

She was aware of his deep chuckle before his smile grew, and she wondered if he could read her thoughts.

"You don't care what people think," he said.

She couldn't tell from the way he emphasized the words if he was asking a question or making an observation. Still, she felt obliged to answer.

"Of course I care. To a certain extent we all care, but we can't care to the point that we live in fear of others' opinions, that we allow them to change who we are. We must be willing to stand up and defend what represents the very core of our being. Otherwise what is the purpose of individuality? We'd be nothing but imitations of each other, and I daresay we'd all be rather boring."

"I don't think anyone with any sense could ever accuse you of being boring. As a matter of fact, you are the least boring person I know."

His admission made her uncomfortable, because it pleased her far too much. Shouldn't his love be the least boring person he knew?

She looked down at her gloved hands, nestled in her lap. He shifted until he was sitting directly in front of her. He took her hands in his. His were so large. With his thumbs, he began stroking her knuckles.

"Is your wound hurting?" he asked.

She lifted her gaze to his. "No."

She wanted to lean into him, wanted to press her lips to his. It was wrong of her to want so much from him, when his heart belonged to another.

"I was thinking that it might be a good idea to have Dr. Graves join us for dinner tomorrow night," she said.

He narrowed his eyes. "Why?"

"It would make it seem more like a true social dinner, rather than simply you and Frannie dining with me looking on."

He released his hold on her, leaned back, and crossed his arms over his chest. "Do you fancy him?"

She was taken aback by his tone; it had taken on an unfriendly edge, as though he were—heaven forbid—jealous. "I like him. Of all your friends, he seems the most polished."

"You don't like Jack?"

"Not particularly, no."

"Why?"

"I'm not exactly sure. I don't"—she shook her head—"I don't quite trust him."

"And Jim?"

"Jim?"

"Swindler."

"Ah, yes, the one with the unfortunate name. I really formed no impression of him. Rather he seemed to blend in with the woodwork."

"He's good at that."

"How does he make his living?"

"He's an inspector with Scotland Yard."

"So everyone is reputable except for Mr. Dodger."

"Jack doesn't force people to sin."

"But he makes it very easy for them to do so."

"Save your sermons, Catherine, for someone who cares to listen to them."

"I wasn't going to preach about the evils of drinking, gambling, and fornicating—"

"I would hope not. That would make you a bit of a hypocrite after gambling tonight. And you've drunk whiskey . . . which leaves but one sin. Have you indulged in it?"

"That, my lord, is none of your business."

He smiled, seeming far too pleased with her answer.

"Shouldn't we be home by now?" she asked.

"I'm having my driver take us on a circuitous route. We'll take different streets every night. Lessen the chance of being set upon—if the attack before was planned. It could have been random. Some lads looking for a quick bit of coin."

She hoped that's all it was and that it would never happen again.

"About dinner tomorrow evening. Will you ask Dr. Graves?"

"If that's what you want."

"It is. And Frannie gave you the menu. I can have myself delivered—"

"I'll send my coach around. What time did you want dinner served?"

"I would like it at eight, but that time of evening it might be more difficult to be unseen. I truly think it would be better if I arrived on my own."

"And what about the gent who's been following you?"

The fury in his voice caught her by surprise. Apparently it did him as well, because he looked toward the window as though he could see through the curtain. She watched as he struggled to regain control of his emotions. He was angry, she realized, not at her, but for her. Wanting to protect her, but that wasn't part of their bargain.

"I'll be careful," she assured him. "I've eluded him before. I shall do so again."

He shifted his gaze to her. "You worry me, Catherine. You seem to think you're quite invincible."

"I'm well aware that I'm not. But I'll not spend my life cowering. That would be no life at all."

He was studying her again, as though she'd revealed something monumental.

The coach stopped. He blew out the flame in the lantern. The door opened, and they went through their usual ritual. She said good night to him at the gate.

Only this time as she closed the gate behind her, it seemed harder to leave him.

Chapter 13

"Whatever happened to your hand?" Winnie asked.

"Whatever happened to your chin?" Catherine responded.

They were in the library at Winnie's residence where they'd planned to address the invitations to their ball. But Catherine was still having difficultly holding a pen, and she was no longer in the mood to discuss the plans for the ball anyway.

Winnie rubbed her chin. "I ran into a door."

"Oh, Winnie, how stupid do you think I am? Where else are you hurt?"

Winnie squeezed her eyes shut. "Nowhere else. He slapped me because I didn't want to perform my wifely duties."

"Slapped? More likely punched. Is that his idea of the best way to entice you into his bed?"

"Please, don't say anything more. It should be gone by the ball. And if it's not, you're the only one who won't believe I ran into a door. Everyone else thinks I'm clumsy."

Because she'd so often blamed any visible bruises on small accidents that hadn't happened.

"I detest Avendale," Catherine groused.

"So you've said on more than one occasion, but he is my husband and I must honor him. Tell me about your hand."

"I cut it on a piece of glass. It was an accident."

"It appears I shall have to address all the invitations."

"I'm sorry, but yes, I think you will."

"I don't mind. It's a chore I enjoy. I daresay if I were a commoner, I might try to find employment addressing things for people."

"You've always had such lovely handwriting."

Winnie blushed. "Thank you. I like to think so."

"I would like to take one unmarked invitation and envelope for my memory book."

Catherine was bothered by how easily she lied to her trusted friend—about her bandaged hand and about her desire for an invitation. It wouldn't find its way into her memory book. With any luck, it would find its way into Claybourne's hand.

It was madness. The amount of time he spent obsessing about Catherine.

Even knowing that Jim was watching her more closely, that he would do what he could to discover who was following her, Luke paced his back garden, awaiting her arrival, his body tense, his nerves taut. Bill was going to fetch Frannie in his carriage. They would travel through some rough parts of London—and yet, Luke was not the least bit worried.

But Catherine, traveling from one exclusive part of London to another, had him on edge. He told himself it was because Frannie was born to the streets and could take care of herself, while Catherine would hurl herself into harm's way without thought. He should teach her to defend herself. He should buy her a sword cane. Or perhaps a pistol.

He should entice her into telling him what he needed to know. He should ask her why she wanted someone killed, who she wanted killed. This game of cat-and-mouse was putting everyone in danger.

He heard the latch on the gate give way, and he was there pulling it open, grabbing her arm, and drawing her inside.

"Oh," she gasped. "What's the matter?"

"Nothing. I . . . Did you have any problems?"

Even in the shadows, with nothing but the glow from his garden lanterns to cast light, he could see her amused smile.

"You were worried."

"Naturally, I had some concerns. Perhaps if you were more open about your reason for wanting me to kill someone—"

"Are you ready to do the deed?"

Do the deed? And how would she look at him then? Frannie would never know, but Catherine, Catherine would know the worst that he was capable of: taking a life in order to gain a wife.

What had possessed him to agree to this bargain?

The irony was that he'd keep true to his word. But he wanted to hold on to what remained of his soul for a bit longer. "I'm not convinced Frannie has learned anything."

"Then tonight will be very telling, won't it?" She began walking toward the house. "Have your guests arrived yet?"

"I don't know. I've been out here."

"What sort of host are you?"

"They're friends. I don't have to welcome them into my home. They know they're welcome."

"Tonight is all about presentation."

When she walked through the house and removed her pelisse to hand it over to the butler, Luke couldn't deny that she was presenting herself very nicely. She wore a gown of deep blue that came off her shoulders and revealed a hint of the swells of her breasts.

"Dr. Graves and Miss Darling have only just arrived, my lord. I've shown them to the parlor."

Luke escorted Catherine to the parlor. He'd instructed Fitzsimmons that they were to avoid using the library tonight. Luke would find himself distracted with too many memories of Catherine in that particular room. It just occurred to him that he might experience the same problem when he took Frannie to his bedchamber for the first time. That he would be thinking of waking to find Catherine in his bed. No, that was not going to happen.

"Ah, there you are," Bill said.

Luke noticed that Catherine seemed to light up at the sight of him. Just as Bill's attention toward her had irritated Luke last night, so hers toward the doctor irritated Luke now.

"Don't you look lovely this evening," Bill said,

taking her hand and pressing a kiss to the back of it.

"Did you tell Frannie she looked lovely?" Luke asked.

Bill seemed startled—no doubt a reaction to Luke's tart tone—but he recovered quickly enough. "Yes, as a matter of fact, I did. Are you bothered by my finding the ladies in your life lovely?"

"No, not at all. I just wanted to make certain that Frannie didn't feel ignored." Even as he said it, he realized the only one ignoring her was him. He turned to her. "It's been a while since you've been here."

"Yes, but it all looks the same."

She was wearing a dark blue dress, the buttons done up to her throat. It appeared to be something she'd work in, not dine in.

"I fear as hostess that I don't know what to do," she said.

"How can you not know what to do? It's been weeks," Luke said.

"Hardly," Frannie replied. "Not more than two."

Luke spun around to face Catherine, who jerked back as though to avoid a blow. He could only imagine the frustration his face revealed. "What have you been doing every night? You said she was learning."

"And she has been, but I also said that a gaming hell was not the best environment for learning all that needed to be taught."

"I have an idea," Frannie said. "Why don't we pretend, just for tonight, that Lady Catherine and

Luke are married? Bill and I will come to call and then you can *show* me what to do. I learn much better by example."

"I want to see what *you* know," Luke said.

"I've told you. I've yet to learn how to properly host dinner."

"But, Frannie, we discussed—" Catherine began.

"I know, but I can't remember everything. Please just show me."

"Please do something to move this along," Bill said, "because I'm starving."

"Very well," Catherine said, raising her hands in surrender. "We won't pretend that we're married, but I shall be the hostess. First, we need to check on the dinner preparations."

"Lovely. Let's go to the kitchen shall we?"

Frannie took Catherine's arm. They walked from the room, and Luke strode to the side table, where he poured himself a generous amount of whiskey and downed it in one swallow, before pouring another for himself and one for Bill.

"You seem out of sorts," Bill said, coming to stand beside him.

"I'm supposed to be acting like a damned earl tonight. Do you not think she'll be judging my behavior as closely as she will be Frannie's?"

"What do you care of her opinion?"

Luke took another swallow of whiskey.

"You want to impress her?" Bill asked.

"No, of course not."

"Just be yourself. The old gent taught you that."

Luke feared, when it came right down to it, that he was going to let the old gent down.

"Sometimes, I think I would be much happier moving back into Frannie's world than having her move into mine. What if I do nothing more than make us both miserable?"

"You've loved her as long as I've known you. Everything you've ever done has been to secure her happiness. I can't see you making her miserable."

Luke wished he was as sure.

"Are you nervous about tonight?" Catherine asked as she and Frannie walked down the hallway to the kitchen. She was still trying to figure out Frannie's strange reaction and suggestion.

"A bit, I suppose. It reminds me of when we lived with Feagan and had to learn to take a handkerchief or coins out of a pocket without being noticed. I don't suppose any bell will ring to alert anyone to my mistakes."

"I don't understand," Catherine said. "A bell—"

Smiling, Frannie stopped. "Feagan would hang jackets and bells on a rope. You had to reach carefully into the pocket of a jacket without causing a bell to ring. If the bell rang, you felt the sting of Feagan's cane across your knuckles." She blushed. "Well, I never did. Luke always put his hand over mine, so he took the blow. Oddly, it made me try harder to learn the task, because I hated to see him hurt."

"It seems you two have always been close."

Frannie nodded. "The first night Jack brought him to us, I can't explain it, but something about him was different. He seemed to expect us to do things for him, but Feagan beat that attitude out of him quick enough."

"Do you think it's possible that he's the rightful Earl of Claybourne?"

"Well, of course, he is. The old gent asked him questions, and he knew the answers. I know he doubts sometimes, and I don't understand that. He knew the answers."

No, Catherine thought, he'd somehow managed to *give* the right answers even though he didn't know them. Was he really that good at deception? Then a rather odd thought came to her and a shiver raced down her spine. What if Claybourne hadn't deceived the previous earl? What if he'd deceived himself?

Dinner was an absolute disaster.

Half an hour into it, they'd finished their fish and were to be served their beef when Catherine's patience snapped. She'd been trying to start conversations about the weather, the theater, and the park. Frannie's and Claybourne's answers had all been succinct as though neither of them had a clue how to expand conversation into something interesting. Dr. Graves had given it a halfhearted attempt, but it seemed his life was little more than dealing with the infirm, and they weren't likely to engage in trite conversation. Claybourne was drinking wine as though it were the main course. He narrowed his eyes each time poor Dr. Graves spoke, and Catherine had little doubt that the doctor was aware of the scathing glances, and probably as confused by them as she.

Claybourne was obviously not happy. But then neither was she. She needed him to see that Frannie was learning, because Catherine was growing desperate for him to take care of the problem of Avendale. But Frannie wasn't cooperating. She was acting as though she knew nothing. And Claybourne had his dratted elbow on the table. He looked as though he was going to slip out of his chair.

"We are hosting a proper dinner. One does not lounge during a proper dinner," Catherine finally told him.

He sipped more wine. "It is Frannie who needs the lessons, not I."

"That is hardly evident by observing your behavior now. We either do this properly or not at all."

"I vote for not at all. I'm bored with this endeavor. I'm certain Frannie has grasped the gist of the occasion."

Catherine had gone to the trouble of dressing properly for the occasion. For these people, she'd put aside the nightly reading to her father who was weaker and paler than ever. She'd spent the afternoon reassuring Winnie that Avendale wouldn't kill her. She'd met with her father's man of business only to discover that some of the investments he'd recommended were not going to pay off as well as he'd hoped—they weren't going to pay off at all. She'd heard not a blasted word from her brother, and when he finally did return to England's shores, he might do so only to discover that he no longer had a source of income, that the estates were in decline—because of ventures she'd approved.

And now Claybourne was bored! He was fortunate a length of table separated them or she'd reach out and slap the boredom right off his face. Since she couldn't reach him, she threw words at him.

"You seem to have little understanding of the aristocracy. Do you believe everything we do is for our pleasure? I can assure you, sir, that it is not. We do it because it is required. We do it because it is a duty. We do it because it is expected. How much more difficult it is to do things because they are right, proper, and required. How much easier life would be for all of us if we could go about and do things willy-nilly, however we pleased. It is the very fact that we understand responsibility and adhere to it that raises us above the common man. I am becoming quite weary of your mocking me.

"Do you think this is easy for me? These ridiculously late hours? Perhaps you can lounge about all morning, but not I. I have a household to oversee."

She was suddenly aware of the tears washing down her cheeks.

"Catherine?" Claybourne was no longer lounging. He was coming up out of his chair.

"Oh, forgive me. That—that was not polite at all. Please excuse me, I need a moment." She rose and walked out of the room.

Luke watched her leave. He'd been insolent and rude. He was upset with Frannie for not trying harder. He was angry with Catherine for having the habit of touching the tip of her tongue to her top lip—just a quick touch, barely noticeable, but he noticed—after each sip of wine as though she needed to gather the last drop. He was angry at Bill for smiling at Catherine, for pretending to have an interest in the amount of rain that was falling on London this summer. He was furious with himself because he wanted to gather that wine from Catherine's lips with his own. He was furious because he was intrigued with Catherine, because he was noticing so many things about her—the way the light captured her hair, revealing that it wasn't all the same shade of blond. Some strands were paler than others. He told himself that his interest in Catherine was only because he didn't know her well, while he knew everything about Frannie. They'd grown up together. There was little for them to learn about each other. But Catherine was another matter entirely.

He looked at Bill and Frannie. "I should check on her."

"Of course, you should," Frannie said, "more than a moment ago as a matter of fact."

He strode from the room and looked in the parlor. She wasn't there. Dread tightened his stomach. What if she'd left? What if she was out walking the streets? What if she'd put herself in harm's way?

Walking into the library, he found her standing by the window, looking onto the garden as she'd been that first night in his home. Only this time she didn't jerk around in surprise by his presence. When she faced him, he saw the fury and disappointment in her eyes. She didn't give him time to say a word before she continued her tirade.

"You say you are willing to do whatever necessary to have Frannie as your wife, but I do not see you doing everything *required*. I see you doing only what it pleases you to do and calling it sufficient to gain what you want. Whereas I must—"

He'd covered her mouth with a blistering kiss before he'd thought it through. He could tell himself that he was bored with the dinner, bored with the conversation, but the reality was that it was driving him mad to watch her sip wine, to gaze at her slender throat and shoulders, to see her smiling at Bill when Luke wanted her to smile at him.

As he swept his tongue through her mouth, he knew it was wrong, but he wanted her, wanted her in a way he'd never desired Frannie. He wanted Catherine rough, he wanted her tenderly. He never thought of taking Frannie to his bed. He thought of marrying her, he thought of having her as his wife, but carnal images of them together never filled his mind. With Catherine, he saw a kaleidoscope of their contorted naked bodies.

Tonight he could feel the need rising in him, felt it rising in her as she rose up on her toes and wound her arms around his neck, her fingers scraping into his hair. Her teeth grazed his bottom lip, tugged—

He groaned, considered the location of the nearest settee—

Shoving him, she scrambled back into the shadows of the draperies. "My God," she rasped. "Your betrothed is down the hallway—"

"She's not my betrothed yet, and I have doubts that she'll ever be. Do you think if I asked her tonight that she'd say yes? Have you convinced her that she can handle being a countess? She doesn't even want to be the hostess over a bloody dinner!"

He swung away from her, didn't want to see that he'd frightened her. Frightened Catherine who'd faced a ruffian with a knife.

He plowed his fingers through his hair. "My apologies. My behavior was abhorrent. I don't know what got into me. It won't happen again."

He heard a hesitant footstep, then another. Feeling the touch of a hand on his shoulder, he stiffened. He wanted to spin around and take her in his arms again.

"Frannie told me you've never kissed her."

"I don't think of her that way."

"You don't think about kissing her?"

"She's not a carnal creature."

"You are."

He moved away from her, before he proved her point. "Yes, well, I'm quite capable of restraining myself when the situation warrants."

"And I don't warrant restraint?"

He faced her. "I want to marry Frannie, but I think of you day and night. I'm sitting at that bloody dinner table wondering about the taste of you with wine upon your tongue. And when you vent your fury at me all you do is make me want you more. But it is only lust, Catherine. It is only the physical. I am with you every night. It stands to reason that my body would react to your nearness. It has grown accustomed to it."

It didn't help matters at all that the scent of her lingered in his bed.

"Do you ever do anything with Frannie?" she asked.

The change in subject seemed abrupt, strange, but he was grateful to turn attention away from his acting badly. "What do you mean?"

"Do you ever take her to the theater or the park or boating? Do you know her outside of Dodger's?"

"Well, yes, of course."

"What's something you've done together?"

"When we were children—"

"Not when you were children. Recently. Since you've been adults."

He considered her question. Everything always seemed to involve Dodger's. And before that Feagan.

"I can't remember the last time we did anything."

"You should do something together, don't you think?"

It was embarrassing to admit that he'd never done anything with a lady that wasn't questionable. "What would you suggest?"

"Have you been to the Great Exhibition?"

He could hardly fathom that she was speaking to him with enthusiasm about an outing with Frannie, as though he'd never kissed Catherine. He realized that she was putting up a wall. After all, she was the daughter of a duke, a woman with noble blood. And they both knew nothing about him was noble.

Frannie was the woman he'd marry. He needed to concentrate on winning her over.

"I've not been," he told Catherine.

"Neither have I. They say Queen Victoria has gone five times already. Can you imagine? I'm hoping to go tomorrow. Perhaps you could take Frannie there sometime. It would be a nice outing."

"I'll consider it."

She nodded, her tongue darting out to lick her lip the way it did after she drank wine. He wondered if she was tasting him. She cleared her throat. "We should probably return to our guests."

"Probably." Only he didn't want to. Dinners were tedious.

"We shall forget what happened earlier, and I won't allow it to happen again," she said.

He studied her in the shadows of his library. "Do you mean the kiss?"

She nodded, and so he nodded as well. She might be able to forget it, but he doubted that he ever would, that he would ever forget the smallest detail about her.

"Have you ever known anyone to stand up to him like she does?" Bill asked, before sipping his wine.

Frannie smiled. "No. And I don't think he quite knows what to make of her."

"He's always loved you, Frannie. Why are you making it so blasted difficult for him? You're not meek, you're not cowardly. I daresay if you wanted all this, nothing would stop you from acquiring it."

"That's the thing, Bill. I don't want all this. It's too grand, it's too . . . well, it's simply too much."

"Think of all the good things you could do."

"I can do them now. I *am* doing them now."

"But you could do so much more. As Luke's wife, you'd have influence, you'd—"

"Be snubbed at every turn. I don't understand why he stays in this world. I truly don't. I see how they look at him at the club. He has no friends among the aristocracy. They spurn him."

"Do you not see the irony? You judge them as harshly as they judge us. What do you truly know of them? Don't you like Catherine?"

She pursed her lips. "You're determined to make this difficult."

"You worry about what the aristocracy thinks of you."

"Don't you?"

"No. The one thing I learned in my youth as a grave robber was that everyone looks the same when they're dead. We're all equal then. So when I meet a chap, sitting on his high horse, I imagine him dead. He's not quite so intimidating then."

She giggled. "You're awful."

He smiled at her. He had such a beguiling smile. He'd always been so very quiet, keeping to himself. When she'd first met him, she'd been afraid that she would die if he touched her. She thought all the children had been afraid of him, or at least in awe of him. He was the first one they'd ever known who didn't fear the dead.

A young man came to Luke's residence shortly after dinner to inform Bill that one of his patients had taken a turn for the worse. Bill quickly took his leave.

It was left to Luke to take both ladies home. Because he wasn't quite ready to trust himself alone with Catherine, he took her home first. Frannie didn't give the impression she suspected that anything inappropriate had happened while Luke and Catherine were out of the room. But then she'd never suspect the worst of him.

After he escorted Catherine to the back gate, he was left alone in the coach with Frannie. It was strange to realize on how few occasions they actually traveled together. When he and Catherine traveled each evening they talked about a great many things. Perhaps it was because they were new to each other's lives and knew so little about each other, whereas he and Frannie had grown up together. They knew everything about each other.

"I think Bill works far too hard," Frannie said after a while.

"Who among us doesn't?" he asked.

"I suppose you're right. I rather like Catherine."

"You made it difficult for her tonight."

"I think we all did, but I just really wasn't in the mood for a formal dinner. I'll do it properly when it matters, Luke."

"I know you will. It seemed tedious to me as well. I doubt we'll entertain often."

She lifted the curtain, glanced out. "Jim was telling me about the Great Exhibition. He was rather impressed with it."

"Would you like to go?"

She dropped the curtain back into place. "I would, yes."

"Will tomorrow serve?"

She smiled softly. "Tomorrow will serve very well."

"Splendid."

Once they arrived at Dodger's, he escorted Frannie to her rooms. Then he walked down the stairs and through the back door that led into Dodger's. He walked down the hallway to the room where he knew he'd find Jack. A footman with meaty fists nodded at Luke and opened the door. Luke knew he was more guard than servant. His presence signaled that Jack was counting his money.

That's exactly what he was doing when Luke walked into the room. Jack looked up from his neat stacks of coins and paper currency. "How was your fancy dinner?"

"Tedious and not so fancy."

Jack reached back for a glass, poured whiskey into it, and pushed it to the edge of the desk. Luke sat in the chair, grabbed the glass, downed its contents, and put the glass back. Jack immediately refilled it. Luke assumed his face revealed that he was a man in need of a drink or two.

"What's troubling you?" Jack asked.

He was the only person Luke knew who was better at reading people than Luke was. "Have you ever loved anyone?"

"You mean besides my mum?"

Luke was dumbfounded as he stared at Jack. He knew his friend's story. "She sold you when you were five."

Jack shrugged. "Doesn't mean I didn't love her. Just means she didn't love me."

Sipping his whiskey this time, Luke pondered

Jack's words. He'd always assumed because he loved Frannie that she loved him back. Could love have only one side to it and still be love?

Had anyone ever loved him before he was unofficially adopted by Feagan and his merry brood? If they had, wouldn't he remember?

"That night you found me in the alley, behind the garbage, did I say anything?"

"Like what?"

Luke ran his finger around the rim of the glass. "Something that might have given you a hint as to what I was doing there."

"I didn't need you to say anything to give me a hint. It was obvious. You were dying."

"But how did I come to be there?"

"Looked to me like someone had kicked you out. You were skinny, your clothes torn. Do you really want to know the truth of it?"

Luke rubbed his forehead as pain began to throb. The late hours, the encounter with Catherine were taking a toll.

"You're not thinking you're really Claybourne, are you?" Jack asked.

Luke shook his head. Claybourne, the real Claybourne, would have been worthy of Catherine. Something Luke would never be. She was a lady, and he was a scoundrel.

"Has Lady Catherine taught Frannie what she needs to know?" Jack asked.

Luke sighed. "It's as though she's taught her nothing."

"Is that why you look like a man who's lost his best friend?"

Leaning forward, Luke dug his elbows into his

thighs and held the glass between both hands, studying the few drops that lined the bottom. "I've been with several women through the years, Jack. No matter what I did with them, I never felt disloyal to Frannie. With Catherine, I feel disloyal to Frannie by simply speaking with her."

"No harm in just speaking to her."

He wasn't going to confess that he'd done more than speak to her.

"Sometimes I worry that Frannie doesn't love me, and just doesn't know how to tell me." He studied the way Jack drank his whiskey. "If that were the case you'd tell me, wouldn't you? If you knew? You wouldn't leave me to make a fool of myself."

"Love is a stranger to me, Luke. Other than my mum, no woman has ever held my affections."

"Not even Frannie?"

"I like her well enough, but that's not love, is it?"

Luke was fairly sure that Jack was lying. He certainly wasn't being honest about something.

Luke set his glass on the desk and stood. "No. Like isn't love."

Neither was lust. And that was all he felt for Catherine, a deep, almost uncontrollable lust.

When he returned home, he was walking toward the library for a bit of whiskey to help him settle into the night when his gaze fell on the envelope sitting on the silver slaver on the table in the entry hallway. He recognized the hand that had addressed it—even though it was not quite as neat as usual. Catherine no doubt once again inviting him to one of her silly balls.

He wondered if she'd left the invitation before or after their encounter in the library, wondered if she was expecting him to bring Frannie.

With a sigh, he headed to the library. Her latest invitation was simply one more that would go unaccepted.

From the Journal of Lucian Langdon

Few came to the old gent's funeral. Until that moment I'd not realized what it had cost him to take me in, to announce to the world that I, the suspected murderer of his second son, was in fact his grandson.

A week after his passing, I attended a ball. I knew it was in bad form, that when one is in mourning one does not attend affairs that exhibit gaiety. But I also knew that gentlemen were often forgiven for not adhering to the strictures of society.

Besides, I had a point to make. I wanted no one to doubt that I was taking my place as the old gent's successor.

I remember little about the ball except that from the moment I began descending the stairs, I regretted that I'd come. People stared at me as though I were an unusual-looking creature on display at a menagerie and, with that thought, my head began to pound. I desperately craved a glass of whiskey. I desperately wanted to be at Dodger's.

Ladies lowered their gazes. Gentlemen looked away. Some stepped back as though they feared being contaminated by my presence.

And then I spied her.

Her.

Lovely, elegant, and daring, she not only met my gaze, but she held it as though she was as fascinated with me as I was with her. For the briefest of moments, I contemplated asking her for the honor of a dance, but I knew such an action would tarnish her reputation. That night, for the first time in my life, I understood the sacrifices that were required to truly be a gentleman.

With regret, I turned away, the wonder of her in my arms to remain a mystery that would often haunt me.

Chapter 14

Catherine couldn't sleep and it seemed a waste to lie in her bed alone with eyes open, staring at the canopy. She could at least be useful so she went to her father's bedchamber and told his nurse to go rest for a bit. Catherine would wake her when she was ready to retire.

Her father appeared to be sleeping, but still she found comfort in holding his hand. Even if he were awake, she couldn't tell him that she'd allowed Claybourne to kiss her three times now. Claybourne's reasons for kissing her she understood: intimidation, distraction, frustration.

But her reasons for kissing him—because she had welcomed his kiss, all three times to her shame and mortification—were a mystery. It was only because she'd thought her legs were going to buckle that she'd pushed him away this evening. The truth of the matter was that she'd rather hoped he'd ravish her further. Even as she'd thought that, she'd remembered Frannie and Dr. Graves waiting for them to return to the dining room.

When they had finally returned, Frannie had refused to hold her gaze. Catherine wondered if something in her eyes or her swollen lips had screamed out that she was a wanton woman.

She didn't want to desire Claybourne, but desire him, she did.

She shouldn't have left the invitation, but she thought if she could just have one dance with him, she'd be content for the remainder of her life. Although she couldn't imagine that a dance would be nearly as satisfying as his kiss.

"I've never known anyone like him, Papa," she whispered quietly. "Sometimes I think he'll break my heart. Not on purpose, because he doesn't know how my feelings are shifting, but it will break all the same." She stroked his hand. "Did you love Mother, I wonder? If so, how did you bear it when she was no longer here? I think that's what worries me the most. I've grown so accustomed to being with him that I'm not sure how I'll survive when he's no longer a daily"—or more accurate, nightly—"part of my life."

She pressed her cheek to the back of his hand. She would find a way to survive.

Catherine had thought it would be fun to bring Winnie's son, Whit, to the Great Exhibition. Winnie had wanted to come along as well. Had insisted on it, actually, convinced that Catherine's reputation would be irrevocably ruined if she were seen out in public without benefit of a chaperone, and as Winnie was married, she served nicely in the role.

They'd arrived at Hyde Park shortly after

breakfast to wait in line. It was the cheap-ticket day, the day when tickets were only a shilling, and common folk more than the elite were about. Winnie's bruise was almost gone, but still she didn't want to meet up with anyone she might know. She thought it less likely if they came today.

The iron and glass building known as the Crystal Palace was an amazing twenty-six acres of exhibits, almost overwhelming with everything it had on display, especially for a child of four. The stunning glass water fountain in the center of the building had caused Whit's eyes to widen, and Catherine had to hold tightly on to his hand to keep him from trying to climb in.

Now, three hours later, Whit was growing weary and grumpy because his legs were tired. Catherine had carried him for some time now, hoping to see more of the exhibits before being forced to leave because her arms were growing as tired as his legs. Catherine understood now why the queen had come five times already. It was impossible to see everything in one go.

"Whit is getting so restless. Do you think we should go?" Winnie asked.

Catherine heard the disappointment in her voice, and she wondered if it was leaving the exhibition or returning home that left Winnie with regret. "Why don't we push on for a little while longer? I'd really like to see the Koh-i-Noor diamond."

"Do you think it's really as spectacular as they say?"

"Everything else we've seen so far has been."

"Even the people," Winnie whispered. "Have you ever seen such an assortment? They're from all over the world. Every time I look around—oh, dear Lord."

Winnie had grown ghastly pale.

"What is it?" Catherine asked.

"Claybourne, and he's coming this way." She squeezed her eyes shut. "I knew we never should have spoken of him in Lady Charlotte's garden the other day."

Catherine spun around. It was indeed Claybourne and Frannie. It was quite evident that they were strolling toward them—as though Catherine and her party were themselves an exhibit to be studied. She felt a little shiver of anticipation. She was safe here with people about and Frannie at his side. He'd not tempt her into thoughts of wickedness with a kiss. It would all be very formal, very proper.

"Ignore him," Winnie said, digging her fingers into Catherine's arm.

Ignore him? How could she when he looked so exceedingly handsome in his dark blue jacket and trousers. His cravat was also blue, but his shirt and waistcoat were a gray that almost matched the silver of his eyes. One leather-clad hand held his black top hat and walking stick. She knew what that walking stick was capable of. It was nearly as dangerous as its owner.

"I won't give him a cut direct he hasn't earned." Although she could feel Winnie's horrified gaze on her, Catherine acknowledged Claybourne with a smile and wondered how to best handle this situation without causing Winnie to suspect that she and Claybourne shared more than a passing acquaintance. She should have known Claybourne would have the situation well in hand.

"Lady Catherine Mabry, as I recall," he said lazily, a hint of teasing in his eyes that she doubted Winnie would notice. She suspected Winnie feared the man so much that she wouldn't lift her gaze above his neckcloth. "Our paths crossed at a ball once, some years back, but I don't believe we were ever formally introduced." He bowed slightly. "I'm Claybourne."

"Yes, I recall that ball. It has been some years. What a surprise it is to see you here today."

"I have it on good authority that the Great Exhibition is not to be missed."

"I daresay they'll be talking about it for years to come." She turned to Winnie. "Duchess, allow me to introduce Lucian Langdon, the Earl of Claybourne."

Winnie's fingers were still digging into her arm, and Catherine could feel her trembling. What was it she feared? The man had done nothing threatening.

"My lord," Winnie said succinctly, and Catherine doubted that Claybourne had missed the rudeness in her tone, yet he didn't seem bothered by it.

"Your Grace," he replied. "Allow me to introduce Miss Darling. An acquaintance."

Frannie was dressed very much as she had been last night. Her dress a drab gray as though she wished to draw no attention to herself. Even her bonnet had very little color in it, almost as though she were in a later stage of mourning.

"Yes, quite, I'm sure," Winnie said, haughtily and suspiciously.

Claybourne narrowed his eyes, and Catherine was certain he'd taken offense. It was one thing to slight him, but to slight the woman he loved—

"Have you been here long?" Catherine asked, trying to make up for Winnie's impoliteness.

"No, not long. Miss Darling wanted to rush through and get a lay of the land, as it were. I prefer a leisurely pursuit. Which do you recommend?"

"I believe it's impossible to see everything in one go. At least by going slowly you see everything in more detail."

"My thought exactly."

Whit began rocking against her, his short legs kicking her backside and hip. "Go! Go!"

Catherine set him down before her arms gave out.

Claybourne immediately crouched in front of him. "And who are you?"

Winnie gasped.

"The Earl of Whitson," Whit said, mimicking his mother's earlier haughty tone. As young as he was, already he recognized differences in the classes.

"Did you know they have lemonade, pastries, and lollipops over there? Would you like to buy some for you and your mum?" Claybourne asked.

Whit nodded enthusiastically, his weariness suddenly cured.

"Hold out your hand," Claybourne ordered.

Whit did.

"Fold it up." Claybourne demonstrated, closing

his hand into a fist. Then he snapped his fingers. "Open your hand."

The boy did, his eyes growing wide at the ha'penny resting on his palm. Winnie gasped again.

"Hmm. I'm not certain that's enough," Claybourne said. He looked up at Frannie. "What's your opinion on the matter, Miss Darling?"

"Definitely not enough. I should think he'd need at least a shilling."

"I suspect you're right." He turned back to Whit. "Close your hand around the coin and say, 'Please, sir, may I have more?'"

Whit closed his hand around the coin. "Please, sir, may I have more?"

Claybourne snapped his fingers. Whit opened his hand, his eyes wider than before. The ha'penny was gone. A sixpence rested on his palm.

Frannie tapped Claybourne on the head. "You silly man. That's not a shilling."

Catherine realized they were performing, and she wondered how often they'd worked together on something similar. Was this how they'd fleeced people? Was this performance a remnant of their childhood? They seemed so natural, so comfortable with each other.

"You're quite right, Miss Darling. What was I thinking? Shall we give it another go, Lord Whitson?"

Grinning broadly, Whit bobbed his head up and down and closed his pudgy fingers over the coin. "Please, sir, may I have more?"

"Why, yes, sir, I think you may," Claybourne said, snapping his fingers.

Whit opened his fist and crowed. "Look! A shilling!"

Catherine realized he wasn't the only one with a wide smile. Winnie was grinning as well, as though her troubles had disappeared as easily as the coins.

"How did you do that, my lord?" Catherine asked.

"Magic."

"Why, yes, I could see that. But what's the secret?"

"I'm afraid I can't tell you that. It'll ruin the fun."

"Your Grace, may I take your son over to get some refreshments?" Frannie asked.

Winnie bobbed her head, then said, "I'll come with you."

Catherine watched as the threesome strolled toward the refreshment booth. "We should probably go with them."

"Probably," Claybourne said, offering his arm.

It would be rude to ignore it, so she placed her hand on his arm.

"You do realize you're creating a scandal having Frannie with you without a chaperone."

"Good Lord, Catherine, we grew up sleeping together, spooned around each other. Do you really think our relationship warrants a chaperone?"

Catherine was hit with an unexpected spark of jealousy and imagined them doing a good deal more than innocent spooning. "Appearance is everything."

"Very well, but she's nearly thirty. Isn't that the

magical age when a woman no longer needs looking after?"

"She's that old? She doesn't look it. Still, seeing you together out in public, people will assume she's your mistress."

"I've never bedded her."

Catherine was surprised by the relief that hit her with that inappropriate confession. "Are you going to wear a sign on your back stating so?"

"You're the one who suggested I do something with her."

He didn't bother to mask his impatience with her.

"I assumed you'd have common sense enough to realize you needed a chaperone."

"There's no hope for it then. We'll have to spend the rest of the day with you and the Duchess of Avendale, who as a married woman can serve as her chaperone in order to save Frannie's reputation."

Catherine narrowed her eyes at him. Had he just pulled some sort of trick on her in order to be included in her party?

"If I didn't know better I'd think you'd arranged this meeting on purpose, deliberately not bringing along a chaperone so I'd feel obligated to protect Frannie's reputation."

"Does it make me a scoundrel to enjoy your company?"

"You're a scoundrel simply because you're a scoundrel."

"I suppose I can't deny that, but Frannie learns by imitation. I thought a day of observing you out and about would serve her well."

"So today is a lesson, not an outing to enjoy each other's company. It defeats the purpose."

"How can it defeat the purpose when it brings you and me one step closer to obtaining what we each desire?"

Catherine's attention was drawn to the pounding footsteps. Whit approached, holding a lollipop.

"Sir, are you going to come with us now?"

Claybourne crouched. "Would you like me to?"

Catherine was astounded by his rapport with the child.

"Yes, sir."

"Have you ever seen an elephant?"

Whit shook his head.

Unfolding his body, Claybourne extended his hat and walking stick toward Catherine. "Do you mind?"

She took them. Claybourne turned his attention back to Whit. "Come on then, my young lord." He hoisted Whit upon his shoulders and the boy crowed once again, his lollipop becoming lost in Claybourne's thick, curling hair.

When Winnie and Frannie joined them, they all began walking, Claybourne leading the way. He seemed to know where they were going, and even if he didn't, he was keeping Whit occupied, which allowed Catherine to enjoy the exhibits a bit more.

Or she would have if her attention hadn't been focused on Claybourne.

It occurred to her that this was the first time she'd seen him when it wasn't night. He seemed less sinister with the light pouring in through the glass ceiling and windows, illuminating him. She'd known he was tall, but he somehow looked taller. She'd known he was broad, but he appeared broader. He strode with confidence, pointing things out to Whit.

She'd never before been able to imagine him with children, and now she couldn't imagine him without. He'd been gentlemanly toward Winnie and utterly charming with Whit. He'd told Catherine that he knew coin tricks, but she'd never imagined one such as he'd performed. Removing a coin from behind someone's ear—even her father had been able to do that. But what Claybourne had done required very clever hands.

She tried not to think what other wondrous things those very clever hands might do—to the buttons on a lady's bodice or the lacings on her corset. She felt the heat rush to her face with those inappropriate musings.

Seeing him in the daylight was quite literally allowing her to see him in a very different light, which she feared—for the sake of her heart—might not be a good thing, because she found herself longing for something she couldn't have.

The Great Exhibition was fascinating, but it paled when compared with Catherine and Frannie staring in awe at the massive Koh-i-Noor diamond. It was locked inside a cage, lit from below with gaslight. Luke was as intrigued by the enclosure as he was by the diamond itself.

But still it couldn't hold his attention for long.

His head had begun hurting as soon as he'd dropped the boy on his shoulders. It had spiked at the stuffed elephant exhibit. He suspected because the boy's enthusiasm had him fairly bobbing up and down, hitting Luke's head.

But he fought back the pain because he wasn't going to give up these moments of watching Catherine and Frannie together. Talking, smiling. He wondered if they'd become friends once he married Frannie, if perhaps they'd go on outings together.

He found an interesting contrast between the three women. The Duchess of Avendale's gaze kept darting around as though she feared being attacked any moment. He thought perhaps she wasn't comfortable in crowds, although her reactions were more along the lines of someone doing something she wasn't supposed to and fearing discovery. Catherine seemed oblivious to the fact that she was being watched. Jim had been there for a while, until Luke arrived with Frannie. Then they'd taken over, striving to determine who was following Catherine. It was possible the man couldn't afford admittance. Frannie was observant, her gaze wandering, measuring people, looking for an easy target. Not that she'd take advantage. They'd stopped fleecing when the old gent had taken them in off the street. But habits born in childhood were difficult to break.

His attention kept drifting back to Catherine and her delightful smile. He'd probably never have another day with her such as this one. Their relationship would once again become confined to the shadows.

It was where people such as he and Frannie belonged, while Catherine Mabry walked in the light.

Chapter 15

Luke sat at the desk in his study, the taste of whiskey still bitter on his tongue, his gaze focused on the invitation resting in front of him.

It had been more than a week since his visit to the Great Exhibition, a week during which Catherine had seemed to distance herself from him. They rarely spoke in the coach anymore. Their meetings didn't reflect awkwardness or unfriendliness, but he did sense a strain in their relationship. He suspected it had more to do with the kiss in the library then their tour of the Crystal Palace. She'd been pleasant enough there, probably because she'd felt safe with the crowds and the lack of shadows.

He knew no lessons would take place this evening. Frannie had seemed quite relieved at the prospect of a night without learning the intricacies of his aristocratic life. By now, shouldn't she be more at ease with the notion of becoming his wife? He'd always envisioned his life with her, living in this house, sharing the small and mundane details of his day. He saw them with children. He saw himself, at long last, being happy.

He was so damned tired of being alone, of snatching moments with his friends around a gaming table, of knowing they were no more comfortable in his world than he was.

None of them were like Catherine, comfortable with dinners, balls, and morning calls. They didn't carry themselves with the cool confidence that she did. They didn't challenge him at every turn. They'd stopped considering him their equal when he'd stepped onto the pedestal of the nobility. It was subtle, the discomfort they each exhibited around him.

Jack, always reminding him that he wasn't the rightful heir.

Jim, always doing Luke's bidding, regardless of the hour, as though it were Luke's right to expect a man to live his life inconveniently to please him.

Bill, never failing to come when called, taking care of business, then leaving. Never lingering for a sip of whiskey, never sharing the burdens he must surely carry as a purveyor of life and death.

And Frannie, terrified of becoming his wife, not because of the intimacies they'd share, but because of the daily struggles they'd face, because of the damned balls they might be required to attend.

Catherine's invitation sat there, mocking him, mocking his life, daring him to show his face—

Damn her!

He poured more whiskey into the glass, brought it to his lips, inhaled the sweet aroma of courage . . . and slowly set the glass back down. He picked up the invitation and ran his finger over the lettering. Had she experienced discomfort when writing it? Did she want him there *that* badly?

He thought of the night they'd played cards.

Obviously, my lord, you don't know what I'm thinking.

But he knew what she was thinking when she'd written his name across her fine invitation: that he wouldn't show.

Perhaps he would call her bluff.

Perhaps tonight, he would make her regret that she'd ever made a midnight visit to his library.

Catherine had known Claybourne wouldn't come, but still as the clock ticked toward midnight, she was disappointed. It was so terribly difficult to attend this ball and not reveal how much she loathed her host. He seemed so pleasant. No one could see the monster that lived within his skin.

Even Winnie gave nothing away, keeping a stiff upper lip, and pretending that all was right with the world. Sometimes Catherine was as angry with Winnie as she was with Avendale.

But she smiled and laughed and flirted with all the gentlemen who danced with her, not revealing to any of them that he was not the one she longed to waltz with. Just once, she wanted to be held within the circle of Claybourne's arms and hold his gaze while her feet whispered over the dance floor. Just once, she wished he would look at her the way he looked at Frannie. The depth of adoration that he showered on Frannie was something that every woman should have at least once in her life.

He might be a scoundrel, with many faults, but he had a heart far more giving than some of the men she'd spoken with tonight.

She glanced at her dance card. The next three dances weren't taken. She was relieved, having grown weary of pretending to enjoy herself. She was too worried about Winnie, too worried that Avendale might find fault with the evening, but all seemed to be going along splendidly. Even her hand was better. Her father's physician had removed the stitches. The scar wasn't too unsightly. Since she always wore gloves in public, few people would ever see it.

But she welcomed a small reprieve from being hostess. She was walking toward the doors that would lead onto the terrace when Winnie stopped her.

"Where are you going?"

"For a bit of cool air. Would you care to join me?"

"No, I don't think so. I'm basking in Avendale's praise. He's ever so pleased with how things are going this evening."

"I'm glad, Winnie."

"I should tell him that most of it is your doing."

"No, don't. You helped with the planning. Allow him to think it's all you." *If it makes him easier to live with,* she added to herself. She squeezed her friend's hand. "Go enjoy yourself. I won't be long."

She walked onto the terrace. With the lanterns in the garden, she could see a few couples strolling along the numerous paths. She'd never had a gentleman take her on a turn about the garden. Not entirely true, she realized. Claybourne had walked through a garden with her the night they agreed to their bargain.

She wandered over to the side of the terrace where the glow from the lights didn't reach. She wanted solitude, she wanted—

"Will you honor me with this dance?"

Her heart very nearly stopped at the sound of Claybourne's voice. She spun around to see him lurking in the shadows like some miscreant.

"What are you doing here?" she asked.

"I was invited."

"No, yes, I mean, I know you received an invitation, but you've not made your entrance."

"Why should I go through that bother when you're the only one I care to dance with? I assumed sooner or later you'd step outside, so I've been waiting."

And Luke had almost given up on her coming out. He'd been peering discreetly through a window, watching her. She was so beautiful this evening, her gown revealing the gentle swells of her breasts. The music drifted onto the night, and for the first time in his life, he *wanted* to dance with a woman.

He was aware of her watching him, studying him. He'd dressed as though he intended to attend, but once he'd arrived he'd no longer seen the point in going through the annoyance of actually being in the company of those he didn't favor. All he truly wanted was a dance with Catherine. And now he would have it.

"You've been waiting in the shadows"—she peered around the corner—"looking in the windows, like some sort of voyeur?"

"It's not as bad as all that. I was simply waiting for you to appear, and my patience has been rewarded." Taking her hand, he drew her nearer. "Dance with me."

"My God, you're a coward."

She might as well have slapped him. He released her hand. "Don't be ridiculous."

"Walk in through the front door. Dance with me on the dance floor. Attend this ball like a gentleman."

"I have attended a damned ball like a gentleman!" he hissed. "I know what they think of me. I saw the way they all looked away . . . except you. They think I'll steal their souls and their children."

"Because they don't know you. You've not given them a chance to come to know you. I daresay all they know of you is that you take their money at Dodger's gaming hell. Of course, gossip, speculation, and unease circles you. Your past guaranteed that it would be so. As long as you cower, as long as you hide and run—"

"I am not a coward," he ground out.

She raised her chin. "Then prove it. Or do you need Frannie by your side first? Is that what you're waiting for? To have a wife strong enough to stand beside you so you are strong enough to step out of the shadows? Do you think it will make it easier? Will you honestly lead her into the lion's den without first making certain that it's safe?"

"You know nothing at all about this, about what I will or will not do."

She wrapped her hand—the hand that had possibly saved his life—around his, offering comfort, support. It was almost his undoing. He didn't want her sympathy, he didn't want her understanding. He didn't even know any longer why he was there.

"It's like drinking whiskey," she said quietly. "The first sip is bitter, the second not so much. And eventually, you come to anticipate the flavor."

"You can drink whiskey in the privacy of your own home. Let me dance with you here in the privacy of the garden."

She studied him for a moment while the music drifted into silence, and another refrain finally began to waft out into the garden.

"Very well. If that's how you wish it to be," she said softly.

And he saw in her eyes, heard in her voice, the disappointment that he would choose the easier road.

"Even if I were to make an appearance, I'd not be able to dance with you."

"Why ever not?"

"Your reputation would be ruined."

"Perhaps in the beginning, but once they come to know you better, I daresay I'd be viewed with a great deal of awe, as a visionary."

"You have an inordinate amount of confidence in my ability to win them over."

"I do." She touched her gloved hand to his cheek. "You've won me over."

She held his gaze for only a heartbeat longer, before it wavered, as though she'd revealed too much.

"Damn you," he growled.

Then he spun on his heel and strode away. How dare she challenge him? How dare she—

How dare she make him regret that he was not a better man.

As she returned to the ballroom, Catherine realized that she'd pushed too hard, and in the pushing, she'd shoved him away.

She should have taken the dance in the garden—joyfully, gratefully, but she was weary of everything involving him being done in the shadows as though their relationship was shameful. Even their encounter at the Crystal Palace was not without its deceptions. They'd pretended they were nothing more than passing acquaintances.

Worse, she felt silly for continuing to invite him to affairs that he had no intention of attending. Even now, knowing that he'd not make an appearance, she still kept hoping—

"Lucian Langdon, the Earl of Claybourne!"

The announcement echoed through the room like a death knell. With her heart pounding furiously, Catherine jerked her gaze to the stairs.

And there he was, standing so incredibly proudly with defiance etched in his stance.

"Oh, dear God, what's he doing here?" Winnie asked, suddenly at Catherine's side, clutching her arm. "I didn't send him an invitation."

"I did."

"What? Why? Whatever were you thinking?"

"That he intrigues me."

She watched as he descended the stairs with an air of arrogance that she now realized was nothing more than a ruse. Growing up, he'd been taught how to deceive, how to trick—but he didn't just apply it to gain what he wanted. He wrapped it around himself like a finely tailored cloak in order to protect the core of his being.

He'd come here to prove to her that he wasn't a coward.

His face was an unreadable mask, just as it had been the first night that she'd ever set eyes on him. He prowled now as he had prowled then. He dared anyone to refute his right to be there—and she knew now that he dared *them*, because he doubted his own place so much.

He wanted—needed—them to accept his position among them because he was unable to accept it himself.

As she watched him, she was struck with the realization that somehow, in spite of all the odds, she'd come to care deeply for this man. That she didn't want him hurt. That she didn't want him to lose that last bit of soul that he clung to.

"Since I invited him, I'll welcome him," Catherine said, and before Winnie could object, Catherine began walking toward their new guest.

The music had halted with the announcement and had yet to resume. As Claybourne made his way into the room, people stepped back as though a leper walked amongst them. She knew Claybourne had to be aware of the reactions, the lowered gazes, the fear, the dismay. And yet, he didn't retreat. He strode forward with the elegance of a king, so much more worthy of respect than those who surrounded him.

When she was near enough, he stopped. If she'd not come to know him so well, she'd have not realized what this moment was costing him. Nearly every ounce of his pride. He was not a man to bow down, and yet for her, he almost had.

She curtsied. "My Lord Claybourne, we're so pleased you could join us tonight."

He bowed slightly. "Lady Catherine, I'm very honored to have been invited."

"My dance card is presently blank, but it is not the custom for a lady to ask a gentleman to dance."

"A coward might not ask for fear of being rebuffed."

"But then you are not a coward, my lord."

She watched his throat work as he swallowed. "Will you honor me with a dance?"

"The honor, sir, is all mine."

She extended her hand toward him, and as he took it, she signaled the orchestra. The strains of a waltz began to fill the room.

"I do hope we won't be dancing alone," he muttered.

"I don't care one way or the other. I only care that I'm dancing with you."

He took her in his arms then, and it was as she'd always imagined it would be. She was aware of his strength as he held her, the warmth in his eyes as he gazed upon her.

Very slowly, cautiously, others began to join them on the dance floor. Catherine suspected they were vying for nearness so they might overhear what the scandalous Devil Earl and Lady Catherine Mabry were discussing.

"Gossip about us will abound tomorrow," he said quietly.

"I suspect it will abound tonight."

"And you don't care."

"Not one whit. I have wanted to dance with you since the first ball I ever saw you attend."

"You looked so young and innocent that night, dressed in white. Who would have thought you were such a hellion?"

She wasn't certain whether he was striving to compliment or insult her, but it didn't matter. What mattered was that he appeared to recall as many details about that night as she did. "You remember what I was wearing?"

"I remember everything about you that night. You wore pink ribbons in your hair and pearls against your throat."

"The pearls were my mother's."

"You were standing amongst a gaggle of girls, and you stood out not because of your beauty—which far exceeded theirs—but because of your refusal to be cowed. No one has ever challenged me as you do, Catherine."

"No one has ever intrigued me as you do, my lord."

She feared they were skirting the edges of flirtation gone too far.

The final strains of the music wafted into silence. Catherine took a deep breath. "I've grown rather warm. Would you be so kind as to escort me onto the terrace where the air is cooler?"

"If that is your pleasure."

She wound her arm around his and strolled through the room, holding her head high, meeting gazes that were quickly averted, watching as her reputation was irrevocably destroyed. Her father would never know, but if—when—her brother returned, he'd be furious. She would deal with the repercussion when it happened.

Once they were outside, she led Claybourne to the corner of the terrace, where they could find a measure of privacy, but were still visible. Her reputation was in tatters but still she held on to what fraying threads she could.

"I have decided not to have you dispense with someone of my choosing. But I am determined to redouble me efforts in convincing Frannie that by your side is where she belongs, and where she'll be comfortable. I'm convinced that it's not so much that she needs to be taught, but rather that she simply needs to be accepted, so I intend to change strategy and bring her into this world, slowly but with more success."

"You're going to keep your part of the bargain without me keeping mine?"

"As strange as it seems, I feel that in the past few weeks we've become . . . friends of a sort, and I'd like to assist you in your quest for a wife—out of friendship." Regardless of the cost to herself, which would be high. She thought she'd never come to care for another man as she'd come to care for Claybourne, that she'd never respect another as she respected him, that she'd never be as fascinated by, as impressed with, any other man as she was him.

But his heart had been given elsewhere, while hers, she feared had been given to him.

"That's extremely generous of you. I hardly know how to thank you."

"It's barely anything at all. As you so aptly pointed out the night we struck our bargain, I'm doing little more than instructing her on the proper way to host an afternoon tea."

"On the contrary, she's acquiring a confidence under your tutelage that she was lacking before. I almost fear she'll become as headstrong as you."

"Do you really want a trifle of a wife? You'd become bored in no time."

"You think you know what I desire in a woman?"

"I credit myself for knowing what you deserve from a woman. As tonight proved, obstacles remain to be overcome, but I have no doubt you will overcome them."

"You remind me of the old gent. He never doubted. I never quite understood what he saw in me."

"He saw his grandson."

Chapter 16

He saw his grandson.

Luke considered those words as his coach rattled over the cobblestone streets. He'd been wandering aimlessly through London for more than two hours trying to settle his thoughts.

He'd left the affair shortly after Catherine and he had returned to the ballroom. He saw no reason to stay. He suspected no other lady would dance with him, but more than that he had no desire to dance with anyone other than Catherine. And he'd not further risk her reputation by having a second waltz. He'd already placed her reputation at risk with one dance and a turn about the garden. Why was she willing to risk so much simply to see that he was accepted?

Friendship? God knew he'd risked everything—including his life—for his friends. They'd risked no less than that for him. But Catherine—what did she gain? If he spent any more time in her company, no decent man would take her to wife.

Tonight she'd done away with the purpose for

their association. For some reason, she'd decided the bloke wasn't worth killing. Luke supposed he should be grateful he'd not taken her at her word that first night and done the gent in.

Still, he was bothered by her change of heart. She wasn't a mindless chit, and she was certainly no one's fool. If she thought someone needed killing, he most likely did. And there was still the matter of the man who was following her. He needed to have a word with Jim, but first he wanted to see Frannie.

The coach came to a halt outside Dodger's, and Luke alighted. He went through the front door. No tension reverberated here as it had at Avendale's. But then this was his home, this was where he belonged.

Jack approached him. "Luke—"

Luke held up his hand. "Not now."

He was a man with a purpose. He opened the door to the backrooms and went down the hallway to the room where he knew he'd find Frannie. She was hard at work on her books. He rapped on the doorjamb. She looked up and grinned at him. As always, her smile warmed him as nothing else did.

"Aren't you dressed rather fancily?"

"I attended a ball hosted by the Duchess of Avendale," he said.

"I didn't think you were one to attend the aristocracy's affairs."

"I thought it time I begin making the way clear for us."

She looked down at the ledgers. "So we'll be attending balls?"

"I think you'll enjoy them. There's gaiety and lovely gowns. Food and drink and people."

"Yes, lots of people I'll not know."

"You'll come to know them. And best of all, we shall dance." He strolled into the room and held out his hand. "Dance with me now."

She snapped her head up. "Are you daft?"

"Probably. But I want very desperately to dance with you."

"But there's no music—"

"I can hum."

Whatever was wrong with him? Why was this need to dance with her so strong?

Laughing sweetly, she rose. "Very well."

She came around her desk. "As I recall, I'm supposed to stand on your toes."

He chuckled. It was the way the old gent had danced with her. He'd seen that they had lessons, so many lessons. Why did Frannie feel as though she needed more now? Surely she'd not forgotten everything they'd been taught.

"The movements are the same but you keep your feet on the floor." He placed one of her hands on his shoulder, took the other in his, settled his free hand on her waist.

He began to hum the tune that had been playing while he'd danced with Catherine. And he moved Frannie in rhythm to his horrendous humming. The space was small. He couldn't sweep her across the area, but it was enough.

With Frannie in his arms, his body didn't tighten, his mind didn't bring forth carnal images. He told himself it was because when he looked down on her, all he saw was buttons and cloth. When he looked down on Catherine, an entirely different portrait emerged. He saw clearly the swell of her breasts, the gentle slope of her throat. He saw her smile. The joy reflected in her blue eyes.

He stopped waltzing and very subtlety drew Frannie a fraction nearer. He cradled her chin as though it was made of the finest porcelain, as though it could so easily shatter. He watched as her eyes widened slightly, as her tongue darted out to dampen her lower lip. He felt a pleasant thrumming low in his belly.

He lowered his head, her eyes slid closed, and he, very gently, brushed his lips over hers, before drawing back.

"There, that wasn't so bad was it?" he asked.

Nor was it particularly satisfying, but that would come in time, as she became more familiar with the physical nature of men.

She shook her head. "No, not at all."

"I adore you."

"I know."

He stroked his thumb over her bottom lip. He should want to lean back in for another kiss. Lord knew he could never seem to get enough of the taste of Catherine. And yet what he and Frannie had shared seemed to be quite . . . adequate.

Adequete. Not passionate, not fiery, not all-consuming.

Civilized. Not barbaric, not beastly, not untamed.

Proper. Not scandalous, not to be whispered about, not disgraceful.

"What's wrong?" Frannie asked.

And he realized he was scowling, his brow furrowed so deeply he was going to give himself another one of his blinding headaches.

Shaking his head, he released her and stepped back. "Nothing. Nothing at all."

But something *was* terribly wrong, because he was doubting his affection for Frannie, something he'd never done.

"Was Catherine at the ball?" Frannie asked.

"She was."

"Did you dance with her?"

He turned away slightly. "I did."

Why did he feel guilty? It wasn't as though he'd bedded her. It had been an innocent dance. But it hadn't felt innocent.

"What was she wearing?"

"What all ladies wear. A ball gown."

"You'd make a horrendous society writer." Frannie returned to her chair behind her desk. "I'll wager she looked beautiful."

"I'll not take you up on that wager as she always looks beautiful."

"Why has she not married, do you think?"

"Because she is too opinionated, willful, argumentative. A man wants peace in his household, and with her, a man would never find peace."

"So you think marriage to me would be peaceful?"

"I do."

"And that's what you want? Peace?"

"I want contentment."

"Do you find me boring?"

"Of course not."

"Sometimes I wonder, sometimes I fear that I

am. I sit here with all these numbers, and they seem so unexciting."

"Nothing about you is unexciting. I look forward to the time we spend together." He sat in the chair across from her. "There just seems to be so little of it of late."

As though to punctuate his words a rap on the door sounded. Luke glanced over his shoulder to see Jim standing uncertainly in the doorway. "Didn't mean to interrupt, but Jack said he couldn't get your attention earlier, and I've got something I thought you might be interested in."

"What is it?" Luke asked.

"The man who's been following Lady Catherine."

Luke's heart slammed against his ribs and everything else suddenly seemed unimportant. "Where is he?"

Jim jerked his head to the side. "Jack's office."

Luke hurried out of the room. "How did you find him?"

"Lady Catherine was running around like an insane woman this morning, taking care of the things for the ball she was hosting tonight." Jim stepped into the room and pointed at a battered man with dark hair sitting in a chair, working the brim of his hat. "Mr. Evans here could barely keep up with her."

Jack's burly footman had obviously been keeping guard. He nodded once and discreetly left the room, closing the door behind him.

"He's been ever so cooperative since he spent a few hours in gaol," Jim explained.

"Abuse of power is wot it was. Locking me up when I ain't done nuffin' wrong."

Luke sat on the edge of Jack's desk, studying the man. "Do you know who I am?"

"Claybourne," the man fairly spit.

"Do you know that I've killed a man?"

"So have I. It's not that hard to do."

"My point, dear fellow, is that I'm fond of Lady Catherine and I don't like that blackguards such as yourself are following her."

"I never 'urt 'er."

"That's the only reason you're still breathing. I want answers and if I don't get them, I won't be nearly as gentle as Scotland Yard. Have I made myself clear?"

Evans swallowed, nodded. He was a bully, and bullies were easy to put in their place.

"Why did you follow her?" Luke asked.

"I was paid to."

"By whom?"

"Fancy gent."

"Who?"

"Don't know his name. He hired a bunch of us."

"Hired a bunch of you to do what?"

He lifted his shoulders in the way a man would to avoid a blow. "Follow people around."

"Come on, mate," Jim said, his voice riffed with authority. "Tell his lordship everything without him having to ask all the questions."

"What people exactly were you following?" Luke asked.

"The Lady Catherine, loike 'e said,"—he pointed to Jim—"a duchess, and you."

"Which duchess were you following?"

"Dunno. I didn't follow 'er. Me mate followed

'er. I know she was the gent's wife; he thought she was up to no good."

"Why did he have you follow Lady Catherine?"

"Dunno. Just wanted to know where she went, who she met, wot she did. So I told 'im. Mostly borin' stuff, shoppin' and the loike."

"There, you see?" Jim asked. "I'm not the only one who thought she was boring."

Luke jerked his head around and glared at Jim.

Jim held up his hands in surrender. "Sorry. But I felt a need to point it out."

Luke turned his attention back to Evans. "Are you one of the gents who attacked me one night?"

The man's cap almost disappeared in his large hands he was wringing it so hard. It was answer enough for Luke.

"Were you supposed to kill me?"

Evans gave a brusque nod.

"And Lady Catherine?"

Evans's head came up, his eyes round. "No, I swear. Didn't know she was even there 'til she popped outta the coach. I didn't follow 'er at noight, 'er being a lady and all. I figured she was already abed."

"Did you tell your employer?"

Evans shook his head quickly. "'E was mad enuf that we didn't get the job done proper. Didn't want to borrow no more trouble."

"Where did you meet him?"

"Nowhere in particular. 'E always found us."

"And you don't know who he is?"

"Sorry, mate."

"Yes, I'll just bet you are." Luke considered what he knew. Nothing made sense. Something was missing. Why would he follow a duchess? And which duchess? "The duchess you were following—did you ever see her with Lady Catherine?"

"Almost every day. They were tighter than two peas in a pod."

"You didn't think that was worth mentioning?"

The man shrugged.

"If they were together, only one of you needed to follow them, but two of you were still getting paid, right?" Jim asked.

Evans sighed and nodded as if he were a child caught pilfering a cookie. But Luke had greater concerns on his mind. He eased off the desk, walked to Jim, and said in a low voice, "Catherine spends a good deal of time with the Duchess of Avendale. Have you seen her in the company of any other duchess?"

Jim shook his head. "If I had, I would have told you before now."

"Makes no sense. Why would Avendale—"

The door opened and Jack strode in, extending a piece of paper. "This just came for you."

Luke took it. The seal was broken. "You looked at it."

"I needed to know if it was as urgent as the man who delivered it claimed."

Luke scowled at him, then unfolded the note. His stomach dropped to the floor.

I need you at Avendale's.
Bring Dr. Graves.
Quickly.

—C

Luke had left Jim to see to Evans and headed to Avendale's, with a quick stop by Bill's residence to alert him that his services were needed. Bill had come in his own conveyance so he wouldn't be dependent upon Luke for transportation. Frannie had come along as well. Luke hadn't known what to expect, but had feared the worst. He'd almost fallen to his knees with relief when he'd realized it was the duchess and not Catherine who needed Bill's services.

Now Luke sat on a bench beside Catherine outside the Duchess of Avendale's bedchamber. He'd caught only a glimpse of her before Bill had ushered everyone except Frannie out of the room. If Luke hadn't known who she was because of Catherine's concern for her, he'd have never recognized her as the duchess.

"The name you'd have eventually given to me, if you'd not changed your mind this evening—would it have belonged to Avendale?" he asked quietly.

With tears welling in her eyes, Catherine nodded.

"I assume this isn't the first time he's taken his fists to his wife."

Taken his fists to her, then fled. No doubt to Dodger's.

Catherine shook her head. "But it's the worst. And it's my fault. He was unhappy that you were in his residence. I should have known better. He's such a controlling beast. Winnie has to account for every minute of every day. And your name wasn't on the guest list, but I wanted to dance with you on a ballroom floor. How stupid and selfish. I should have lied and told you he'd taken my virtue and then this matter would be done."

"It's not an easy thing to live with a lie, Catherine." He knew that truth well enough.

"Do you think it is an easy thing to know you are responsible for your friend's death?"

"She's not dead yet. Don't give up on her so easily. Bill is very good at what he does."

"Two of Avendale's wives have died. I shall never forgive myself if Winnie does as well. Because I was a coward and waited. As much as I wanted the deed done, I began to worry about how I would feel afterward, how I'd live with myself. And now look what's happened to her."

"Catherine, it's not your fault."

"It is. As I explained."

"What did you do, sweetheart? You sent out an invitation to a person he'd not anticipated. I killed a man and no one took a fist to me." He put his arm around her, drew her near, and pressed a kiss to her temple. "His punishment doesn't fit your crime."

Catherine took such comfort from Claybourne's nearness. From the moment that Winnie's lady's maid had shown up at Catherine's residence weeping, Catherine had feared the worst, and she'd not hesitated to send for Claybourne, for herself more so than Winnie. She knew she could draw from his strength. Knew she would find comfort in his presence.

"How many stab wounds would it take to kill a person?" she asked.

"One if you do it right. But using a knife makes it very personal, Catherine."

"A pistol would be better then."

"Only if you're a very good marksman."

She moved out from beneath his arm and shored up her courage. "Can you teach me to be a good marksman?"

"I could. But I see no need. I'll take care of this matter."

He took her hand, rubbed his thumb across her knuckles, then circled it over the back of her hand. It felt so lovely, so tender, so reassuring.

"I thought you were a beast," she said quietly.

"Closer to the devil, don't you think?"

Ah, yes, the Devil Earl. She couldn't recall the last time she'd thought of him in those terms. "Why did you kill the man you did?"

"Because he hurt Frannie."

Catherine tried to remember when everything had taken place.

"She would have been a child at the time."

"Indeed, she was, and in spite of the life she'd led, up until that moment, she was a very sweet and innocent child."

"Have you killed anyone else?"

He slowly shook his head.

"But you'll kill Avendale?"

He gave one brusque nod.

"Will you be able to live with it?"

With his thumb, he wiped the tears from her cheek. "That's for me to worry about."

"You said I was asking you to give up the last of your soul."

"There's only a small bit left. Giving it up will be no hardship."

But she feared it *would* be a great hardship, that

it would change him irrevocably into a man she could no longer love. Oh, dear Lord, when had she fallen in love with him? Had there been a precise moment or had it been simply an accumulation of many?

"It was easier for me to ask you do this before I knew you," she said.

"And it's easier for me to do now because I know you better."

The bedchamber door opened. A somber Dr. Graves and Frannie stepped out. Catherine came to her feet, expecting the worst.

"She's going to recover, but she's going to require a lot of care," Dr. Graves said. "She's been terribly abused in very personal ways."

Catherine nodded. Winnie had been conscious for a while, in pain, suffering, weeping over the atrocities her husband had made her endure: raping her, beating her, striving to break her spirit. She feared he'd succeeded with the last. "I can see after her."

Claybourne urged everyone closer. "Can she travel?"

Dr. Graves widened his eyes. "Not far, not far at all."

"She doesn't have to go far." Claybourne sighed. "Avendale has been having Catherine followed. He's also responsible for the attack on us that night."

"What?" Catherine asked. "How do you know all this?"

"Jim caught one of the ruffians he hired to follow you. We were discussing the matter with him when I received your missive. Avendale must be dealt with but not here, not in London, where he may have resources of which I'm not aware. My plan is this. We will lead people to believe that we are taking the duchess to my country estate. You should come with us, Catherine. Avendale will come to you first, searching for his wife."

"But my father—"

"He'll be watched. No harm will come to him."

She believed him, absolutely without question.

"We'll do a switch," he continued, "take the ladies to your residence, Bill, where you and Lady Catherine can look after the duchess. I shall travel on to Heatherwood. Avendale is sure to follow me there if we leave enough clues. At which time, I shall put the matter to rights."

"What about Whit?" Catherine asked.

Graves looked at her. "Who's Whit?"

"Avendale's heir," Claybourne responded before she could. "We'll bring the lad with us. I suggest we move quickly. Bill, can you help me prepare the duchess for travel?"

"Yes, certainly."

"Catherine, you get the lad," Claybourne said. "Remember, we want it to look as though we're all going to the country."

Catherine nodded, her mind racing.

"Good girl," he said, just before he quickly disappeared into Winnie's bedchamber with the doctor.

"I'll help you get the lad," Frannie said. "We want to talk loudly as we move through the house about our going to Heatherwood."

Catherine grabbed her arm. "Claybourne is going to face Avendale alone."

"It would seem so, yes."

"I can't let him go alone, Frannie. I brought him into this mess."

"He's not going to put others at risk. It's not his way. He won't let you go with him if that's what you're thinking."

"I'll not give him a choice. Will you look after Winnie for me?"

"Catherine—"

"I've come to care for him, Frannie. I'm no threat to you. I know you hold his heart, but I can't bear the thought of him facing Avendale alone. I know there will be little I can do except to stand by him, but stand by him I must. Can you understand?"

"Have you considered your reputation if you go through with this madness? If you travel with him alone?"

"Who will know that I have gone if we simply say that I am with you and Winnie? His servants shan't know who I am. They'll think I'm some trollop. My name need never be associated with him." Reaching out, she squeezed Frannie's hand. "Do you really want him to face this alone?"

Frannie shook her head. "No, I'd planned to go with him, actually. But you're right. You're the better choice. I'll take care of Winnie and you take care of Luke." She squeezed Catherine's hand so hard that Catherine nearly cried out. "Don't leave him alone, especially at night. For some reason, he doesn't do well at Heatherwood. Avendale won't be the only demon he'll face."

Catherine detected an urging in Frannie's voice, saw an understanding in her eyes, that was giving

Catherine permission for something beyond what they were discussing, but before she could ask for confirmation, she heard the door to the bedchamber opening.

"You get Whit," Frannie said. "I'm going to travel with Bill to his residence so all is ready when Luke feels it's safe."

Catherine nodded and headed down the hallway to the nursery. There was so much to get done, and for this plan to work, they needed to get everything in place before Avendale returned home.

Things moved at a rapid pace. Catherine found Winnie's lady's maid and instructed her to pack a small bag of clothing for the duchess, that she was going to Claybourne's country estate to recover. Then Catherine packed a smaller bag for Whit. While servants put the bags into Claybourne's waiting coach, she woke Whit and carried the small boy outside. Claybourne joined her there, carrying Winnie bundled in blankets.

Now he held Winnie on his lap, trying to provide an extra buffer between her and the rattling coach. Periodically, Winnie groaned and Whit sniffled.

They'd stopped at Catherine's residence, and she'd stuffed a simple dress, nightclothes, and undergarments into a satchel for herself. Then she'd gone to see her father. He'd been awake, or at least his eyes had been open.

"Winnie's been hurt. She's going to the country to recuperate, and I'm going with her. Please don't worry. I'll be fine. And I'll be back in a few days." She'd kissed him on the forehead. "Don't go while I'm gone."

She'd left instructions for his care with her servants—not that they truly needed any. They'd been taking care of him for longer than a year now.

Now Catherine slipped her finger beneath the coach curtain and peered out. She could see tenement houses. "How certain are you of your plan?"

"As certain as I can be," Claybourne said.

The coach came to an abrupt halt. The door opened. Dr. Graves was standing there. After Claybourne shifted Winnie into his arms, Graves turned away. Then Frannie was in the doorway, holding her hand out to Whit.

Claybourne turned to the boy. "Don't be afraid. They're going to take care of you and you're going to take care of your mother. Do you understand?"

The boy nodded.

"Good lad." Claybourne ushered him to the doorway where Frannie took him in her arms. She looked at Catherine, gave a barely discernible nod, and moved away.

And then the footman was there, holding out his hand to Catherine. She took a deep breath, released it. "I'm going with you."

"Don't be daft," Claybourne said.

She reached out, grabbed the door handle, and slammed the door closed—almost nipping the footman in the process. She settled back, hands folded primly. "I'm not going to allow you to face him alone."

"Dear God, Catherine, he's not going to be in a pleasant mood."

"I don't care."

"I'm likely to do things to him of which you will not approve."

"Do you honestly think, after seeing what he did to my friend, that there is anything you could do to him of which I wouldn't approve?"

"Your reputation—"

"The servants here all believe that Winnie is traveling with us. As for the servants at your estate, I assume they'll be discreet. As far as I can determine, Avendale is the only one who might cause us any problem, and I assume you'll deal with him."

"I should toss you over my shoulder—"

"And kiss my bare bottom? You don't frighten me, Lord Claybourne. You wouldn't harm a woman if your life depended on it. Unlike Avendale who would strike his wife simply because he didn't fancy the color of her gown. I'm not staying behind."

He cursed soundly, signaled his footman, and a few seconds later, the coach sprang forward.

"You're the most irritating woman I've ever had the misfortune to know," he ground out. Then he shifted, took her hands, and pressed his mouth to her bare knuckles. "And the most courageous."

"If I were so courageous, I'd have never involved you."

He moved until he was sitting beside her and had her nestled against his side. "It should have never fallen to you to see to the matter to begin with."

"She's my dearest friend in all the world."

"We will do what we can to salvage your reputation."

"I care only that Avendale is dealt with. What are your plans for him?"

"I need some answers from him. Depending on what they are, I may try to reason with him."

"And if he'll not provide the answers or be reasoned with?"

"Heatherwood is a rather large estate. A man can easily get lost and never be found."

Chapter 17

The coach came to a stop outside Claybourne's ancestral residence the following night, long after dark. The footman opened the door

"Stay here," Claybourne ordered.

"I'll not be bullied—"

He sighed with impatience. "Catherine, do you trust me?"

"Do you trust me?"

"With my life," he said.

Oh, dear Lord, she'd not expected him to place that burden on her. What was she doing here? How had she brought them to this moment?

"I think things between us would go much better if you'd simply explain the reason for your orders," she told him. "I don't mean to be difficult, but I don't want to be kept in the dark either."

"Very well. I'm going to send most of my servants to the village for two reasons. I want them out of harm's way and it'll increase the likelihood of preserving your reputation, so I need you to stay hidden until they're gone. A butler and a few footmen are all who will stay behind."

Nodding, she settled back. "I shall wait patiently like a good little girl."

He chuckled low. "I have a feeling you've never been good a day in your life."

Before she could castigate him for that erroneous assessment of her, he'd disappeared out the door. He'd not allowed her to be seen at any of the inns where they'd stopped to change horses and purchase food. He always bought an inordinate amount of food as though he had several people to feed. If Avendale stopped where they'd stopped, if he made inquiries, he'd think Winnie was in the coach. Winnie and Whit.

He would be furious when he discovered he'd been duped.

Catherine heard the whinny of horses and the rumble of carriage and wagon wheels. She supposed the servants would use whatever means possible to travel to the nearby village. She'd not meant to put everyone out. But Claybourne was right. They would be safer there.

The minutes dragged slowly by. Finally, she heard movement in the boot and assumed the footman was gathering Claybourne's satchel and hers. The door opened, and she released a tiny squeal.

"Are you all right?" Claybourne asked, and she thought she detected humor in his voice.

"Yes, quite."

He held out his hand. "Come on, then."

She put her hand in his, felt his strong fingers close around hers, and all her doubts and worries dissipated. This was Claybourne. He'd survived much worse than a cad like Avendale.

Together they would see that Winnie was safe forever.

She stepped out of the coach. Although she could only see the silhouette, she could tell that his residence was grand. She placed her hand on his arm and allowed him to escort her with the footman scurrying ahead with their bags.

"Under normal circumstances, the guests sleep in the east wing, the family in the west. But these circumstances are hardly normal. I've instructed the footman to put your belongings in the bedchamber next to mine. I want you near, Catherine, so I can assure your safety. I'll not take advantage."

The last was said quietly, almost with a measure of regret echoing through it. She couldn't deny that she felt a bit of disappointment.

"Well, it's not as though I haven't spent the night in your bed," she said.

He lost his footing, and suddenly she was reaching for him to help him keep his balance. When he was again standing tall, he said, "You play a very dangerous game, Lady Catherine Mabry."

Too late she'd come to realize that fact. But she'd not retreat now. She'd do whatever necessary to achieve her end.

"Don't you think I should have a false name while I'm here?"

"Did you have something in mind?"

They'd reached the steps and were climbing toward the door.

"What was your name when you were a lad? Before the Earl of Claybourne discovered you?" she asked.

"Locke. Luke Locke. I was very skilled at picking locks. Most of us were orphans, didn't know our real names anyway. But even for those who did, Feagan always insisted on changing their names. When they came to him, they started life anew. So what would you like your name to be?"

Now that it was upon her, she couldn't think of anything. "I have no skills. What would you suggest?"

"Heart. Because it is your generous heart that has brought us this adventure."

He opened the door.

"Is that how you see it?" she asked. "As an adventure?"

"For now."

She walked into the foyer. The wooden floor gleamed. Busts and statuettes decorated tables. Paintings hung on the walls. No butler stood at attention.

"I've told the remaining servants to remain scarce unless called for."

"Oh. You might have said so instead of playing along with my desire for a false name."

He smiled warmly. "You never know when you might need a false name."

"I think you're mocking me."

He grew serious. "I would never mock you, Catherine."

"Aren't you the least bit concerned about what awaits us with Avendale?"

"We have a while yet. No need to fret until it's time to fret. Let me show you to your room."

It was exactly as he'd told her—right next to his. She knew because the door separating their rooms was open and she could see the footman putting away Claybourne's things. She wondered if he had put hers away as well.

"I assume you left no women servants behind," Catherine said.

"No. The fairer sex is called the fairer sex for a reason." He held up a finger. "I know you're an exception. If you need assistance undressing"—he cleared his throat—"I'll do what I can."

"I should be fine. I was already abed when Winnie's maid came to fetch me." She held out her arms. "As you can see I dressed as simply as possible in order to dress as quickly as possible."

"If you'd like to bathe, I'll have the footman bring up warm water."

"I would like that," she said, "before bed. Right now, I must confess that I'm rather famished."

"I'm afraid I sent my cook to the village. Would an omelet suffice?"

She smiled. "Very nicely. Thank you."

Luke knew he should have protested more. He should have insisted Catherine stay behind, but what was done was done. He couldn't deny that he took some pride—undeservedly, of course—in showing her various rooms as he escorted her to the kitchen. The Claybourne legacy was grand.

Nor could he deny the pleasure it brought him to prepare her an omelet or how much he enjoyed having her watch him from her place at the large table where servants usually enjoyed a quick meal or a bit of gossip. He planned to confront Avendale alone. He just had to convince Catherine to leave. But he was in no hurry to do so.

"When do you think Avendale will arrive?" she asked.

He heard the worry in her voice. He didn't think she was frightened. Apprehensive perhaps. He poured a glass of red wine and handed it to her. "Drink that. It'll help you relax."

She did as he bade without arguing. Oh, yes, she wasn't nearly as calm as she appeared.

"He won't be here for a while," Luke assured her, remembering another time when he'd prepared her an omelet. "I sent word to Jack. He's going to ply him with liquor. That should set him back a day, and I suspect it'll take Avendale another day or so to work up the courage to come here."

He placed the omelet on a plate and set it on the table.

"You still haven't mastered preparing two at a time?" she asked with a raised eyebrow.

"I'm afraid not."

She took a bite of the omelet and studied him. "You're not at all worried, are you?"

"About facing Avendale? No. I would be more comfortable if you weren't here."

"You won't convince me to leave and I'll not drink enough wine to lose my wits."

"Have you *ever* drunk *that* much?"

Nodding, she gave him an impish smile. "The night before Winnie married Avendale, actually. I stayed with her and we took several bottles from her father's wine cellar. The next day I was so miserable. I thought I might be ill at the church."

He gave her a sardonic smile. "I've had many

occasions where I have been ill." He sliced off a section of omelet. "Did she love him?"

"I think he fascinated her. He can be quite charming. Quite honestly, he'd given me reason to believe that he had interest in me, before he shifted his attention to Winnie."

Luke's stomach tightened and his appetite fled. When he thought of Catherine with the likes of Avendale—

"Then that night after you came to the ball he stopped calling." She released a little cry of surprise, her eyes wide. "Oh my goodness, you don't suppose he changed his mind because I didn't cower when you looked at me?"

"I suppose it's possible."

"More than possible I'd say. He wouldn't want someone who'd stand up to him. It seems I owe you more than I realize."

"You don't owe me anything, Catherine."

"That wasn't our arrangement."

"As you said at the ball, we've become friends of a sort. So as a friend, I shall rid you of the problem of Avendale."

An hour later, as Catherine brushed her hair following her bath, she admitted to herself that she'd enjoyed their late-night repast in the kitchen, relaxing as the minutes progressed, not so much because of the wine—she'd drunk more than she'd intended—but because of Claybourne's ability to distract her from what they would soon face. They'd spoken of inconsequential things: the rain that had started to fall while they ate, the finely crafted furniture that he'd been told had been in the family for three generations, the portraits painted by the most famous of artists. He promised to show her the grounds the next day.

"There'll be time," he said.

She was grateful that she'd come, that she had this little bit of time with him—alone. Just the two of them.

She kept thinking about Frannie's comment that Catherine was the better choice to accompany him and her urging Catherine to take care of him. She didn't doubt that Claybourne loved Frannie, but she did question whether or not Frannie loved him as deeply as he deserved—as deeply as Catherine did.

Setting the brush down, she realized that she'd never have an opportunity like this again. Once they confronted Avendale or he confronted them, once the matter was resolved, they'd return to London. Their bargain would be at an end, and Claybourne would become nothing more than a name handwritten on an invitation to her balls.

After circling the dance floor in Claybourne's arms, Catherine knew her reputation was undoubtedly ruined—even if no one ever discovered that she'd traveled alone with him.

He'd told her that first night that the price she'd pay for waltzing with the devil was residing in hell. Well, she'd waltzed with him and if hell was coming, she wanted a good deal more than a waltz.

He was sleeping in the room next to hers. So close. So very close.

Yet she knew, with absolutely no doubt, that he'd not come to her. That he'd not take advantage of her nearness. He was a scoundrel and a gentleman.

He was the man she'd quite simply fallen madly in love with. And if she could have only one night with him, she would make it enough to last her lifetime.

Luke stood at the window in his bedchamber, staring out at the night. He'd bathed earlier and now wore nothing except a silk robe. He'd hoped the warm bath would bring slumber, but he never slept well here. To make matters worse, he couldn't stop thinking about Catherine being in the next room. What had possessed him to give in to her demands and allow her to accompany him?

He didn't think she'd be in danger. He felt quite confident that he could handle Avendale. But it had been reckless to bring her. Even more so when he considered the truth of it: he wanted her near.

She'd brought him into this situation and should face it with him.

Oh, if only his reasons were that selfless. But no, they were completely selfish. Once he saw to Avendale, Luke's portion of their arrangement would be completed and Catherine would become little more than someone he saw occasionally at a ball—if he and Frannie attended balls. He'd not force her if she remained reluctant. So perhaps Catherine would no longer be in his life at all.

He was taken aback by the despair that particular thought brought.

He couldn't deny that he cared for her. He enjoyed her company. He admired her courage, her loyalty to her friend. He admired the manner in which she carried burdens with no complaint. He admired the slope of her throat, the plumpness of her lips—

Groaning, he dug his fingers into the edge of the window. He'd hurl himself through it before he dishonored Frannie by taking another woman to his bed now that he'd asked her to marry him. But Frannie was not yet his wife. She was not even his betrothed. She was simply the woman he adored, the one he'd always envisioned spending his life with. He pressed his forehead to the outer corner of the window. Was adoration love?

He'd known her more years than he'd known Catherine, yet at that precise moment he couldn't remember the shape of Frannie's lips. The hue. Were they a dark red or pink? Catherine's were the red of an apple, freshly fallen from a tree.

It made no sense that Catherine occupied so much of his mind when Frannie was the one he wanted as his wife.

But God help him, Catherine was the one he desired.

And not only physically. She was the one he looked forward to talking to each evening. She was the one whose smile made his heart beat a little faster. She was the one he wanted to explore—not only every curve of her body but every facet of her mind. She fascinated, tempted, and beguiled him as he'd never before been fascinated, tempted, or beguiled. He told himself it was because she was new while Frannie was familiar—yet Catherine didn't feel new. She never had. From the first moment he'd spotted her at that ball all those years ago, when he'd gazed into her eyes, he'd thought that if he still possessed all his soul it would have found its mate in hers. But his soul was but a remnant, and in very short order it would be gone completely.

He wasn't even certain that he could ask Frannie to marry him then. Like Catherine, she deserved a better man than one who could so easily give the devil his due.

The door clicked open, and before he turned he knew who'd come into his room. He should have ordered her out. He should have leapt through the window.

Instead he stayed as he was and began praying that he would have the strength to resist what he feared she was about to offer.

On silent bare feet, Catherine crossed the room to where Claybourne stood before the window. "I couldn't sleep. I thought perhaps you couldn't either. Are you watching for Avendale?"

"No, simply watching the rain. I've never slept well here, never been comfortable. I tend to suffer numerous head pains."

"Are you suffering now?"

"Not yet."

"But you will."

"Most likely."

She gazed out the window as well, finding it much easier to speak looking outside rather than directly at him. "I suspect I'll never marry," she said quietly.

"Indeed?"

"I know I'm strong willed, outspoken, and that

men prefer a biddable woman when it comes to a wife. I'm not very skilled at being biddable."

"Indeed?"

She heard humor laced through his voice.

"If you're not going to converse don't be patronizing."

"My apologies. There is little I can expound on when the truth is spoken."

He was going to make this difficult or perhaps he was simply too dense to follow where she was leading with this. She twisted her head to look at him and discovered he was watching her, his eyes smoldering as they had that night at the first ball he'd ever attended. He wanted her. She knew it as surely as she knew that she wanted him.

He had the appearance of a gentleman but he was a scoundrel at heart, and she was depending on that aspect of his character now, hoping beyond hope that it'd not let her down.

"I don't wish to die without knowing what it is to lie with a man—"

"You're not going to die," he ground out, his voice fairly seething, and she realized that he thought she was referring to her imminent demise when they faced Avendale.

Although she realized it was a very real possibility and made her decision to come to his room seem all the more right. "I'm not expecting an early death," she assured him. "I know you'll see to Avendale. I'm talking years from now, and I'm talking tonight. I want my first time to be with a man of passion. I know you love Frannie, but you are not, as yet, officially betrothed, so I thought perhaps you would . . ." She lowered her gaze. "I care for you. I don't want to be alone tonight."

He placed his knuckles beneath her chin and tilted her head back until he could hold her gaze. "I can't have you in my bed without having you, Catherine. I'm not a saint."

"I don't want a saint. I've always been of the opinion that if a woman were going to stray from the righteous path and seek out wickedness, she would be far more satisfied lying in bed with the devil."

His fingers unfurled and he cradled her face. "Be certain, Catherine, because once this is done, it can't be undone."

Very slowly, very deliberately, she unbuttoned her dressing gown and slid it off her shoulders, very much aware of it slithering along her bare body and pooling on the floor, very much aware of his breathing turning ragged, his eyes darkening with desire.

Reaching out, he cradled her face between his large hands. She knew the strength they held, knew the comfort they could deliver. His thumbs circled her cheeks, stroked the corners of her mouth, while his gaze never left hers, as though he were measuring her readiness, as though her standing there bare-assed was not proof enough.

"I don't know if I've ever known a woman as beautiful as you, Lady Catherine Mabry. You humble me by coming to me tonight."

"Do you have to talk so much?"

He grinned at her, a warm grin, filled with understanding. "I don't have to speak at all."

Then he lowered his mouth to hers, and any

semblance of civility between them was washed away as his tongue plundered. There was a rumble deep in his chest, a growl that required from her an answering moan. He moved his hands to the back of her head, scraped his fingers along her scalp, threaded them through her unbound hair, angling her head so he could kiss her more deeply, as though he would devour her, as though he could never have enough her.

Lord knew she'd never have enough of him. She closed the small gap that separated his body from hers, her hands seeking and finding the knotted sash of his robe, her fingers frantically working it loose until the sash fell away and the robe parted. Without thought, without shame, she pressed her bare breasts against his bared chest. The warmth of him, the velvetiness of his skin felt so marvelous. Her nipples hardened into tight little buds that pulled at the core of her womanhood. She wrapped her arms around him, holding him close, running her hands up and down his broad back.

All the while, his mouth clung to hers.

His muscles rippled beneath her fingers as he shrugged out of the robe. Now nothing separated them. She was aware of his heat burning against her belly. Hard. Hot. Growing damp.

He tore his mouth from hers. "I shall spill my seed all over you before I ever get you to bed."

"Is that a good thing?"

"It will be," he rasped. "I have no doubt it will be."

He lifted her into his arms and began carrying her to the bed. She ran her hands over his shoulders, his chest. She wanted to know how he came to have every scar that she pressed her lips to, ran her tongue over. He had only the lightest smattering of hair in the center of his chest, and she wove her fingers through it. She kissed his neck, damp with sweat, nibbled on his earlobe, heard him growl, and bit lightly. His growl deepened.

He laid her on the bed. The covers had already been turned down. The sheet was cool against her back. She was hot, so very hot. The rain continued to patter against the pane, so they couldn't open the window. There was no hope for it. Tonight she'd burn in hell, and she'd never wanted anything more.

She scooted over so he could join her, but instead he sat on the foot of the bed where he ran his hands over her ankles, her calves. He kissed her toes, her knees, the inside of her thighs, her stomach, stretching his body over her before rising up above her and gazing down on her. She thought she should feel shame at the way he looked at her so blatantly, but all she felt was joy because she could see that he found her pleasing.

"You're so beautiful," he rasped. "More so than I imagined."

"You've thought about me?"

He gave her a deliciously wicked and sensuous smile. "Oh, yes, Catherine. That night at the first ball, I imagined you just like this, spread out over my bed in all your naked glory. And you have haunted me ever since."

He lowered his mouth to hers, his tongue meeting no resistance, because she wanted to taste him as much as he wanted to taste her. Whiskey was ripe upon his tongue, a flavor that intoxicated her, reminded her of the night when she'd almost lost him. Desperation fueled her passion, desperation to know him in every way that a woman could know a man.

Luke didn't know if he'd ever lain with a woman as enthusiastic as Catherine. She touched him everywhere as though she couldn't get enough of him. Not only with her hands, but with her mouth, her lips, her tongue. She kissed each of his scars with tenderness, then ran her tongue over his chest as though she were a cat and he were the milk to be lapped from the bowl. She was by turns, bold and shy, looking to him for approval, her lovely blue eyes darkening with desire when he granted it.

She was everything a man could wish for in a lover.

Claybourne was everything a woman could wish for in a lover, Catherine thought as he skimmed his hands along her body. By turns, he was considerate and gentle, rough and demanding.

She'd grumbled at him for talking so much, and he'd told her that he didn't have to speak at all, but he did. Near her ear, he urged her boldness on with a raspy voice that more often than not sounded as though he were strangling.

Touch him there and there and *there.*

Hold him tightly. Stroke him slowly.

And when her fingers faltered, he laid his hand over hers, guiding her motions, his gaze holding hers, daring her not to look away, daring her to see the smoldering passion and to know what she was capable of doing to him. She was capable of driving him to madness. He was not a quiet lover and each sound he made was music to her ears, enticed her into giving him more so that she might receive more.

A fine sheen of sweat coated his throat. Sweat belonged to laborers, not gentlemen, but she kissed his throat anyway, felt his pulse jump beneath her lips. Felt her own pulse leap when he buried his fingers in her hair and blanketed her mouth with his own.

She didn't know what she'd expected. Something quick, painful, but still somehow exquisite. But this was more than she'd ever imagined. Beautiful in its intensity, frightening because she didn't know how she'd live without it when it went away.

He touched her everywhere, intimately, with his fingers, his mouth as though he cherished every inch of her, as though she could possibly mean as much to him as he did to her.

He moved back down to her feet, and this time when he kissed his way up her body, he managed to wedge himself firmly between her thighs.

"I wish I could do this without hurting you," he rasped.

She eased her back off the bed and pressed a kiss to the center of his chest, before falling back to the pillow. "You'll only hurt me if we don't finish what we've begun."

She felt him pushing, seeking entry, felt her body welcoming him, watched the concentration on his face, almost blurted out that she loved him—

And then the pain came, sharp and quick, and he groaned so loudly that she thought it had hurt him as well, but when he opened his eyes, there was naught there but supreme satisfaction.

"You're so tight," he gasped, "so hot. Marvelous."

He kissed her then, his tongue darting and swirling as his hips thrust and circled. She couldn't deny that she felt discomfort, but it gave way to sensations that rippled through her in undulating waves of pleasure.

Their bodies slick, grew slicker. Their flesh hot grew hotter.

He grabbed her hands, intertwined their fingers, held them in place on either side of her head as he pumped his body into hers, his deep feral groans echoing around them.

"Oh, Lord!" She'd never known sensations such as this, thought she might fall apart as he ground his hips against hers.

Then the cataclysm came, wondrous in its intensity, as she tightened around him, mewling sounds echoing around her. She was vaguely aware of his body shuddering, hers pulsing around him. They were both breathing harshly when he kissed the curve of her shoulder and rolled off her. She barely had time to feel bereft at his leaving, before he slid his arm around her and drew her up against his side, guiding her head to the crook of his shoulder, the perfect place to listen to the wild thudding of his heart. And listen to it she did, felt it as well, with her hand touching his chest.

"Are you all right?" he asked.

"Perfect." *Breathless, languid, tingling all over, but perfect.*

He laughed, a deep rich sound of pure satisfaction. "Good."

His breathing began to even out. She tilted her face up slightly, saw his closed eyes, and realized he'd gone to sleep. If she didn't feel so lethargic herself, she might have been disappointed that their night together was already over.

Instead, she pressed a kiss to his chest and joined him in slumber.

Luke awoke with a start. Usually he didn't sleep when he came to the estate because the dreams were so disturbing. He was always being chased, trying to hide—

But it wasn't a dream that woke him this time.

He looked down on the woman sprawled halfway over his body, her small hand curled in the center of his chest. If he'd not encountered her maidenhead, he'd have thought she was as experienced as any courtesan. But then he wasn't surprised that she hadn't been timid. Not his Catherine.

His Catherine. She wasn't his. At least not beyond their time at Heatherwood.

True to the brand that marked him as a thief, he was stealing moments with her, moments that didn't rightfully belong to him. He should have resisted her, but he had no regrets. He'd have always wondered. And now he knew. In all things, she was incredible.

Her eyes fluttered open and she smiled at him. "I was right. A devil is better than a saint."

He rolled until she was on her back, and he was on his side. "How do you know? You've never had a saint."

"But I can't imagine that he could bring me as

much pleasure." She took his hand and pressed a kiss to the scar that marred the inside of his thumb. "I hate that they did this to you."

He took her hand, unfolded it, and looked at the angry red scar. He ran his tongue over it, thought of all she'd risked in order to save him. "I hate that they did this to you."

"I'm not. You might not lick my palm otherwise."

"I shall lick your palm and a good deal more again before the night is done."

"I think you talk a good deal more in bed than out."

"Not usually." He grimaced. It was bad form to refer to being with other ladies, but the truth was that tonight had been very different from any previous encounter with a lady that he'd experienced. Catherine was remarkable. He wasn't certain that he could ever have enough of her.

He cradled her breast, flicked his thumb over her nipple, took delight in watching it pearl. "It shouldn't hurt so much the next time."

"Will there be a next time—with you, I mean."

His stomach knotted with the thought of her having a next time with someone other than him, but he thought he successfully managed to keep his thoughts from showing. Instead, he grinned at her and said, "If I have my way."

"Tell me what I can do to make it better for you."

"If you make it any better for me, Catherine, I'm likely to die from the attention."

She smiled, and he saw how his words pleased her.

"But it would be a lovely way to go wouldn't it?" she asked.

"I'd rather stay around if you don't mind."

"I don't. Not at all. But I want to know that I please you."

"You do. Very much. You never struck me as a woman who needs reassurances."

"Whether or not a woman needs them, she likes to have them." She skimmed her fingers over his chest. "I like touching you."

"I like you touching me."

She furrowed her brow. "I wish you hadn't had such a harsh life."

"There are those who had it much harsher. Some still do."

"That's the reason you're working toward prison reform."

He shrugged. "I will once my peers accept me, but that's not pleasant bedchamber conversation."

"Well, then, what is?"

"This." He lowered his head and kissed her, relishing the eagerness with which she returned his attentions.

She knew the very worst about him, and yet still she came to him. Knew the very worst about him, yet still she welcomed him. No hesitation, no turning him aside because she feared his world or worried that she wasn't good enough.

He didn't want anyone else in this bed with them. Catherine deserved to be the only one on his mind, the only one he thought about, the only one he wanted to please.

She *was* the only one he wanted to please.

At that moment, no one else mattered. Nothing else mattered. Not the possible danger that might be rushing toward them. Not the innocents who needed to be protected. Nothing mattered except Catherine, now, in his bed.

The musky scent of heated sex mingled with her sweet rose fragrance. He inhaled deeply, filling his nostrils, savoring the unique perfume they created together. Kissing her deeply, he slid his hand along the concave of her stomach, tangled his fingers in the springy curls nested between her thighs. She was wet and hot, ready for what he had to offer her.

He ran his hand up to her hip, trailed his mouth along her throat.

"Oh, God, please don't stop," she gasped.

He nestled his face in the curve of her shoulder, pressed a kiss just below her ear, and rasped, "Have you fantasized about this?"

"More than you'll ever know."

"How did you know what to fantasize?"

She rolled her head from side to side as though lost in ecstasy. "Instinct I suppose. Must we talk?"

Chuckling low, he embraced her and rolled to his back, bringing her with him, listening to her tiny squeal as she landed atop him, straddling his hips, looking down on him, while her glorious, abundant hair formed a curtain around them. He threaded his fingers through the golden strands, brought her mouth down to his, and kissed her eagerly, hungrily.

He loved the way she held nothing back, didn't pretend timidity. She wasn't embarrassed by her nakedness. Somehow he wasn't surprised by that. His dear, bold Catherine was in this bed with him now, just as she'd been in Dodger's back room beating him at cards, just as she'd been in that alley fighting to save him, just as she'd come to his library in the middle of the night to make him a daring proposition in order to protect a friend.

He'd never known anyone like her, never known anyone who mesmerized him as she did. Had never known anyone he wanted more.

Tearing her mouth from his, breathing heavily, she stared down at him. "Can we make it work this way?"

He grinned. "We can make it work any way we want."

She ran her hands over his chest. He cradled her breasts, adoring the weight of them in his palms. There was no aspect to her that he didn't adore.

Raising her hips, she wrapped her fingers around him. He groaned low in anticipation.

"Does it hurt?" she asked.

"God, no."

She slid down, enveloping him in her silky wetness. He almost spilled his seed then and there. Instead he clenched his jaw, fought for control. He ran his hands up her slender back, slid them back around to her breasts, and began to knead her soft flesh.

Dropping her head back, she moaned. Then she began to ride him as though her life depended on it.

He thought he would die from holding back—but he'd not give in to his own release until he'd given her hers. But she felt so wonderfully good, her passion igniting the blood rushing through his veins.

She rocked against him, her cries escalating. He pumped his hips as she drove herself down. Her fingers were digging into his shoulders, his fingers were holding her hips, each of them holding on for dear life. He'd never experienced anything this intense.

He had to hold back, for her, for her—

But his body wouldn't be held back. He bucked beneath her, his deep feral groan nearly drowning out her cry of satisfaction, her back arched, her face carved in an expression of awe and wonder. Shudders wracked his body as the pleasure coursed through her.

She went limp, falling to his chest, spent. He wasn't sure where he found the strength to wrap his arms around her, but he wanted to hold her close too much not to find the energy. He thought he could lie there forever. If he died this moment, he'd die content.

Never in his life had he ever known such peace, such joy. He'd thought once more with her would be enough. But as he held her, and listened to her breathing, he feared he might never have enough of her.

Chapter 18

They walked from the house in the early hours of the morning, with him carrying a picnic basket, while she carted a blanket. She wore a servant's dress that he'd located for her in the servant's quarters, because she'd brought so little of her own clothing. It wasn't confining and in a way, she preferred it to her usual attire. She was surprised that she could feel so relaxed knowing what awaited them.

That morning, after another rousing session of lovemaking, Claybourne had tried to convince Catherine to go to the village and wait for him there, but she'd brought them to this moment. She wasn't about to retreat now. He thought it would be another day or so—possibly longer—before Avendale made an appearance. Catherine wasn't certain that he'd show at all.

But she was delighted with the prospect of having a picnic with Claybourne.

They walked for some time before they reached a pond. While Claybourne spread out the blanket, she asked, "Are there fish in there?"

He stilled, looked at her, looked at the water. "I think so."

"Have you never fished in it?"

He closed his eyes, shook his head. "I don't think so. No."

"Is your head bothering you?"

He opened his eyes and smiled. "Only a bit. It'll go away."

"I wonder what makes it hurt."

"People have headaches all the time. It's nothing in particular."

"I don't."

"Then you're very fortunate."

He took her hand and helped her to sit on the blanket. She glanced around. "Are you certain we shouldn't be more alert?"

"We'll become more vigilant this evening, and I have men watching the roads. For just a bit longer, let's pretend that all is right with the world."

He poured them each some wine and removed a block of cheese from the basket.

She took a sip of wine. "Do you want to hear something silly?"

Leaning over, he gave her a quick kiss. "I'd never consider you silly."

"It could just be wishful thinking, but I don't think Frannie would find fault with all that's happened between us."

His jaw tightened. "I don't intend to tell her."

"No, I wasn't expecting you to. It's just something she said."

He narrowed his eyes. "What?"

"When I told her that I didn't want you to be alone, she encouraged me to come with you.

She even said that I shouldn't leave you alone at night. I think she was giving me permission to be wicked." Voiced aloud, it sounded even sillier than it had bouncing around in her head. "That sounds so ludicrous, doesn't it? If you were mine, I certainly wouldn't give another woman—" She stopped, glanced around. "The hole I'm digging is getting rather large, isn't it?"

"Do you feel guilty about last night?" he asked.

"Strangely, no. Do you?"

"I know I should, but I don't. I suspect because Frannie doesn't really consider me hers, yet. I'm beginning to realize that I'm simply one of Feagan's lads, and that you had the right of it. I need to spend more time with her. Our feelings, I fear, are based on our childhood, not our adulthood."

Oh, yes, the hole she'd dug was monstrously large now, large enough to bury her. She wished she'd kept her thoughts to herself.

"If I ask about your childhood will you tell me that it isn't proper picnic conversation?"

He grinned. She did so love it when he looked as though he hadn't a care in the world. She imagined that he had so few moments like that and she relished each one he shared with her. He stretched out on his side, raised up on his elbow, and studied her for a moment, before asking, "What do you want to know?"

She was almost giddy and . . . *Drat it!* She couldn't think of a single question, or at least a single question that she didn't think would ruin his good humor. But she wanted to know so much.

"You killed Geoffrey Langdon."

He swirled the wine in the glass, took a sip, nodded.

"How?"

"I stabbed him."

"How did they know it was you?"

"There was a witness."

"Are you going to make me ask all the questions? Why can't you just tell me the story?"

He finished off his glass of wine and poured himself another one. "It's not pretty, Catherine."

Reaching out, she skimmed her finger over his scar. "There is nothing you can tell me that will make me think less of you."

"But it is not only my tale."

"Please. I know you killed him for Frannie, so I know something awful happened to her. I can imagine what it was."

"But I doubt you can imagine how brutal it was." He took another sip of the wine as though he needed it to shore up his courage. "Some men prefer virgins. Less chance of catching the pox that way. Young girls are usually virginal. Sometimes a young girl on the streets is taken, against her will, to a brothel, where she is tied to a bed so that it's easier to take her virginity."

Catherine was horrified. "And that's what happened to Frannie?"

He shook his head. "Geoffrey Langdon untied her because he favored girls who fought, and Frannie, bless her, fought. We knew where she was, Jack, Jim, and I, but we got there too late. She was hurt and bleeding. I carried her all the way back to Feagan's. She never wept. It always seemed to me that she should have wept. But she didn't."

She wished she hadn't asked for the details, and yet knowing them helped her to understand him so much better, and not only him but his relationship with the others. The strong bond they shared. "How did you learn who the man was?"

"When Frannie was stronger, Jack and I took her back to the brothel. We hid on the street and watched who came and went. Jack knew what I was going to do, but Frannie thought we were just going to beat him up. When she pointed him out, I did what I'd planned to do. Walked across the street and put a knife into him before he could open the door. Unfortunately, he'd knocked on it and the madam opened it. She saw me. Screamed. And as fate would have it, a damned bobby was right around the corner.

"I didn't even try to run. Jim found out later that Langdon visited the brothel every Wednesday night for a virgin. But his sins weren't as grave as mine. He was the heir apparent, so my offense was much worse."

"He deserved what you did to him."

He gave her a self-mocking grin. "I always thought so. Now you know my sordid past. When the old gent came to Scotland Yard to confront the boy who had murdered his son, he decided I was his grandson."

"Why?"

"My eyes. Silver eyes run in the family."

"I've met Marcus Langdon. His are silver."

"Yes."

"But surely there was more than that."

"The old gent asked questions. 'Do you remember a tall man with dark hair?' 'Oh, yes, sir, yes indeed.' 'Your father?' 'Oh, yes, sir. He held my hand.'" He shook his head. "He made it so easy."

"You didn't have any of those memories."

"Of course not." He began rubbing his brow.

"Is it your head?"

"Yes, I think it's the flowers here. Their scent is so strong."

"Come and put your head on my lap."

He didn't hesitate to move closer, to rest his head on her thigh. She began to massage his temples. He moaned low. "Almost makes the head pains worth it to have your tender ministrations."

"I worry about these headaches you're getting."

"I've had them for years, Catherine. They come. They go. They're of no importance. If they were, surely I'd be dead by now."

She smiled down on his rugged face, took a moment to trail her fingers over his nose. "What happened to your nose?"

"I got into a fight. In gaol, they don't segregate children from adults while we're awaiting trial, so we were at the mercy of big bullies and the worst society has to offer. Some individuals in gaol deserve to be, but that's not pleasant picnic conversation. Tell me about your brother."

"Sterling?"

"Have you another?"

Bending down, she kissed the tip of his nose, before returning to rubbing his temples. "I told you. He and Father had a row, but I don't know what it was about."

"How is your father?"

"Not well. He grows paler and thinner every day. He can't speak, can't tell me what he wants. I thought to take him out to the garden for a spell, but his physician doesn't agree."

"I should think if given the choice between spending his final days in bed or in a garden, an Englishman would always choose his garden."

"You think I should disregard the physician's advice?"

"I think you should do what you know in your heart is right."

She brushed her lips over his. "Thank you for that."

He rose up, twisted about, and latched his mouth onto hers, kissing her hungrily, laying her down in the process. He tasted of wine. She thought she'd never again sip on red wine without thinking of him.

She ran her hands up into his thick, curly locks. She thought of him as a child, how unruly his hair must have been as he'd raced over the bleak and rugged moors. She thought she could hear the sea in the distance and assumed if they walked farther, they'd eventually meet up with the cliffs.

She drew back from his lips. "Are there any portraits of you as a child?"

"No."

Sometimes it was difficult to get information from him, not because he was being obstinate—although he was certainly that—but because when she looked at him she saw the Earl of Claybourne. When he looked in a mirror, he saw an imposter.

"Are there any portraits of the earl's grandson—before you came into his life?"

He gave her an indulgent smile. "You're trying to find something in me that simply doesn't exist."

"So there is one."

"In the room that the old gent referred to as the Countess's Sitting Room."

"Will you show me?"

"Catherine—"

"Please. I'm not trying to prove you're Claybourne. Honestly. But the old gent must have seen something in you, so it's the closest I'll come to seeing you as a lad."

"Why would you—"

She pressed her finger to his lips. "Do I really ask for so much?"

He arched a brow, causing her to smile while rolling her eyes. "All right. I suppose I do."

He pressed a kiss to her forehead, her nose, her chin. "But you don't ask for anything I'm not willing to give."

She liked this aspect of him, when he wasn't quite so dark and brooding, when he teased her, when he made her so terribly glad to be with him.

He rolled off her and helped her to her feet. They began packing away their picnic.

The wind picked up, rustling the leaves in the trees. She glanced toward the distant road, and a sense of foreboding sent a shiver through her. She didn't know if it was the prospect of looking at the true Earl of Claybourne as a child or something more sinister that disturbed her.

* * *

Luke had visited this room only once and it had given him a blinding headache then.

The old gent had brought him here, to show him the portrait and to explain how his wife had died in this room, died with grief over the loss of her firstborn son and grandson. The room had carried a heavy flowery scent back then—no doubt the lingering presence of the countess—and Luke had attributed that to causing his headache.

But the room now smelled of furniture oil, and yet still his head began to pound as he watched Catherine trace her fingers over the faces in the portrait without actually touching the canvas. She took a step back. "They look to be very happy."

"The old gent thought they were."

She turned to face him. "Have you ever considered growing a mustache?"

"Like the man in the portrait? No." Nothing he did would make him look like the man in the portrait.

"I can see similarities—"

"Catherine."

"I know you don't think you're Claybourne, but there are similarities. The hair, the eyes . . . even the chin I think."

He shook his head.

"How old were you—was he—when this portrait was done?"

"Six. It was completed just before they were killed."

"Why would someone kill them?" she demanded to know.

Luke had no answer for that. "Robbery most likely."

"But the boy, what happened to him?"

Luke shook his head. "Sold. Put on a ship. Perhaps he died elsewhere. There's no way of knowing."

"It just seems so very odd. And it also seems that quite possibly you could be—"

"Catherine, as you say, they were happy. Why would I not remember that? Why would I have no memory of him or *her*? You were young when your mother died. Have you no memory of her?"

Sighing, she looked down at the floor. "I remember her. Vaguely." She lifted her gaze back to his. "I see your point, I suppose."

"Good." He plowed his hands through his hair, pressing on his scalp, trying to relieve the pain that had begun without giving away that it was there. "I need to see to some matters."

"Am I free to roam the house?"

"You're free to do anything you want, although I advise you against leaving. Avendale could show up at anytime."

"I won't leave these walls."

He took a step nearer and stroked his thumb over her lips. He wanted to carry her to his bedchamber, he wanted to spend every moment that remained to them here making love to her. But the truth was that he was no longer certain how to define their relationship.

She'd asked for a night in his arms. Had it been enough for her? It certainly hadn't been for him, but it was wrong of him to pursue more when he couldn't give her forever. It was wrong when Frannie—

He dropped a quick kiss on her lips. "I'll see you at dinner."

Then he strode from the room, praying that Avendale would make his appearance soon, before Luke went mad with wanting Catherine again.

The rain began near dusk, the wind whipping off the moors, the thunder rumbling.

In the library, Luke stood at the window, his hip against the windowsill, gazing out on the darkness, the land occasionally illuminated by the flashes of lightning.

Catherine sat in a nearby chair, a book in her lap. She'd read the same passage three times now and still hadn't a clear understanding of what Jane Austen was trying to say. It wasn't a complicated point. She simply couldn't concentrate.

"I've been pondering something you told me once," Claybourne said quietly.

Catherine welcomed the opportunity for conversation and closed the book. "And what was that?"

Claybourne was studying something beyond the window. "You said that the first Earl of Claybourne had earned the right to pass the estates and title on to his heirs."

"I have a vague recollection—"

He turned from the window. "When we return to London, I'm going to appear before the House of Lords and denounce my claim to Claybourne."

Slowly coming to her feet, Catherine felt as though all the air had been forced from her lungs. "Why would you do that?"

"Because I'm weary of living a lie. Because a time existed when I didn't fully appreciate what I'd been handed—I saw only my life not the legacy behind the title. All of this truly belongs to Marcus Langdon, and I shall see that he comes to have it."

She saw so many problems and difficulties with his plan that she hardly knew where to begin. "They'll hang you."

"I doubt it. The witness to my crime died several years ago. What evidence do they have? Besides, I can well afford to pay the sharpest legal mind in all of England to defend me if it comes to that."

"But Marcus Langdon—he isn't you."

He chuckled low. "Yes, that's quite the point."

She took a step nearer. "No, I mean, I truly can't see him as the Earl of Claybourne. You seem so well suited to the role."

"That, too, is the point, Catherine. It's been a *role* that I've played. I've been playacting all these years."

But she knew his reasons encompassed more than he'd revealed. His being the Earl of Claybourne was preventing him from obtaining the one thing he truly wanted: Frannie.

She took a step nearer, felt the tears sting her eyes. Reaching out she touched his cheek. "You are a remarkable man, Lucian Langdon. Frannie is incredibly lucky to have your affections."

"I'm not doing this for Frannie. I'm doing it because of you. When I see my reflection in your eyes, I don't want to see it tainted by deception and as long as I'm the Earl of Claybourne, I'm not a man worthy of any woman."

"I know of no man more worthy." Stretching up on her toes, she kissed him, unable to believe how deeply she loved him. She wanted to do more than kiss him. She wanted to show him that he'd managed to claim not only her body, but her heart and soul.

She wondered how much time remained to them before the devil would appear. She drew back from the kiss. "When do you think he'll come?"

She saw regret in his eyes, knew he understood what she was asking, what she wanted. "It could be any time now."

"How long will we wait before we decide he's not coming?"

"He'll come."

"How can you be so certain?"

He gave her an indulgent smile, which might have pricked her temper before she knew him well enough to know that he wasn't mocking her curiosity, but rather he was amused by her interest, perhaps even a bit impressed that she'd care. "I've played cards with him for a number of years. I know how the man thinks."

"You misjudged me when we played cards."

His smile disappeared. "He can't be that good at hiding the sort of man he is."

"Did you know he beat his wife?"

He shook his head. "No, but he hates to lose. He especially hates to lose to me. He shall come here to reclaim his wife. I have no doubt."

"What will you do when he arrives?"

"I'm not going to kill him if that's what's you're wondering." He took her hand, kissed it, then began stroking his thumb over the scar on her palm. "It's not an easy thing to live with the death of a man on your conscience, even when you know he deserved it. You see his face when you close your eyes to sleep—and there are times you won't sleep because you don't want to see his face."

"Then how shall you ensure that he'll leave Winnie in peace?"

"By making certain he understands that she is under my protection, and if he ever touches her again, I *will* kill him. Without remorse. Without regret. Without mercy."

A shiver raced up her spine, caused her scalp to prickle. She nodded.

"He's a bully," he said quietly. "It usually takes only standing up to him to make him back down."

With her free hand, she skimmed his hair off his brow. "But what if he threatens you?"

He pressed a kiss to her palm. "I have my guardian angel."

The library door opened, and the butler walked in. "My lord, the Duke of Avendale has come to call."

"You see," Claybourne said, grinning at Catherine. "Civilized." He looked at his servant. "I'll see him. And under no circumstances are we to be disturbed. I don't care what you hear or think you hear happening inside this room. As a matter of fact, once you've delivered him here, dismiss the remaining servants for the evening."

"Yes, my lord."

Claybourne released her, walked to his desk, leaned against it, crossed his arms over his chest, and met Catherine's gaze. "I don't suppose you'd leave while he and I discuss—"

"I'll not leave you to face him alone."

"Don't interfere."

She opened her mouth to speak—

"I mean it, Catherine. This is going to be like a very complicated game of cards, and I intend to do a great deal of bluffing."

She nodded, heard the click of determined footsteps. Her stomach roiled. She walked so she was off to the side, near the shelves, far enough away not to be bothersome, but close enough to offer what support she could.

Avendale strode in, and once he was clear of the door, the butler closed it behind him. Catherine could sense the fury emanating off the duke in waves. She was also very much aware that Claybourne seemed completely unaffected.

An extraordinary number of lamps had been lit as though Claybourne wanted a clear view of his adversary, or perhaps he wanted Avendale to have a clear view of him. Unfortunately, they also gave Avendale a clear view of her.

He sneered at her. "I should have known you were at the heart of this travesty."

"You'll address me, not Lady Catherine," Claybourne said, his voice firm, his manner that of a man who knew no fear.

Avendale shifted his attention to Claybourne. "We're not among my peers where I must pretend politeness, so let me speak frankly. You're nothing.

You're not the rightful earl, and I'll not recognize you as such. I am here for my wife and heir. You will bring them to me and you will bring them to me now."

"I have some questions I want answered first."

"I do not answer to you."

"Why were you having Lady Catherine followed?"

"Where is my wife?"

"Answer my question and I'll answer yours."

Avendale looked at Catherine, not bothering to disguise his low opinion of her. She just didn't know if it was a recently acquired opinion. "She is a bad influence on my wife, and so I thought it worth keeping an eye on her."

"And the reason you tried to have me killed?"

"Because I don't like you, you insolent dog. You're a blight on the aristocracy. Now bring me my wife and son!"

"It's a bit difficult to do your bidding when they're not here."

"You're lying."

"I've not lied since I was fourteen. Search my residence, every room, every nook and cranny. You'll not find them here because they never left London."

"You think to keep them away from me?"

"If I must in order to protect them. You and I are going to come to an understanding—"

Avendale dropped his head back and yelled, his hands balled into fists. When he again looked at Claybourne, the fury he'd brought into the room with him was tenfold. "I'll not allow you to take anything else that rightfully belongs to another!"

He swung his fist one way, knocking a lamp onto the chair, swung it the other way, sending another lamp flying toward the draperies. Before anyone could react, he flung himself toward Claybourne.

The lamp on the desk hit the floor, shattering, spilling kerosene and fire. Catherine grabbed a cushion from a chair, made a move toward the flames in order to beat them out—

Suddenly dark eyes, insane eyes, were in front of her. Without warning. She felt blinding pain shooting through her jaw into the back of her skull, more pain as her head collided with something. The floor she realized. She felt a jerk on her arm, heard a roar, and the hold on her arm was gone.

Forcing her eyes open, she could see Claybourne and Avendale crashing around the room, with flames dancing around them as though they were in some macabre form of hell. Flames. Fire. She had to get up. She had to get help.

She struggled to her knees. The room spun around her. Crawling to the desk, she pulled herself up. How long had she been on the floor? She screamed for help, but already the flames were circling the room, blocking her way to the door, the windows. She considered trying to leap across them, but her skirts would surely catch on fire.

Reaching beneath her hem, intent on removing a petticoat so she'd have something to slap at the fire, she looked toward Claybourne. He had Avendale pinned to the floor. He punched him, once, twice—

Avendale bucked, throwing Claybourne off. Something else shattered. Another lamp. Catherine pulled off her petticoat and began beating at the flames that were racing up the shelves devouring the books, the papers, the wooden shelves—

Dear God, was there a worse room for a fire to be let loose? So many flames rose higher and higher. And they were hot, so hot. The gray, billowing smoke made it difficult to see. Her eyes stung. Her lungs hurt.

Hearing a grunt, she looked back over her shoulder. Avendale had Claybourne bent backward over the desk, pummeling him. Catherine picked up a nearby statuette. Coughing and gasping, she staggered over—

Avendale turned away from Claybourne and with an unholy glow in his eyes, punched her again. Staggering backward, she landed once more on the floor. She'd forgotten how he relished striking women.

Growling, Claybourne flung himself at Avendale, knocking him down. Avendale's head hit the edge of a low table and he lay still, unmoving. Claybourne bent over him, pressed his ear to his chest. "He's alive."

"We've no way out, nowhere to hide," Catherine yelled.

It seemed only then that Claybourne realized the dangerous predicament they were in. "This way," Claybourne ordered. He pulled Avendale upright, folded him over his shoulder, and lifted him up as he rose to his feet. In long strides, he reached the fireplace.

"What in the bloody hell do you think we're

going to do?" Catherine yelled. "Climb up the chimney flue?"

"No. We're going to climb down. Grab a lamp."

She was surprised that a lamp still remained, but she spotted one on a small table in the corner. Grabbing it, she watched as he did something along the side of the fireplace—pushed something, pressed, pulled, she couldn't see clearly with all the smoke—and a grinding, groaning began to echo through the room as one of the great shelves shifted forward, creating a passage behind the wall.

Something crashed. She felt as though her blood were beginning to boil.

"Come on. Quickly." He pressed his hand to the small of her back, urging her into the darkened passage.

The lamp illuminated a set of stairs.

"Go down," he ordered.

"Where does this go?"

"I don't . . . I don't bloody well know. I just know it's safe. Go!"

She dashed down the stairs. It was cool here, the air while musty was easier to breathe. At the bottom she reached a tunnel.

"Keep going," he ordered.

She ducked cobwebs, thought she heard a rat squealing—but facing a rat was better than facing a fire. She came to a fork in the passage, stumbled to a stop.

"Keep right," Claybourne said.

She glanced back at him. "Where does the other go?"

"Back into the house."

"I certainly don't want to go there."

She followed the fork as he'd indicated. After a while she began to hear the rush of the ocean and smell the salt air. She walked out into the darkness, onto the shore. Dark clouds moved across the moon, but still the light glowed off the nearby sea. Had the family made its original fortune as smugglers?

Claybourne dropped Avendale onto the shore, then staggered over to a boulder. He sat on it and stared at the waves rushing in to cover his boots before darting back to sea. A light rain continued to fall, but it was the least of their concerns. Catherine knelt before him, lifting the lamp so she could see his face. "Luke?"

"Catherine, how did I know? How did I know about the passage?"

"I don't understand."

He shook his head. "I didn't know it existed. I didn't know it was there."

"How could you not know? Someone must have shown you."

"No, no one has ever shown me."

"The previous earl."

"No."

He sounded so certain, so sure.

"But you went right to it. You knew what you needed to do."

"Only after you said we had nowhere to hide. Until that moment"—he pressed the heels of his hands against his brow—"dear God, my head. I feel like it's trying to split in two."

Breathing heavily, he dropped his head back.

"I'll have to worry about this later. Right now, we need to decide what to do with Avendale. And make sure the servants are safe."

He stood up, fell to his knees. She crouched beside him. "Luke, you're frightening me."

He lifted his gaze to hers, cradled her face with his palm. "My courageous girl." Leaning in, he kissed her.

When he drew back, she asked, "What are we going to do about Avendale?"

"Find a way to kill him—without either of us being sent to the gallows for doing it."

"If that was your intent, why not just leave him in the fire?"

"Because I want his death to serve a purpose. I need him alive for that to happen."

"I don't understand what you're talking about."

"Do you trust me?"

"With my life." Suddenly she was in his arms, shivering and crying, feeling like such a ninny but they were alive, Claybourne was alive, and that was all that mattered.

Chapter 19

Using strips torn from Catherine's underskirt, Luke bound and gagged Avendale after taking great satisfaction in delivering a blow to the man's jaw when he'd begun to stir. Luke was not of a mind to be gentle or forgiving. It didn't help matters that his head had begun to pound mercilessly. He actually envied Avendale his unconscious state.

With great effort, he hoisted Avendale over his shoulder. With Catherine at his side, they began making their way back to the manor. No path marked the way, but the terrain wasn't too rugged. The rain, however, had increased in intensity, but Luke didn't mind. With any luck, it might reduce the fire's damage to the manor.

"If the house were still burning, don't you think we'd see fire in the distance?" Catherine asked.

"Yes. The servants and village's fire brigade no doubt got it under control."

"Your head's bothering you, isn't it?"

"I'll be all right."

"What are you going to do with Avendale tonight?"

"If the manor still stands, put him in the wine cellar. It has a door with a lock and a bar."

"And after that?"

"You and I will return to London. I'll come back for Avendale once I've made arrangements. Until then, my most trusted servants will keep him imprisoned and fed."

"What will the arrangements entail?"

Groaning, he shook his head. "I can't think clearly right now, Catherine."

She wrapped her hand around his upper arm as though to steady him. "You're in a great deal of pain."

"It's never been this bad." It was all he could do to put one foot in front of the other. He was still baffled by how he knew about the passage, but concentrating only made his headache worse and he thought if it got much more painful that he might actually lose consciousness. Instead he focused on Catherine's hand on his arm. He thought about her silky body beneath his and the pain eased a little. He concentrated on remembering how wonderful it had felt to sink into her. The pain in his head eased a little more, but he began to ache elsewhere.

Better to simply concentrate on walking.

Eventually they reached the manor. It appeared undamaged until they went around to the wing where the library had been. A portion had collapsed and little remained except charred remnants.

"My lord!" His butler rushed over. "We feared the worst."

Claybourne dropped Avendale onto the ground. "What's the damage?"

"We were fortunate. Only this wing sustained any real damage. The other wing and the main portion of the house are unscathed and habitable."

"Good." Luke stepped over what remained of the wall near the chimney that had withstood the assault. The secret door was gone. A gaping hole revealed the stairs leading down into the passage. "Were you aware this passage existed?"

"No, my lord," the butler said. "I'm sorry. Where does it lead?"

"To the sea. Ask the other servants."

"Pardon?"

Luke pressed his fingers to his forehead. "Ask the servants if anyone knew about this passage. I need to know who told me about it."

"Yes, my lord." He hurried off.

Luke looked around. The old gent had taken such joy in his books and now they were destroyed. Luke felt an irrational anger at the useless destruction. The charred stench on the air was nauseating.

A sound caught his attention and he turned just in time to see Catherine stumble. Reaching out, he grabbed her and kept her from falling.

"So much lost," she murmured, and he heard the sorrow in her voice.

"It could have been worse. I'll see that Marcus Langdon has the funds to rebuild all this to its former glory."

"You may not be the true Earl of Claybourne, but it's obvious you care about this place."

He couldn't deny that he had come to care for it. Giving it up would be more difficult than he'd realized, but it was because he'd come to care for it that he was determined to see it returned to the rightful owner. A good many things would change with his decision—including the fact that Frannie would no longer have an excuse not to marry him.

Someone had set tall torches in the ground. Their burning flames illuminated Catherine, and Luke could see the soot and dirt covering her face. No, it wasn't all dirt. A bruise was forming from where Avendale had struck her. Luke had a strong urge to kill him for that alone. Tenderly he touched her cheek. Strangely he found himself thinking about the man who would have the honor of touching her cheek when she was old. He hoped the man would appreciate that her strength and beauty would never age.

"Our chambers are supposedly habitable. I could use a hot bath."

She smiled at him, stunning him that after all they'd been through, she could still smile.

"I would like that very much," she said.

And he realized she was granting permission for him to have one more night with her.

As the water lapped around her, Catherine thought she would be forever spoiled when it came to bathing. It was simply delicious to be immersed in warm water while snuggling against a man, especially when that man was Claybourne. Fortunately the tub was large. Legend had it that it had been made especially for the men of the family, because they tended to be tall and they liked room to move about. She also suspected that they liked not taking baths alone.

They'd locked Avendale in the cellar, with two guards to keep watch. Portions of the library continued to smolder, but the few servants he'd not sent away when he and Catherine had first arrived were keeping watch there as well, putting out any small fires that erupted. It was strange to suddenly have so few worries, yet Catherine relished the peace. She just wished that Claybourne's head would stop hurting.

He wasn't complaining, but his furrowed brow and tightened jaw told the tale of his discomfort. He'd been unable to find any servant who knew of the secret passage. He was bothered by the fact that he'd known about it, but Catherine was convinced that the previous earl had shown it to him at some point and Claybourne had simply forgotten. It was the only explanation that made sense.

With his hand, he lazily stroked her arm while she skimmed her fingers over his chest. She wished she could wash away the scars, the evidence of his harsh life, yet his life had shaped him into a man who stood strong for others. Even if he weren't a lord, he'd still be a man to be admired.

Selfishly she wished they could delay their leaving, because once they began their journey back to London, everything between them would change, would come to an end. Unselfishly, she was anxious to see Winnie and her father. She knew they were being well cared for, but the knowledge didn't make her miss them any less, didn't make her not want to do what she could to bring them comfort.

"What are you thinking?" she asked Claybourne.

"I'm trying not to think."

With the water splashing around her, she eased up; and not finding room enough along the side of the tub, she straddled him. His body reacted immediately. With a groan and a smile, he opened his eyes. "I think you found the cure for my head pains. Send the ache elsewhere."

"They can't have gone away that quickly."

"Not completely, no, but I'm not going to let them stop me from having what I want."

She gave him what she hoped was a seductive smile. "And what is that?"

His eyes darkened. "You."

He threaded his fingers through her damp hair and brought her nearer. She leveraged herself so she could welcome his kiss. The hunger of his mouth on hers sent desire spiraling down to her toes. He eased her back, took the soap, slicked up his hands, and began rubbing them over her body, coming back to her breasts over and over as though they were the center of her being, the city from which all roads led and returned.

In his eyes she saw appreciation and pleasure.

Reaching for the soap, she imitated his actions, enjoying the feel of silkiness on velvet. Dropping her head back, she moaned from the incredible sensations created by his touching her, the joy of touching him.

His hands dug into her hips and he lifted her.

"If this water weren't so filthy, I'd take you

right here," he said. Instead he moved her aside, stood, and pulled her to her feet. Pitchers of water surrounded them. He lifted one and poured the water over her, removing the soap and any lingering dirt. Another pitcher, another dunking. Then he did the same for himself.

"Stay," he ordered as he stepped out of the tub.

"I'm not a dog to be commanded about."

Chuckling low, he grabbed a towel and vigorously dried himself off. "Must you always be so difficult?"

"You're not acting as though you truly find me difficult."

He flung the towel around her and lifted her into his arms. "I find you adorable."

He carried her to his bed and very gently dried her off, then he flung the towel aside. With one smooth motion, he sank into her and stilled. "When I saw him strike you, when you fell—" His voice was rough with emotion.

"Don't think about it," she urged.

"Why do you have to be so damned courageous?" he asked as he kissed her neck, her ear, her throat, her chin.

She wondered if he'd want her if she weren't, but she wasn't brave enough to ask, so perhaps she wasn't as courageous after all.

"Don't talk," she murmured as she kissed his temples.

He took her slowly, as though he realized this would be the last time, savoring each thrust, creating memories with each touch. There was nothing frenzied about their joining. Rather it was simply an appreciation that they'd escaped the fire, a celebration of survival, and perhaps in a way, a farewell.

As the pleasure peaked, she shivered in his arms, he shuddered in hers. Breathing heavily, he pressed a kiss to her temple before rolling off her and drawing her near. Nestled up against him, she fell into a deep sleep.

"Mummy!"

"Shh, darling, shh, we have to be quiet. We're playing a game. We're going to hide from Papa."

"Scared."

"Shh. Don't be frightened, darling. Shh. Mummy will never let anything bad happen. We're going to have fun. Do you see the magical lever? It's our little secret."

Catherine awoke to an agonized groaning. At first she thought it was the thunder, but then she became aware of being in the bed alone, of harsh breathing in the room. Reaching out to the bedside table, she turned up the flame in the lamp.

It chased back the shadows to reveal Claybourne, naked, kneeling on the floor, rocking, his arms wrapped around his stomach as though he were suffering intense pain. She scrambled out of bed and crouched before him. "Luke, Luke, whatever's wrong?"

He lifted his face, and she saw the tears trailing down his cheeks.

"I remember," he rasped. "Dear God, I remember."

Feeling powerless to stop his agony, she touched his shoulders, his face. "Remember what?"

She heard him swallow, felt him shudder beneath her fingers. "My parents. Ah, it hurts!"

"Your head?"

"No, my heart. It was my uncle."

"Luke, darling, I don't understand."

"They took me to a menagerie. So many animals. A lion. And a giraffe. And a striped horse. I didn't want to leave. But it was growing dark and the crowds were thinning—there had been so many people that the carriage was parked far away. I grew tired of walking. My father lifted me onto his shoulders. And then the boy . . ."

His voice trailed off, but she was still confused. What was he saying?

"What about the boy?" she asked.

"A street urchin. Said his mother was dying in the alley, needed help. My father took me off his shoulders and hurried after the boy. My mother grabbed my hand and rushed after them. But my father's legs were so long, mine so short that we couldn't keep up. When we turned the corner, we saw my father being attacked by men—it looked as though they were savage animals. Clubs and knives. And my uncle standing off to the side laughing, as though it was his favorite prank. My mother screamed for me to run, and I did. But I was still near enough to hear her cries as they descended on her."

Catherine cradled his face between her hands. "I'm so sorry, Luke, but I don't understand what you're trying to tell me, I don't understand what it means."

Her heart ached at the devastation in his eyes.

"It means I'm Claybourne. I knew about the

secret passage because my mother and I used it to play a game—we'd hide from my father, but he was always there, waiting at the entrance." He gave her a heart-wrenching smile. "He'd sweep her into his arms, and they'd laugh. Then we'd play in the sea as though we hadn't a care in the world."

He took a deep breath, and swiped at his tears.

"Why would your uncle kill them?"

"Why else? For the title and all that came with it."

She sat back on her heels. "And you're remembering it all now?"

"Just snatches of the past. I remember the secret passage, the menagerie, the alley. I remember my uncle and his hideous face. And I remember running like a coward."

"You were a child."

He rubbed his hands up and down his face. "I couldn't save them."

"They didn't expect you to. Saving yourself was your greatest gift to them."

"Why couldn't I remember any of it?"

"Why would you want to? It sounds horrendous."

He held her gaze. "I've longed to know the truth of my past, and now I want nothing more than to forget it."

He forged his mouth to hers as though she had the power to return to him the innocence he had lost. For even though he'd grown up on the streets, had seen the worst of men, it was clear to Catherine that until tonight, he'd not truly known the worst of his family. He'd killed his uncle, his uncle had killed his parents. Deception, hatred, betrayal, greed . . . all the elements for family scandal and destruction had resided within the bosom of Claybourne's family. His life on the streets—in spite of the crimes he'd committed—had been more honest, and those with whom he lived more trustworthy.

Somehow, they managed to get back into bed, mouths locked, arms and legs in a tangle. He wanted to forget what she thought it was crucial he remember. Yet, she couldn't deny him a few moments of solace. If she could, she'd give him a lifetime of comfort in her arms.

His mouth was hot, desperate, eager. She was more than ready for him when he drove himself into her, like a man possessed, a man running from his past, a man unable to see his future. He pumped fast and furious. She met his eagerness with her own, digging her fingers into his firm buttocks, riding him as he rode her.

His powerful thrusts had the headboard knocking the wall, the pleasure rippling through her in undulating waves. There was madness here, and she didn't care. She cared only about him losing himself in her, and her losing herself in him.

She expected each time they came together for it to be the last—each time was a gift: a giving, a joining, a receiving, a taking. They were equals. If she could have given him more, she would have. Instead she rode the waves until they crested, calling out his name, aware of him growling hers, aware of his violent shudders, his face buried in the curve of her shoulder.

Holding him close while their breathing slowed, she relished the weight of his body. She'd wanted to know what it was to lie with him. Now she had to find the strength to give him up, to give him to another, to give him to Frannie.

She felt the tears sting her eyes because she wouldn't be the one to share his joys or his troubles. She wouldn't bear his children. She wouldn't be the one who stood beside him as he left his mark on the world. And she had no doubt that he was a man capable of leaving behind a magnificent legacy. He'd been forged in the fires of hell—and the man emerging, all of London would soon learn, was one to be reckoned with.

It was dark when the coach finally reached London. Catherine was still dressed in the clothes of a servant, and Luke didn't look much better. He knew he should go home first, make himself presentable, but he had a matter that he needed to see to—urgently. He'd told his driver where to go, and as he recognized the buildings signaling that they were nearing their destination, he felt the fury raging within him.

"Aren't we going home?" Catherine asked.

The coach came to a halt.

"Stay here," Luke ordered. He opened the door and leapt out of the coach before his footman could assist him. He strode into Dodger's, a man with a purpose. He spotted Jack straightaway.

The man known as the Dodger turned away from a gaming table and smiled brightly. "Ah, there you are. Have you put matters—"

Luke smashed his balled fist into Jack's face, sending him tumbling to the floor, overturning the table in the process. There were gasps from the gentlemen customers, squeals from the ladies who were trying to entice them up to their rooms.

"Get up!" Luke demanded.

Jack wiped the blood from his mouth, looked at the back of his hand, before peering up at Luke. "I'm not quite certain—"

"Get. Up."

Jack pushed himself up until he stood straight, and Luke punched him in the stomach. Jack staggered back, and Luke pounded his fist into his chin, snapping his head back and sending him sprawling to the floor.

"Luke!" Frannie cried from somewhere behind him. "What are you doing?"

She knelt beside Jack and looked up at Luke, horror in her eyes.

"It's all right, Frannie," Jack said. "I'm sure he has a good reason for punching the bloke who saved his arse on more than one occasion."

Luke took a step forward, taking satisfaction in Jack's flinching. "You found me hiding behind that garbage in the alley, because you followed me. You followed me from where my parents were attacked. All these years, you knew the truth. You knew I was the old gent's grandson, but you held your silence because to do otherwise would reveal your part in the murder of my parents. You knew my torment and yet you left me to suffer with my doubts. I should bloody well kill you."

It was as though a veil had dropped from Jack's eyes. Luke saw the truth there, saw that what he'd remembered was exactly what had taken place.

"Please do," Jack snarled. "By all means. Ever since that night we were in gaol and I offered myself up to those blighters so they'd spare you, I've prayed for death. So do it. You killed your uncle. So kill your friend! I bloody well dare you!"

Luke was suddenly aware of the cane in his hand, the sword unsheathed. He'd not remembered bringing it with him, but it would serve him well now. He took another step forward, felt a hand squeezing his arm, looked back—

Catherine. With tears swimming in her blue eyes. "You're not a murderer."

"I killed my uncle. Let there be no doubt."

"He took a young girl's innocence. But you are not a murderer."

He pointed at Jack. "He led us to the alley. He was the urchin who claimed his mother was dying. He's the one—"

"I'll not let you give up the last bit of your soul. I will stand in front of you if I must."

But it was enough that she stood beside him. He looked back at Jack. "What did he pay you?"

Jack just glowered at him.

"Damn you! Answer me."

To his surprise, Jack didn't avert his gaze in shame. "Sixpence."

Luke slammed his eyes closed.

"I didn't know what he had planned," Jack said quietly. "You have to believe that, Luke, I didn't know."

Luke opened his eyes. He'd been blind with rage, and only now did everything around him come into focus. Chesney and Milner staring at him, mouths agape. Other lords and common gentlemen—vice made them equal.

Frannie staring up at him as though she didn't know him.

"Did you know what he'd done?" Luke asked quietly.

She slowly shook her head.

Catherine clinging to his arm as though she alone had the power to stop him from doing something rash and irrevocable. Catherine, dressed in the clothing of a servant, her hair askew. Catherine who'd not stayed in the coach as he'd ordered. Catherine standing in the midst of a gaming hell.

What had he been thinking to come here first? What had she been thinking to follow him inside? Was there a chance in hell that no one would recognize her?

He felt a need to do something, to say something, to bring this moment to a deserving end. But there was nothing inside him, nothing except grief and loss. The past twenty-five years of his life had been filled with lies. And the truth offered no comfort.

It terrified Catherine how quiet Luke was in the coach. He'd walked out of Dodger's without another word being spoken. She sat beside him, holding his hand, a hand that was so cold it was as though he'd died.

"You shouldn't be alone tonight," she said.

"I am who I'm supposed to be, and suddenly, inexplicably, I feel so unworthy. I have been an imposter all these years, but not in the way I thought."

"You've not been an imposter."

"I thought I was a scoundrel masquerading as a lord; instead I was a lord masquerading as a scoundrel. I thought I was one of them, I thought I was one of Feagan's children. I thought we had the streets in common."

Her heart was breaking for him. "You did. For a while you did."

He looked at her with a gentleness in his eyes that she'd feared had been lost forever. "Do you think there is any chance that any of the nobles in Dodger's tonight did not recognize you?"

She sighed. "A small chance perhaps."

"You shouldn't have tried to stop me, Catherine. Your reputation is not worth the scandal that will erupt."

"Let's see. My father lies at death's door, my brother is traipsing around the world. I have no husband, no children. My reputation matters only to me, and you mean a great deal more to me than it."

He cupped her face, brushed his lips over hers. The passion between them had cooled, as it should have. When all of this was behind him, he'd once again return to Frannie's side. She had no doubt of that.

"We need to get you home," he said quietly. "And I need to determine what I'm to do about

Avendale." They'd left him in his cellar prison at Luke's estate until everything could be arranged. Luke sighed deeply. "I'd have never thought that remembering would bring with it far more trouble than forgetting."

Chapter 20

Catherine was drained as she slowly made her way up the stairs toward her bedchamber. She wanted desperately to see her father, but she didn't want him to see her dressed like a servant, looking as though she'd spent a few days being ravished. Which she had, but still. He didn't need to know that.

Jenny prepared the bath and Catherine sank into the steaming water. She was sore and miserable. And that was the good news. While nothing would remain of her reputation, she would deal with that problem later. Right now, her main concern was Claybourne. She didn't want him to be alone tonight.

But she was so exhausted that it was all she could do to continue breathing.

When she was finished with her bath, Jenny began drying her. "Shall I help you prepare for bed?"

"No, I want to visit with my father for a while, and as he's not seen me in a few days, I think a simple dress would be appropriate."

She felt a little more herself as she walked down the hallway to his bedchamber. His nurse rose as Catherine stepped into the room.

"How is he?" Catherine asked.

"Doing well, my lady."

He couldn't speak coherently, he couldn't move about on his own. He had to be fed and bathed—how in the world could he be doing well?

But he lifted his withering, shaking hand, and Catherine could have sworn that a welcoming light appeared in his fading blue eyes. Sitting in the chair beside the bed, she took his hand and pressed a kiss to his fingers. Then she combed her fingers through his thinning silver hair.

"Did you miss me?"

He gave her the barest of nods.

"Tomorrow, if the sun favors us, we're going to go out to the garden. I have it on good authority that it won't harm your health at all. As a matter of fact, it might improve it." She felt the tears sting her eyes. "Oh, Papa, I've done something terribly silly. I've fallen in love with someone, and he loves another. The strange thing is, as much as it hurts, I only want him to be happy. And if she'll make him happy, I want him to have her."

He squeezed her hand. She moved up and laid her head on his chest, felt his hand come to rest on her hair. "I think you'd like him."

She heard a low rumble in his chest. "I know you don't think he's good enough for me, but then you don't think any man is good enough for me."

She sat up. "Avendale has been beating Winnie, Papa. Some friends and I hid her away, so he couldn't find her. But I want to go see her tonight.

I don't want you to worry. I think I have an inspector from Scotland Yard watching over me. So I'll be fine. And tomorrow we'll go into the garden, and I shan't stop reading to you until we've finished Oliver's story."

Leaning up, she kissed her father's forehead and whispered words she'd never be able to say to Claybourne, "I love you, with all my heart."

The portrait of his father hadn't changed, but it seemed that it had. Or perhaps it was only he who had changed. Or maybe it was because he looked at it through a drunken stupor, his first bottle of whiskey drained, the second dangling between his fingers. He'd have to find a new supplier.

Strange how different *everything* looked. Things that had once seemed foreign, no longer did. After he'd returned home, he'd walked through every room, looking at things through different eyes, through the eyes of the Earl of Claybourne. He remembered how the lion's head on the fireplace poker had frightened him as a child. He remembered riding the wooden rocking horse in the nursery.

Usually when he looked at the portrait for too long, cataloging the features, his head would begin to hurt. But not tonight. Tonight there was nothing except the calming liquor swirling through his blood. Even that was unusual. Normally, he sought oblivion. Tonight he just wanted peace.

His hand ached from striking Jack. His heart ached from Frannie's defending Jack. Why had Luke thought she'd unquestionably side with him? Frannie's reaction was natural, though. Luke had come in like a madman, and unlike Catherine, Frannie didn't know everything that Luke had remembered. She hadn't witnessed the pain his memory had brought.

Luke had lived in the squalor and wretchedness of that one small room with Feagan and his band of child thieves, and he'd felt safe. They'd shared their clothing, their food, their beds. They'd taught him how not to get caught. They'd taught him how to hide. And more than anything, in the beginning, he'd wanted to hide. Hide from his uncle, from the yells of his father dying, from the shrieks of his mother begging for mercy. When he'd walked through Feagan's door, he'd done so willingly, wanting—needing—to leave his terrifying other life behind.

Nothing was more frightening than knowing that someone for whom he'd drawn a picture of a pond, someone who'd given him a small wooden carved horse, someone who had tucked him into bed once when visiting, kissed the top of his head, chuckled with his father, danced with his mother—could stand by laughing while others murdered his family. But his uncle was deeply ensconced in all those memories.

Luke heard the door open, heard the light footsteps. He twisted around in the chair, looking back toward the door. He hated the joy that filled him at the sight of Catherine. Despised more the relief that swept through him because she was here. She made him feel weak, because his need for her was so great. He needed her gone from his life and to accomplish that, he needed to take care of Avendale.

Luke swallowed more whiskey and settled back into his chair. "You shouldn't be here."

She knelt on the floor beside him, placed her hands on his knees. "I told my father I was going to see Winnie, but I didn't. I just told him that excuse knowing full well that I was coming here. I didn't want you to be alone tonight."

"Catherine—"

"I'm here only as a friend." She turned her face toward the portrait and rested her cheek on his thigh. "I can see the similarities so easily now."

"I remember so little about him."

"I think he would have been proud of his son as a man."

Luke chuckled low. "Where do you find your faith in me, Catherine?"

"From coming to know you."

She stayed with him, just as she'd promised. In his bed. Doing nothing more than holding him, allowing him to hold her. Something more than friendship, something less than lovers. But it was comforting. And while Luke didn't sleep, neither did he drift into the realm of memories. Rather he concentrated on how it felt to have her in his bed: the feel of her, the fragrance of her, the sound of her breathing.

Before dawn, he escorted her home with the promise of seeing to her problem posthaste. He returned to his residence for breakfast and to read the *Times*. He was grateful to discover that the front page did not announce that Lady Catherine Mabry had been spied at a gaming hell, even more grateful to discover no tidbit of news whatsoever about all that had transpired last night. It would come, though. Surely it would come.

It was late morning by the time Luke arrived at Marcus Langdon's residence. Luke was dressed in his finest, and he knew, with no doubts, that he appeared every bit the lord that he was.

The butler told him that the master and his mother were in the drawing room. Luke found them there. Marcus was reading a book. His mother was concentrating on her embroidery. What a harsh life they led.

Mrs. Langdon put down her needlework, obviously disgusted that Luke had made an appearance in her sanctuary. Marcus closed his book.

Luke cleared his throat. This was harder than he'd thought it would be. "I wanted you to know that my memories have returned to me. If you continue your efforts through the courts, you will be wasting your money, for I am the Earl of Claybourne."

"Quite convenient that they would return now, when your position is threatened," Mrs. Langdon said. "But that will not stop us. My son is the rightful heir."

"No, madam, he is not. My parents were murdered by your husband."

She gasped, paled. "That's a lie!"

"I wish it were. I have a witness." Jack. He'd drag Jack into court if need be in order to testify about what he'd done. "But I have no desire to bring more shame to this family than it has already experienced these many years. One murderer in the family is enough, and as I've never denied my deed, I see no reason to cause you further embarrassment by revealing what your husband—my uncle, my father's brother—set into motion."

"You were raised to lie, cheat, murder, and steal, to take that which does not belong to you—"

"You lost a silver necklace that had three red stones in it."

She stiffened. "What do you know of my precious jewelry? It was a gift from Geoffrey, on the day we wed."

Luke looked at Marcus, with his gaping mouth and the stunned look in his eyes that signaled he remembered the jewelry. He knew what was coming next. They were the only two who did.

"You'd read *Ivanhoe* to us, Auntie Clara," Luke said quietly, rushing on before she could object to the intimate name he'd used. "Marcus and I took the necklace—"

"That's not true," Marcus said, coming to his feet. "I alone took it. You were only six, I was eight." He looked at his mother. "We embedded the stones in our wooden swords, but after Father got so furious and was questioning the servants about the missing piece, we threw away the evidence of what we'd done. He took the cane to me more than once. I wanted to avoid another blistering."

"What does all this prove?" his mother asked.

Marcus looked at Luke. "It proves he's my cousin. I never told anyone what we did."

"Neither did I," Luke said. In truth, before yesterday, he'd not remembered. He turned his attention back to Mrs. Langdon. She seemed to be in shock. He could hardly blame her. "I have no intention of revealing the true nature of your husband, but if you persist in trying to take from me what is rightfully mine, it will all come out. I will not give up easily what my father fought to hold, what my grandfather entrusted to my care."

Marcus cleared his throat. "I shall talk with my solicitor this afternoon and see that our claim is removed from the courts."

Luke nodded. "Very good." He turned to go—

"Claybourne?"

He looked back at Marcus.

"May I have a word in private?"

"Certainly."

"You can't possibly believe him," Mrs. Langdon said.

"We'll talk when I get back, Mother." He followed Luke into the hallway and studied him as though only just then really looking at him. "It truly is you. I think I knew, I think I always knew."

"I didn't," Luke admitted.

"I'll speak with Mother. She'll come around."

"I appreciate it. It's been a difficult few years. I'd like to put all the difficulties behind us."

Marcus licked his lips, darted his gaze around the hallway as though he expected danger to be lurking about. "That's what I wanted to talk with you about. You said you were attacked one night."

"Yes."

"It was Avendale's doing."

Luke knew that, but how had Marcus known? Luke stared at him, suspicion creeping in. "Avendale? What would make you think that?"

"Apparently, he's lost a good deal of money to you. He's in financial straits and he's quite angry about it."

"And how do you know all this?"

"Because he approached me and told me that he would help me regain my title if I promised to pay him what you'd stolen from him once I inherited."

"Help you regain it by having me murdered?"

"I didn't know that was part of his plan. I told him that I wanted to do it legally through the courts. I thought he understood, but I learned too late that he is quite the madman."

"And you didn't think I needed to know this when I came before?"

"I was ashamed that I'd become involved with him. And quite honestly, I was terrified. He indicated that he'd killed before, and I have little doubt he spoke the truth."

"I appreciate your honesty."

"For what it's worth, I always thought you were a decent chap—well, except for killing my father, of course."

"He brutally raped a twelve-year-old girl. That's the reason I killed him. And while until recently, I had no memory of my parents' murder, maybe a part of me did recognize him—for I hesitated not at all in delivering what I considered justice."

"You can't always tell from looking at a person what he's really like."

Luke placed his hand on Marcus's shoulder. "I don't think you're like your father."

"Thank you for that. I'd best get back to Mother.

While it's not obvious, I suspect she's taken all of this news rather hard."

After watching his cousin disappear into the drawing room, Luke turned his thoughts to the problem of Avendale. He was going to take a great deal of pleasure in dispensing with the fellow.

Chapter 21

Midnight.
My library.
–L

The missive went out to three of them. There was a time when it would have gone to four.

They slipped into Luke's library as quiet as the night, coming into the residence through their various preferred entrances. Bill entered through the kitchen. Jim climbed a tree and came in through a bedchamber window. Frannie preferred slipping in through a door that led off of the terrace.

Catherine was there. She'd come in through the front door as though she no longer had a need to hide what they were doing. But Luke knew the truth of it. What they were about to do they would have to carry with them to the grave.

They all sat in chairs in a circle.

"Let's begin," Luke said.

"Shouldn't we wait for Jack?" Bill asked.

"He's not invited."

Bill looked at the others, as though he expected someone to object, to defend Jack, and when no one did, he settled back. He was the healer among them. He always wanted to fix things, make them right. But some things, once broken, would never be the same.

"As you're aware, I set up an opportunity to confront Avendale at Heatherwood. Presently, he is my prisoner, being kept in the manor's cellar. The man is a danger. To his wife, his son, Catherine, and me. If it were only me, I'd let it go and deal with him one on one, but I'm not willing to risk the others." He especially wasn't willing to risk Catherine.

"So what's the plan?" Jim asked.

"If any of you have doubts, you should walk out now."

They all stayed seated.

Luke felt the tightening in his chest, cleared his throat at the demonstration of their faith in him. Apparently Jim wasn't the only one who would follow him into hell without asking why they were taking the journey. "Thank you for that."

Taking a deep breath, he gave his attention to Bill. "We need a body. A man, recently buried, would no doubt be best. We'll want him dressed in these items, as well as the two rings. I've included a note that tells which ring goes on which finger on which hand." Luke took a bundle from where it rested beside his chair and extended it to Bill. He'd taken Avendale's clothing and jewelry before leaving Heatherwood.

Bill took the parcel without hesitating. "It's been

a long while since I've done any grave robbing, but it's a skill once learned, never forgotten."

"After he's dressed, we'll want him burned beyond recognition."

Bill nodded. "I'll see to it."

"Take comfort in the fact that his final resting place will be very grand indeed." Luke turned to Jim. "I'm looking for someone being transported to a penal colony for life. Age doesn't matter, as long as the documents can be changed to reflect a man of thirty-four."

Jim nodded somberly. "A boy of fourteen was recently sentenced to transportation to Tasmania. I believe it was for life, for picking pockets."

"Bloody hell, that could have been any of us," Bill said. "Whose pockets did he pick? Prince Albert's?"

"That was my thought—but for the teachings of Feagan, there go I." Jim looked at Frannie. "Can you make a fourteen look like a thirty-four?"

She grinned cockily. "In my sleep."

"I'll get his papers to you."

"We'll also want to arrange respectable employment for the lad," Luke told her.

She gave him an odd look before nodding. Probably because that would have been Jack's job, to see that the lad was placed somewhere safe.

"I'll take care of it," Frannie said.

Luke looked at Catherine, sitting beside him. He wanted to take her hand, but it seemed wrong with Frannie sitting there. "Now then, here's the hard part."

Taking a deep breath, she nodded. "Whatever it is, I'll do it."

"I never questioned for a moment that you wouldn't." Still, he knew it would be difficult for her. He sighed. "You need to inform the Duchess of Avendale that her husband died in the fire at Heatherwood, a fire that was started when an ember jumped out of the fireplace unobserved, until it was too late."

"But that's not what happened."

"Which is why I said yours is the hardest part. You're going to have to lie to her, Catherine, to everyone. Once we've all seen to our tasks, it'll be as though what you told her is the truth. We'll present her with an unrecognizable burned body wearing Avendale's clothes and rings. And she will never see him again."

"I don't understand why I can't tell her the truth."

"Because the fewer who know, the better. Laws are being broken here, Catherine. We're all at risk. And while it's possible she could hold her tongue on this matter, he was her husband. With distance and time, she may forget what marriage to him was like or she may decide she prefers marriage to a beast over widowhood. She may try to find a way to bring him back. It would have been easier all the way around if I'd left him in the fire, but I didn't, so we must make the best of it and leave no doubt that the Duke of Avendale is dead so his son might inherit."

"But shouldn't we at least let them know how the fire really got started? The things he said, the things he did—"

"His son will live with the legacy of his father's actions, Catherine. It will be easier not knowing the kind of man he was. If you doubt me, ask my cousin."

Nodding, she tipped up her chin, showing her resolve. "I shall do better than speak with Winnie and Whit. I shall help them arrange the funeral." She looked at Bill. "And it shall be very grand indeed."

"Very good." Luke looked around the circle. "Are there any questions?"

"I have one," Catherine said.

Luke arched his brow.

"What task is left to you?"

"The best one of all. I have the honor of arranging Avendale's delivery to the ship for transportation to his new life on the far side of the world."

Catherine insisted on going with him. Luke had known she would.

The fog was thick and heavy, chilling the bones. The great ship creaked and moaned against its moorings, as though she were anxious to be off, but she had to wait for her guests to finish shuffling aboard, their leg irons clanking in the predawn stillness.

"How did the duchess take the news of her husband's demise?" Luke asked.

"She actually wept. I'd not expected that." She peered up at him. "You don't seem surprised."

He shook his head. "People fear loneliness. They prefer living with an unpleasant person to living alone."

"I don't know if this is enough. It seems as though he got off rather easily, after all he's done."

"He's a man accustomed to someone tying his neckcloth for him. He'll be down on his knees scrubbing the deck. His hands will blister, his feet will toughen, and I suspect before the journey is done, he'll find himself flogged on more than one occasion. I don't know if there is hell after death, but I do know there is hell in life. I have waited in its antechamber. It is not a pleasant place. Avendale will rue the day he was born. He will be punished, Catherine. Every day, for as long as he lives.

"Although he's actually managed to do a bit of good with his life, switching places as he has with Thomas Lark, giving the lad an opportunity for a better future."

"One lad. It seems so little when there are so many."

"We can't save them all, Catherine, so we take satisfaction in saving those we can."

They watched the two hundred and thirty prisoners march up the gangplank and onto the deck of the ship.

"There he is," Luke said quietly. "The one in the gray coat, with the shoulder so badly torn."

"I thought he'd resist more."

"Bill gave me something to pour down his throat to make him as gentle as a lamb."

"Still, I'm surprised he's not yelling out his name and rank."

"Bit difficult to do with a broken jaw."

She snapped her head around to look at him. He shrugged. "He wasn't being cooperative."

They stayed until the last prisoner took his place aboard the ship, until the ship set sail.

Luke heard Catherine breathe a sigh of relief. "I can't believe it's over."

"Believe it."

Dawn was just beyond the horizon when Claybourne's coach pulled to a stop in the alley behind Catherine's residence.

Claybourne. She didn't think he'd yet grown comfortable with the realization of who he was, but she had no doubt that he would in time. He was the proper earl. She wished she could help him, reassure him, stand by his side as he truly took his place among the aristocracy, but she wasn't the one he wanted at his side. She knew that. Had accepted it before she ever entered his bedchamber at Heatherwood.

They'd talked of nothing personal since the night of his revelation. That, too, was how it should be.

The coach door opened. Claybourne climbed out, then extended his hand to her.

For the last time, she placed her hand in his, felt his strong fingers close over hers. For the last time, she stepped out, inhaling the masculine scent that was his alone. For the last time they walked side by side to the gate, speaking not a word, as though too much remained to be said and so little time remained to say it.

She cleared her throat. "I'll arrange a tea for Frannie, begin introducing her into society."

He nodded. She swallowed. "So we're in agreement there'll be no more evening lessons."

He nodded. She extended her hand. "Then, thank you, my lord. Our arrangement has been . . . gratifying—"

Grabbing her hand, he pulled her into his arms and kissed her, almost savagely, as though this moment was as painful for him as it was for her. Of their own accord, her arms wound around his neck. She didn't want to let him go. She didn't want another woman in his bed, in his life, in his heart.

She almost told him that she'd do anything, anything he wanted if he'd only choose her, but she loved him too much not to grant him the fulfillment of his dreams—and Frannie, not Catherine, was part of those dreams.

He broke away, stepped back, breathing harshly in the pre-dawn stillness. "Our bargain is complete. Nothing else is required of you."

He spun on his heel and strode to the coach. She stood as she was while the driver cracked the whip, setting the horses into motion, and the coach rumbled by. When she could no longer see it, she opened the gate and walked inside.

After closing the gate behind her, the pain of lost love overtook her and she dropped to the cool grass and wept.

Nothing else is required of you.

He was mistaken there. One more thing was required of her: to survive the breaking of her heart.

Chapter 22

It was a lovely day for sitting in the garden, and Catherine took advantage of it, having her father brought down and settled in a chaise longue while she sat in a chair beside him.

It had been nearly a month since Catherine had stood in the pre-dawn with Claybourne and watched as Avendale boarded what was certain to be a ship bound for hell. She should have slept well, knowing that Winnie and Whit were safe for all time. It wasn't guilt that kept her from peaceful slumber. It was worrying over her father, whose health was diminishing rapidly now.

And it was longing for Claybourne to be there to ease the burden that was weighing on her.

Catherine scoured the papers every morning searching for the announcement of Claybourne's betrothal to Miss Frannie Darling, but she had yet to see it. No matter. It would come, and when it did, it would be like a knife through her heart.

One morning she'd told her father the tale of the Earl of Claybourne. He'd seemed as entertained by the story as he was by *Oliver Twist*. As feeble as he seemed, she suspected he was well aware that Claybourne was the man she'd been silly enough to fall in love with. But she saw no condemnation in his eyes.

The focus of her life had narrowed to her father, enjoying his company as much as possible during what she was certain were his final days. She'd written to her brother, beseeching him to return home. Lord only knew if the letter would find him in time.

Now she read the final words of *Oliver Twist* and very gently closed the book. She smiled at her father. "So Oliver found a home. I'm glad of it."

He blinked slowly. She combed her fingers through his hair. "My heart did go out to the Artful Dodger, though. I was sorry he was transported. I hear it's a very harsh life, although I suspect there are those who deserve it."

His gaze shifted past her, and his eyes seemed to fill with gladness. She glanced over her shoulder where he looked, halfway expecting to see Sterling there. Instead, she saw a beautiful white lily.

"Where did that come from? I'd not realized the gardener had planted lilies. It's rather late in the season for one to bloom." She turned her attention back to her father. "Would you like me to pluck it for you, bring it nearer so you might enjoy it a bit more? I know they're your favorite."

He gave her a very small nod. She rose, leaned over, and kissed his cheek. "I love you, Papa. I'll be right back."

She walked to the table where she kept her slender cutters. She was often nipping off blossoms to share with her father. In a way she hated to cut the lily, knowing it would wither that much sooner, but she was willing to do whatever would bring her father joy.

"I do believe this is the most perfect lily I've ever seen," she said, turning back to her father. Her heart caught, tears welled in her eyes. Even from this distance she knew. And she was left to wonder if it was truly the lily that had caught his eye or if he had seen something more divine.

She walked back to where he was, kissed his cheek again, and knelt beside him. "If I'd known you were going to leave, I'd have not left you to take that final step alone. Sleep in peace, Papa. Your journey is done, and I have a feeling mine is just beginning."

Luke thought he'd always known the comings and goings in London, but since the night he'd gone to Dodger's and confronted Jack, it seemed he was privy to a good deal more. Fitzsimmons had to purchase a larger bowl for the table in the entry hallway, a bowl large enough to hold all the invitations that Luke was suddenly receiving: to balls, dinners, and afternoon recitals—as though he cared whether or not a man's daughter could play the pianoforte. People acknowledged him on the streets now. Women asked his opinion on the selections they were considering in the shops if he happened to be in there perusing possible gifts for Frannie.

And they shared their gossip.

So it was that he knew Lady Catherine Mabry had spent the past month in seclusion with her ailing father. He also knew, within hours, when the dukedom had passed to her wayward brother.

Not calling on Catherine had been one of the hardest things he'd ever done, but he'd not risk her reputation further. Speculation was rife that Lady Catherine Mabry had been spied in Dodger's gaming hell. Conflicting rumors also abounded—that no indeed, it had simply been Claybourne's latest mistress, a woman he had so little respect for that he dressed her as a servant. Luke never commented on either argument, in hopes that in time both would die a quiet death.

Marcus had assured him that was the best approach. Lord knew their family had suffered enough scandals that the man was fairly an expert on how to lessen the damage.

But still, Luke couldn't ignore the death of her father.

The shades were drawn when he arrived at her residence late that evening. The butler led him to the withdrawing room where the casket rested. Catherine sat on a chair near it. Several people were there. He recognized a few of the lords, the others he assumed were family, paying their respects. Catherine was dressed in black, her face haggard. She looked as though she'd lost weight.

He realized how hard the past month had been on her, and he cursed himself for caring more about society's expectations than hers. In striving to protect her, he'd failed her. He'd never known a deeper regret.

She rose as he approached and he took both of her gloved hands in his.

"My Lord Claybourne, it was so kind of you to come."

"My condolences on your loss. I know your father meant a great deal to you."

Tears welled in her eyes. "He died in his garden, surrounded by the flowers he loved so."

"I suspect you were the blossom he loved most of all."

She released a tiny bubble of laughter, and quickly covered her mouth while those surrounding them raised brows. "My lord, I'd not realized you were a poet."

"When the situation warrants, I can rise to the occasion."

He held her gaze for longer than was proper. He didn't want to leave, but he knew that etiquette dictated that he go.

"Truly, Lord Claybourne, thank you for coming. Your presence here means more to me than you'll ever know."

"I wish I could do more."

She smiled softly. Something must have caught her eye, because she turned her attention elsewhere. Her eyes widened, and she grew pale, as though she'd seen the ghost of her father. She pulled her hands free of Luke's and took a step away from him. "Sterling?"

Luke turned to see an impeccably dressed man with blue eyes as hard as stones standing near. His hair and thick beard were a dark blond, the bronzed hue of his skin reflecting a man accustomed to the outdoors.

Suddenly out of the corner of his eye, Luke saw Catherine's head loll back, her eyes roll—

As her body went limp he caught her and swept her into his arms.

The man took a step forward. "I'm her brother. I'll take her."

"I think not. Simply show me to her room."

"That, sir, would be inappropriate."

"I don't give a bloody damn."

Luke edged his way past him. In the hallway he found a servant whom he dispatched to fetch Bill and another whom he ordered to show him to Catherine's room. His legs were feeling so weak that he wasn't certain he'd make it up the stairs.

All these weeks of striving to preserve her reputation, and he'd managed to undo it all in a matter of seconds.

But it didn't matter. All that mattered was Catherine.

Catherine thought she should have been embarrassed being examined by someone she knew as other than a physician, but Dr. Graves had the uncanny ability to put her at ease.

One moment she'd been moving toward Sterling, and the next she was in her bed, staring at her canopy. Now she was resting on that bed, in the dressing gown Jenny had helped her change into.

"Lord Claybourne insists that you be examined," Jenny had told her.

As though Claybourne had the authority to issue such a demand. Oh, her heart went out to Frannie. The woman would no doubt find him impossible to live with.

While Catherine was fairly finding it impossible to live without him.

"Well?" Catherine asked now, watching as Dr. Graves began putting instruments back into his bag.

"You swooned, which isn't unusual when one is dealing with grief."

"And the unexpected arrival of my brother after so many years certainly didn't help," she added.

"Quite so, but I suspect your fainting had more to do with your condition."

Catherine swallowed. "Which is?"

"You're with child."

Sliding her eyes closed, she unconsciously pressed her hand to her stomach. Then she opened her eyes and met his concerned gaze. "I feared as much," she said. "No, that's not true. I rather hoped as much."

With his arms crossed over his chest, he leaned against the bedpost, no longer the physician, but a friend. "Are you going to tell him?"

"You say that as though you know who the father is."

"I have my suspicions. He'll want to know."

"There's no need for him to know."

"You don't think he'll hear of it?"

Oh, he would. Claybourne knew everything that involved the aristocracy.

"Not until after he's married. I'll do what I can to conceal my condition until he's married."

He nodded. Straightened. "Very well then."

"Promise me you won't tell him."

"I won't. Although he'll probably take a fist to me when he finds out. As Jack learned, Luke doesn't take well to discovering secrets are kept from him."

"Mr. Dodger was harboring a rather large secret."

"And you don't think this is?"

"I'll not deny him his happiness with Frannie."

"As you wish."

A few moments after he left her, she wished she could call him back. Apparently Sterling had insisted that Claybourne take Dr. Graves's word for it—that grief had caused Catherine to swoon—and had refused Claybourne admittance to Catherine's bedchamber. She'd always known Sterling's absence had allowed her a measure of freedom she'd not have had otherwise. She simply hadn't realized exactly how much.

"That was quite the spectacle," Sterling said now, pacing beside Catherine's bed.

Dr. Graves had insisted she remain there at least until tomorrow morning.

"After all these years, your first words to me are chastisement?" she asked, insulted, hurt, and infuriated.

"I'm afraid they're deserved, Catherine. I've heard that you were spotted at Dodger's gaming hell. That you danced with Claybourne, that you took a turn about the garden with him. And now this? Carrying you to your bedchamber as though he were accustomed to ravishing you at whim? Your reputation is ruined."

"Are you saying you engaged in no mischief while you were out gallivanting around the world?"

"No man is going to take you to wife."

"Which works out wonderfully well as I have no intention of taking any man to husband."

"You will marry. I'll see to it. It shall be my first act as the Duke of Greystone, to secure you a proper husband."

"I don't want a proper husband." She wanted an improper one: Claybourne. And if she couldn't have him, she'd have none at all.

"I don't care what you want. I'm lord and master here."

"You're not the young man you were when you left here. What happened to you?"

"We're not here to discuss me. We're here to discuss you and your abhorrent behavior."

If she weren't suddenly feeling lightheaded again, she might have charged out of the bed and smacked him. Instead, she forced herself to calmness and leaned back against the pillows. "Father is dead."

"I'm well aware of that."

"Yet we don't seek to comfort each other?"

"We each grieve in our own way."

"Are you grieving, Sterling?"

He did nothing except clench his jaw.

"Where have you been all these years?" she asked.

"That is not your concern."

"How is it that you managed to hear about all these rumors in so short a space of time? How long have you been in London?"

He suddenly seemed very uncomfortable. "A while."

"And you didn't come see Father?"

"There was much between us that you wouldn't

understand, Catherine, and none of it involves you."

"But you're my brother."

"Which is why I'll see that you're married."

She grabbed a nearby pillow and flung it at him. "I'll not marry a man of your choosing."

"Then you have six months to choose one of your own, before I do it for you."

He strode out of the room, without so much as a backward glance.

Catherine flopped back on the bed and cursed him. Who the devil was that man? It seemed inconceivable that he was her sweet, generous brother.

Chapter 23

"Aren't we somber in our mourning clothes," Winnie said.

Winnie and Catherine were sitting in Winnie's garden, both of them dressed in black as was suitable for their recent status in the world, one a widow, the other mourning the loss of her father.

"Even though you're in mourning, you seem quite cheerful," Catherine said.

Winnie smiled slyly. "I've been speaking with Dr. Graves on occasion, and I'm thinking of trying to raise funds to build a hospital."

"Oh, that would be lovely and would give you something to occupy your time."

"That's what I thought. He's a rather nice man, even if he is a commoner, and I don't think I shall ever get married again. I think you have the right of it. Be independent, do as you like, not be weighted down by a husband."

It all sounded so fine in principle, but in practice, Catherine spent far too much time thinking of Claybourne.

As though knowing where Catherine's thoughts had drifted, Winnie said, "I have it on good authority that Mr. Marcus Langdon has removed his petition to reclaim the estates as his from the courts."

"He'd have not won. Claybourne is the rightful heir."

"So people are saying. I've heard that he's even being issued invitations to various functions. And it's rumored that Mr. Langdon has been seen in Claybourne's company on several occasions—laughing as though they're dear friends. Is that not a strange turn of events?"

"Claybourne can be quite charming when he sets his mind to it. And they are cousins, after all."

"I've also heard that Mr. Langdon is seeing after some of Claybourne's business interests, and his income for his services is more than five thousand a year."

Yes, Catherine could see Claybourne being that generous.

"For a widow who is not supposed to be out and about, you're certainly keeping up with the gossip," she said wryly.

"I have visitors on occasion. Lady Charlotte stopped by just yesterday. She anticipates being betrothed before the Season is out."

"I thought she wanted a titled husband."

"I daresay she'll settle for a wealthy one."

Catherine laughed lightly, enjoying Winnie's company immensely. She was almost as lively as she'd been when she was a younger woman and she and Catherine had their coming out.

"Is your brother settling in as duke?" Winnie asked.

"Oh, yes. Although I'd forgotten how serious he can be. He still hasn't forgiven me for all the scandalous gossip I've caused, which makes him rather difficult to live with."

"I can well imagine."

"Can you?" She leaned across the table and took Winnie's hand where it rested beside the teacup. "Then you'll understand why I can't stay."

"Whatever do you mean?"

"I've decided to go to America."

"For a holiday?"

"No, for the rest of my life."

Winnie appeared horrified. "No, you can't. Whatever will I do without you here?"

"You're stronger than you realize, Winnie, and you'll come to know the truth of that much more quickly if I'm not here."

"But America—it's so far away. What will you do there?"

"I'm not certain. I suppose I shall have to find some sort of employment. Although Father did leave me a small bit of money that isn't part of the entailment. If I invest and live frugally, I think I shall be able to manage."

"Stay here. You can live with me. Two single women—"

"I can't, Winnie."

"Why not?"

There were so many reasons. But only one that truly mattered. She squeezed Winnie's hand. "I'm with child."

Winnie's eyes bugged, her jaw dropped. "Good God, no! Catherine, you're not married."

"Believe me, I'm well aware of that." Still, she smiled, unable to contain her joy and excitement.

"Who's the father? Oh, my God, it's not Claybourne is it? Oh, it is."

Winnie was asking questions and answering them without giving Catherine a chance to respond.

"And the blackguard won't marry you?"

"He doesn't know, and even if he did, he loves someone else."

"It doesn't matter who he loves. He brought this shame to you—"

"I don't feel any shame, Winnie. I want this child, I want him desperately."

"But he'll be a bastard."

She shook her head quickly. "No one need know. I shall wear my mother's wedding ring. I shall tell people I'm a widow. My husband died tragically in a railway accident. Lord knows we've had enough of those of late."

"It seems you've thought this through."

Every night, alone in her bed, yearning to have Claybourne beside her, she'd made plans for all she'd do to protect his son, to give him a kinder life than his father had experienced. She had no doubt whatsoever that she was carrying a boy.

She'd learned a great deal that night in Claybourne's library, included in the inner circle of scoundrels as they'd planned how to arrange Avendale's death. She now knew who to go to if any papers needed to be forged. She had little doubt she could obtain a false certificate of marriage as well as one of death. She nodded. "Yes, I have given it considerable thought and I'll not be dissuaded."

"I could never have your courage."

"Oh, Winnie, I'm not so certain that it's courage as much as it is love." Love for her child, and love for his father.

Luke hadn't seen Frannie since the night they'd arranged to send Avendale on his merry way. It was strange how seldom during these many weeks he'd thought of Frannie, how often he'd thought of Catherine. Bill had assured him that Catherine was fine, but Luke was still haunted by what had happened. After all she'd been through, why would she swoon at the sight of her brother? His return seemed insignificant when compared with the times she'd been in danger of losing her life.

It perplexed him, occupied his thoughts as he waited near the orphanage, waited for Frannie's arrival. The building was completed. She'd sent him a note and asked him to meet her there. She wanted to take him on a tour of it. He supposed this moment, today, would provide the perfect opportunity to ask her to marry him. A children's home was the fulfillment of a dream for her, and marriage to her had always been his fondest dream. It seemed appropriate that he propose today, here.

He spotted the hansom, watched as it came to a halt near the building. The driver helped Frannie climb out. Reaching them, Luke paid the driver.

Neither he nor Frannie spoke until the hansom was headed away.

"You look lovely," Luke said. And she did. There was a happiness, a joy to her. Being under Catherine's tutelage had given her confidence, confidence to become his wife.

"Thank you," she said softly. "You don't come to Dodger's anymore."

"I've been busy."

She gave him a look that said she knew a lie when she heard one.

"Who are we to judge what any of us would do to protect ourselves?" she asked. "He knew if you knew the truth that he would lose your friendship, and your friendship meant more to him than anything. You can't imagine how he suffers these days."

"Do you love him, Frannie?"

She appeared taken aback. "I love all of Feagan's lads."

He didn't doubt the truth of those words. She'd mothered them all, even though she was younger than most of them.

"You know what it is to live as we did, to have so little," she said. "We all have our secrets, none of us are completely honest with the others."

"Not even you?"

"Especially not me. But Jack—"

He was weary of discussing Jack, of having her defend him.

"Eventually, I will forgive him, Frannie. Just not yet."

She nodded. "All right, then. Would you like to see the children's home?"

"Very much."

With her hand on his arm, she led him into the building. It opened into a large room with stairs leading up to other floors.

"The children will sleep in rooms up there. Three floors of rooms." She squeezed his arm. "Can you imagine how many children we'll be able to provide for?"

"Quite a number I suspect."

There were classrooms, a dining hall, a reading room. All of the finest quality. Sturdy. Well-made. Unknown to her, he'd paid the builder a good deal more than she'd originally planned to invest in order to see that it was so.

She led him through the kitchen to the garden, a fence circling the large area. "Children will play here," she said. "They'll be safe."

"When do you plan to start bringing children here?"

"Once I have the furniture."

"Order what you want. I'll pay for it."

"You've done too much—"

"Frannie, please, just do it."

"You're too kind to me, Luke. You always give me everything." Reaching up, she skimmed her fingers along his jaw. "You were always the best of us."

"Not true. I was only very different. My parents taught me right from wrong. It was never a game."

She feathered her fingers over his hair. "You were always special to me. From the beginning, I always knew you'd protect me. There was just something about you."

He took her hand, held it between both of his. "I adore you, Frannie. You know that. I always have."

She gave him the smile that had always warmed him, but it was not one that threatened to bring him to his knees. He would kill to keep that smile on her face. But to keep Catherine smiling, he would willingly die.

"But you *love* Catherine," Frannie said quietly.

He felt as though he'd been slapped, but at the same time, relief swamped him. Yes, this was the perfect setting to ask Frannie to marry him, but he'd known he'd not take advantage of it. "How did you know?"

"If you could see the way you look at her. You've always held your emotions so well, but with her, the love you feel for her, it can't be contained. If a man were ever to look at me as you do her, I daresay, I would marry him—even if he were a king."

He took her hand and kissed her fingers. "Forgive me, Frannie, but after all these weeks of asking you to learn all you needed to become my wife, I can't marry you."

"I never thought you could. Or should. I adore you as well, but as a sister would a brother."

"I did not want to fall in love with her. But you're right. I have. It terrifies me to love her as much as I do."

"I suspect it terrifies her as well. Does she know how you feel?"

"No, God, no. What if she rebuffs me? I don't know how I will live with it."

"You're a coward."

Chuckling low, he squeezed her hand. How

many times had Catherine pointed out that same flaw in him? "When it comes to the heart, yes."

"She won't wait forever, Luke."

"I know, but I fear I'm unworthy of her."

"If I were a petty woman, I could take insult at that. You considered yourself worthy enough for me."

He grinned. "I didn't mean for that to sound as it did. Do you know I struggled for a year before asking for your hand?"

"Don't wait that long to ask for hers. If you truly want her, don't wait another day."

Catherine strolled through the front door, a mixture of feelings dogging her steps. She was excited about traveling to America, sad about leaving England. But she had purchased her ticket that morning. She'd leave from Liverpool and arrive in New York in a matter of weeks. Once there she'd find lodging. It seemed a lot of Englishmen had begun to immigrate to America. She wouldn't be alone and they could help each other along.

She'd removed her hat and gloves and set her purse—with her precious ticket inside, along with the documents Frannie had prepared for her—on the table in the entry hallway.

"Ah, there you are," Sterling said, striding from the hall. "You've a visitor. He's waiting for you in the library."

"Who is it?"

"Claybourne."

Catherine's heart kicked against her ribs. "What's he doing here?"

"Apparently he wants to see you. He's been

here for two hours waiting. What were you doing out and about?"

"I don't owe you an accounting of my actions." She walked into the hallway, and Sterling fell into step behind her. She stopped and faced him. "Nor do I need you to accompany me when I speak to Claybourne."

"A woman does not go into a room with a gentleman by herself."

"Sterling, while you were enjoying your travels, I spent a good deal of time alone with Claybourne. I don't need you now to oversee our meeting. I assure you there is no cause for worry. He'll be a perfect gentleman."

He glanced toward the doorway where the footman waited, then looked back at her. "Catherine, I know I've not been the best of brothers, but I'm determined now to take my responsibilities more seriously."

If he took them any more seriously, she'd find herself locked in a tower.

"There's no need. I'm quite capable of seeing after myself. So, please, don't disturb us."

She left him standing there and swept in through the doorway as the footman opened it. She was reminded of that first night in Claybourne's library, only now *he* stood by the window and the room was filled with the warmth of sunshine rather than the coolness of midnight shadows.

"My Lord Claybourne, it was so nice of you to come to call."

"So formal, Catherine, after all we've shared?"

There was nothing mocking in his tone, rather

it was decidedly sensual. Just the thought of all that they'd *shared* had her body growing warm, and she thought she might be in danger of swooning again. He looked so amazingly wonderful, dressed so formally. Handsome as sin. Her heart was stuttering at his nearness, her hands wanted to reach out for him. She would miss him terribly—but she would always have and cherish the precious memento of their time together that he'd unknowingly given her.

"How is Frannie?" she asked, her words coming out in a rush, her fervent hope that he would leave before she came undone. Even though she'd seen Frannie only that morning, she didn't want to raise his suspicions by not inquiring.

"She's well. I saw her late this morning as a matter of fact."

"Did you ask for her hand in marriage at long last?"

He slowly shook his head. "I apologized to her."

"For what? You didn't tell her what passed between us—"

"No."

With the predatory prowl that she'd come to associate with him, he crossed over to her. "I apologized because I've done all in my power to convince her to become my wife, would do *anything* to have her as my wife, and I suddenly realized that I couldn't marry her, that I had to marry you."

Her heart stammered. "Why?" Before he could respond, the truth hit her. "Damn them! They told you, didn't they? I didn't want this. I didn't—"

"What? Who? What are you talking about?"

"Dr. Graves and Winnie. They've opposed my plans from the beginning. But it's not fair to you, just because I'm with child—"

"What?" Claybourne wrapped his hand around her arm, drew her near, and stood over her with fury undulating off him in waves.

It occurred to Catherine that this might have been how David felt when he confronted Goliath.

"Oh, dear Lord, they didn't tell you."

"You're with child?" he asked, as though what she'd said had finally registered with him. His gaze dropped to her belly. Her condition was not yet evident. Then ever so reverently, he splayed his fingers over her stomach. He lifted his gaze back to hers. "Why did you not tell me? Because of that first night in the library when I told you that I'd not give you respectability if I got you with child?"

"No, no." Reaching up, with tears in her eyes, she cradled his beloved face between her hands, holding his gaze so he'd have no doubt she spoke the truth. "I didn't tell you because I knew you *would* do right by me, and in so doing, you would sacrifice your own dream. You would marry me and give up Frannie, the woman you love more than life itself. And I love you far too much—"

She suddenly found herself crushed against him, his mouth devouring hers, his hand plowing into her hair, scattering pins, the heavy strands tumbling around her.

He tore his mouth from hers. "I love you. I adore Frannie, but I love you desperately, Catherine. You're courageous, bold, and you challenge me at every turn. You're willing to risk everything for those you care about. Your willingness to sacrifice knows no bounds. I am so unworthy, but if you'll marry me, I'll see that you never regret it."

His heartfelt declaration had tears running along her cheeks. "You are the most worthy man I know. You've got a bit of the devil in you, and a bit of a saint, but you're everything I could ever wish for in a man, in a husband. The answer is yes. Gladly."

He was kissing her again, and she felt the fire building between them. She wondered if she could sneak him up to her bedchamber so she could give him a proper answer.

The door suddenly burst open. Catherine simply looked back over her shoulder to see Sterling standing there, his arms crossed over his chest, his expression formidable. "Catherine, you assured me the blackguard wouldn't take advantage. I assure you, sir, a wedding is in order here."

Catherine looked at Claybourne. He smiled down on her.

"As soon as it can be arranged," he promised.

Chapter 24

It was late, long past midnight, when Luke walked the familiar back hallway of Dodger's. He and his friends had gambled there, drunk there, commiserated there. In a way, it was Feagan's dwelling—simply fancier, cleaner, better smelling.

Luke stopped at the open doorway that led into Jack's sanctuary, not surprised to find Jack sitting behind his desk going over his books—not checking Frannie's figures so much as relishing all he'd gained. More than any of them, Jack loved his coins.

Luke cleared his throat. Jack glanced up, and for a heartbeat, Luke thought he saw joy in Jack's eyes before he shuttered his emotions.

"You haven't stopped by in a while," Jack said, leaning back insolently in his chair.

"I had no desire to be here."

"I can hardly blame you for that, I suppose. What brings you here tonight?"

"I've asked Lady Catherine Mabry to become my wife. She's consented to granting me the honor of being her husband."

Jack's eyes widened slightly, before he once again gained control of his thoughts. It wasn't like him to reveal so much, and now he had—twice.

"I thought you loved Frannie."

"I do. But I love Catherine more deeply." And differently. He'd come to realize what he felt for Frannie was the love of a boy for a girl and what he felt for Catherine was the love of a man for a woman. When he'd thought of taking Frannie to bed, he'd never felt any fire, probably because he'd never truly contemplated anything beyond sleeping together, spooned around each other as they'd slept as children. But where Catherine was concerned, he could hardly go fifteen minutes without thinking of falling into bed with her—and sleeping was seldom on his mind.

But these were realizations that he could no longer discuss with Jack. There was now a part of his heart and his soul that he might never again be able to share with his long-time friend.

"Damn," Jack muttered.

Luke arched a brow. "That seems an odd reaction—even from you."

"I have to build Bill a hospital. We wagered"—he shook his head—"it doesn't matter. Congratulations. Shall we drink to it?" He stood up, reached for the bottle—

"No."

Jack looked back at him.

"I'm not drinking much these days."

"I am." Jack poured whiskey into the glass, then held it aloft. "To your health and happiness as well as Catherine's."

He downed the contents in one gulp.

Luke remembered that it was Jack who had given him his first taste of whiskey, rum, and gin. It was Jack who had taught him how to cheat at cards, how to pick pockets without getting caught. Jack who had assured him when he was a small, frightened boy cowering in the alley that everything was going to be all right, that Jack wouldn't let anyone hurt him. In spite of his flaws, of which there were many, Jack had never abandoned Luke. Never.

"I've come to ask you to stand with me," Luke said quietly, "when Catherine and I marry in two weeks."

Jack scoffed. "You're a lord. You should ask Chesney or Milner."

"I'm not friends with Chesney or Milner. I wouldn't lay down my life for them, nor would they for me."

Jack averted his gaze, his voice rough with emotion when he finally spoke. "To stand with you will be the greatest honor of my life."

"You've always stood with me, Jack."

Jack looked back at him, nodded brusquely. "We were quite the pair, weren't we?"

"Too arrogant at times, I think."

"That's because we were so very good and so very clever." He chuckled low. "Well, except for the time when we got caught, of course."

Luke stepped into the room. "I believe I will have that drink."

Jack poured them each a glass. When Luke held his, he tapped it against Jack's. "To Feagan, who taught us how to survive the streets."

"And to your grandfather," Jack said somberly,

"for trying to turn us all into gentlemen, and failing miserably with some of us, I'm afraid."

Luke felt the familiar, painful knot in his chest, near his heart, as he thought of the old gent. He lifted his glass higher in salute. "To my grandfather."

It rained on the day they wed. But Catherine didn't care. She had enough happiness and joy inside her that if it rained for the remainder of their lives, they would always know sunshine. Because she and Sterling were still in mourning over the loss of their father, and Winnie was in mourning over the death of Avendale and etiquette forbade that widows attend weddings, Catherine insisted that the ceremony be small and intimate, held in a chapel.

Claybourne wouldn't allow her to be denied what she requested. She'd always relished her independence, and she drew comfort from knowing that he would never attempt to stifle it. On the contrary, she suspected that he relished it as well.

In spite of the weather, a few among the nobility attended—more out of curiosity than anything. Marcus Langdon was in attendance, his mother notably absent. Frannie stood with Catherine since Winnie couldn't put aside her mourning. Jack stood with Luke. She was glad they'd reconciled, even if Luke had done so with some misgivings.

But what surprised Catherine most was when the bishop asked of Luke, "Do you Lucian Oliver Langdon, the fifth Earl of Claybourne . . ."

Oliver.

Holding his gaze as he gave her his vows, she wondered how much of his youth was contained in the words of the story that she'd recently read to her father. It seemed improbable, but not impossible. But it was a puzzle for another day.

Today she was basking in the love for her that she saw reflected in his eyes. They were the window to a soul she could see so clearly, a soul that had once been dark and now glowed brightly with the promise of their future. She was astounded by how much she loved him, how much he loved her.

They'd journeyed through hell together. She knew no matter what life tossed their way, they would embrace it or overcome it, but they would never be defeated by it.

Later that night, Catherine sat at her vanity, wearing a white cashmere dressing gown, intricately embroidered with pink roses. She brushed her hair, listening intently to the sounds of her husband in the next room preparing for bed. Her husband. She nearly laughed aloud. The one thing she'd never thought to acquire, had never thought she'd want to acquire. The one thing she now knew she could never do without.

She would never take him for granted. She'd always hold him near.

The door leading from his bedchamber into hers clicked open, and he prowled into the room, anticipation lighting the silver of his eyes until they sparkled like the Crown Jewels. She rose and faced him. He'd come to her this time, and she felt unparalleled delight at the thought.

He was still walking toward her when he

reached out and cradled her face between his large hands, tilting her face up, not stopping his forward momentum until his lips were locked on hers. They'd not been together for weeks, and already her body was melting with desire for him.

He slid his hands along her throat as he drew back. He began freeing the buttons of her dressing gown. "I've a good mind to put you over my knee for not telling me you were with child as soon as you realized the truth of your situation."

She peered up at him, saucily. "I was hoping you would."

His joyous laughter echoed through the room, his smile broader than she'd ever seen it, and she could only hope that it would be the first of many.

"I do love you, Catherine Langdon, Countess of Claybourne, with all my heart and what remains of my soul."

He eased her gown off her shoulders until it glided down her body. Lifting her into his arms he carried her to the bed and set her on it. "Roll onto your stomach."

Furrowing her brow, she peered up at him. "Why?"

"I won't risk putting you over my knee in your present condition, but I do intend to kiss your bare bottom."

And kiss it he did. His tongue swirling over her flesh. He kissed the backs of her knees, her thighs. He trailed his mouth along her spine. Heavenly. So heavenly. And unfair. Unfair that in this position she couldn't touch him.

Rolling over, she wound her arms around his

neck and brought him down to her. She thought she'd never have enough of this, of touching him, of having him touch her. It was as if they knew everything about each other, even as they made new discoveries.

He was ticklish under his arms, jerking if her fingers got too close. She was ticklish on the inside of her hips, laughing when he skimmed his fingers over them.

They teased each other, bringing each other close to that moment when the world faded away and there was nothing except the two of them. Only to retreat and start the dance of seduction over.

She thought she would go mad with the wanting. She began urging him to hurry.

"Now," she gasped. "Now. I need you now."

He rose above her and plunged inside her. They were each so ready for the other that they were straining and bucking against each other, leaping over the edge until there was nothing except the pleasure.

Nothing except each other.

Epilogue

From the Journal of Lucian Langdon, the Earl of Claybourne

They say my parents were murdered in the London streets by a gang of ruffians.

I now know that to be untrue.

They were killed by my father's brother, my uncle. And fate, in its mysterious ways, delivered him to my hand for retribution.

My memories have slowly begun to drift out of the dark shadows where I banished them for so long.

I remember standing beside my father at the pond. He was so much taller than I. To me he appeared to be a giant. Yet he always made me feel safe, and I strive now to give my own children that sense of well-being.

And the old gent. I know him now as my grandfather, and I think of him with increasing fondness. I regret that I was not as certain of my place beside him while he was alive—I regret even more that he was aware of my misgivings.

Yet I know he never doubted, and I shall do all in my power to ensure that his faith in me was not misplaced.

When I was small, he would hoist me upon his lap, hold me near, and tell me tales of my ancestors. And on sunny mornings, with my small hand nestled in his larger one, we would walk over the moors, where he taught me to gather flowers to give to my mother.

My mother. I can see her so clearly now. She had the gentlest of smiles. I remember her tucking me into bed at night and whispering that I would become an exceptional earl.

My wife assures me that is the way of it, that I have fulfilled my mother's prediction, but then she is rather biased. She loves me in spite of my flaws. Or perhaps because of them.

My friendship with Jack remains strained. I want to believe that he was duped, but he has always been far too clever to fall for another man's ruse. So we have added yet one more thing to our relationship about which we never speak. Sometimes I think we will break beneath the weight of it, but on those occasions I have but to look at my wife in order to find the strength to carry on. I am determined to be worthy of her and that requires that I be a far stronger and better man than I had ever planned to be.

We see Frannie from time to time, not as often as we'd like unfortunately. She did eventually marry, but that is her story to tell.

Dear Frannie, darling Frannie.

She shall always remain the love of my youth, the one for whom I sold my soul to the devil. But Catherine, my beloved Catherine, shall always be the center of my heart, the one who, in the final hour, would not let the devil have me.

Next month, don't miss these exciting new love stories only from Avon Books

The Mistress Diaries by Julianne MacLean

Cassandra Montrose throws caution to the wind for one night of passion with Lord Vincent Sinclair before she begins her new life. Vincent is a shameless rake, forced to settle down or lose his inheritance. But on the same day he brings his fiancée to meet his family, Cassandra shows up on his doorstep . . . and nothing will ever be the same.

Before I Wake by Kathryn Smith

An Avon Contemporary Romance

In her contemporary paranormal debut, Kathryn Smith weaves a tale of darkness and passion. Dawn is special, able to exist in both the dream realm and "reality." Forced to team up with a mortal, Noah Clarke's unique abilities put them both in terrible danger. Will they be able to overcome this Terror before it destroys them—and their new love?

Too Dangerous to Desire by Alexandra Benedict

An Avon Romance

Lord Adam Westmore is determined to shut himself off from the world. When Evelyn Waye begs for his help, he finds he can't resist her plea—or the lure of her arms. But Evelyn's past holds a dangerous secret, one that could ruin them both . . . forever.

Surrender to Me by Sophie Jordan

An Avon Romance

Lady Astrid Derring is on a mission: to track down her missing, criminal husband. On her wild journey to Scotland, she crosses paths time and again with Griffin Shaw, an arrogant American who makes her feel again. When her trip reaches a surprising end, only Griffin can save her. But is he also willing to save her heart?